FIRST LOVE, SECOND CHANCES

FIRST LOVE, SECOND CHANCES

A Novel

Anita Stansfield

Covenant Communications, Inc.

Covenant Communications, Inc.
American Fork, Utah

Printed in the United States of America
First Printing: February 1995
95 96 97 98 99 00 0 1 02   10 9 8 7 6 5 4 3 2
ISBN 1-55503-776-3

To my parents . . .
Thank you for beliving in me, and for your endless support.
Like Nephi, I have been born of goodly parents.

Prologue

Emily Ladd and Michael Hamilton were college sweethearts, but Emily married Ryan Hall because he could take her to the temple. After a decade of unhappy marriage, Emily's path crossed Michael's again, and he begged her to leave Ryan and go with him to Australia. Her choice? She would stay with Ryan and honor their temple covenants—a decision that humbled Ryan and brought new life to their marriage. Then, just as she was beginning to fall in love with her husband all over again, the Lord took him home. Emily was now alone with three young children—and free to seek the safe and loving shelter of Michael's arms. But would it be so easy—or even possible?

Michael, who had returned to Australia, was unaware of her loss, but he acted on a prompting and left everything behind to fly to the states and make certain that she was all right. Discovering her circumstances, he was determined to share his life with her. He believed that there was nothing they could not overcome.

It was easy for Emily to accept Michael's proposal of marriage. She had rejected him twice before, but the feelings she'd always had for him made sense now. Only the timing had thrown them off.

Emily often wondered . . . if Michael had been a member of the Church, would it have made a difference in her original decision? In her heart she knew she had done the right thing; but she eagerly accepted his proposal now, fully expecting to marry a nonmember. He was a good man, and she knew he would do everything in his power to make her happy and respect her beliefs. His revelation that he had recently been baptized simply put the icing on the cake. Her joy was inexpressibly full at the prospect of putting the pieces of her life back together and sharing it with Michael.

In spite of Michael's need to return to Australia to take care of some business, Emily had every reason to anticipate a bright future. She believed that together they could conquer anything—but she had no way of knowing how intensely her belief would be tested.

CHAPTER ONE

Orem, Utah

Michael Hamilton had been gone five days. It seemed like forever. All Emily could think of was hearing his voice, seeing him again. She cursed herself for being so stalwart when he'd left, and insisting that he didn't need to call every day.

It had all happened so fast . . . he had come back into her life and changed so much in so little time, that it was still difficult to comprehend. Last week she had been a destitute widow with little hope. Now she was engaged to her college sweetheart and the future was bright. Except that he was off in Australia seeing to business, and she missed him desperately.

Trying not to think of Michael's absence, Emily immersed herself in work. She cleaned until the house sparkled, and kept up with such efficiency that not a crumb got ahead of her. By mid-afternoon, she found herself with nothing left to do. She stared at the phone, as if doing so might make it ring.

The doorbell startled her, and she absently moved to answer it. There was no one Emily wanted to see that would ease this ache for Michael. Still, she was not disappointed to see Penny. She was about to ask why her best friend had rung the bell and waited, but Penny didn't give her a chance.

"Have you checked your kitchen table recently?"

"Why, what's wrong with my table?"

"Nothing, I just wondered." Penny closed the door and tried not to smile.

"I was just in there, Penny." Emily's eyes narrowed. "What are you up to?"

"I'm not up to anything. But why don't you go check your kitchen table? I'm taking Alexa and Amee for a walk to the park."

"I go to da pawk," two-year-old Amee shouted as she jumped up from her storybooks and ran to the door. Her little sister, Alexa, crawled after her like a shadow. Emily watched Penny dubiously as she herded them out the door, then stepped into the kitchen and caught her breath. She'd half expected a plate of cookies or a hot loaf of bread that Penny was prone to sneak through the back door. Instead, she found a dozen white roses.

"How sweet," she said aloud as she bent to breathe in their fragrance. She picked up the little card, wondering if Michael had called Penny and asked her to do this. But something intangible made her heart quicken as she read on the envelope, *To my first love, forever.* It was written in his hand.

Emily opened the card and slid it out, unconsciously putting a hand to her heart as she read *I promise . . .*

Smiling, she recalled the way she'd insisted he make a promise without telling him what it was until he returned. She looked up, nearly expecting to see him there, demanding to know what he'd promised. Her heart ached to think of him halfway around the world. She set down the card and picked up the roses, closing her eyes to inhale their sweet aroma.

Carefully she touched the full buds, reminding herself this was proof that he loved her, and he *would* be back. She only hoped it might not be too many weeks.

Emily became suddenly alert to her surroundings as she sensed something unfamiliar. She heard only silence, but as she concentrated on the feeling, she could have sworn she was not alone. Scolding herself for conjuring up ghosts, she turned abruptly to satisfy herself that no one was there.

Suddenly she found it difficult to breathe. She crushed the flowers to her chest with one hand and gripped the back of a chair with the other.

"What *did* I promise, Emily?" Michael said it with a straight face as he casually slid his hands into the front pockets of his faded jeans, topped by a denim shirt of a nearly identical blue.

Emily resisted the urge to run into his arms. She carefully set the flowers aside without taking her eyes from him, perhaps fearing that if she turned away he would be gone. For a long moment she indulged in the luxury of just looking at him, attempting to comprehend the part he played in her life. The anticipation of holding him close was sweet, and she relished it.

"I thought you were in Australia," she scolded lightly.

"I'm not." He smiled and shifted his weight onto one leg.

"Are you trying to tell me you've flown over and back in five days?"

"Actually, I didn't make it past L.A., where I called to check on things and realized it wasn't as bad as they'd originally told me. So I took care of it by phone and came back." He motioned toward the door. "But I could leave again if—"

Emily shook her head. "I'm not letting you go back to Australia until you take me with you."

Michael smiled and stepped toward her. "I was hoping you'd say that."

Emily could hear her own heartbeat as he touched her chin with his finger and lifted her face to his. Michael's kiss was brief but full of promise; then, as if he'd read her mind, he drew her into his arms, holding her as if his life depended on it. Emily silently thanked God for bringing him back to her so soon, and for knowing that he loved her as much as she loved him.

"Well?" he whispered near her ear. "Aren't you going to tell me?"

Emily was baffled, or perhaps just lost in his eyes.

"What did I promise?" he repeated.

Emily smiled. "You promised to come back to me."

Michael chuckled and kissed her nose. "I see." He stepped back and took both her hands in his. "I don't think I could have stood going to Australia without you; not now. Knowing you're mine makes it practically unbearable to be without you."

"My thoughts exactly." She smiled and squeezed his hands. "Will you be staying for dinner?"

Michael grimaced. "Actually," he apologized, "I came straight from the airport, and I've got some business to finish up by phone once I get checked in to the hotel. If you think you can live without me a while longer, I'll come by tomorrow and we can get started on the rest of our lives."

Emily was so glad to know he wouldn't be gone for weeks, that being without him this evening seemed insignificant.

She nodded and he kissed her brow. "Thank you for the roses," she said as he moved toward the door.

Michael smiled. "I'll see you tomorrow, darlin'." He winked. "We have a wonderful life ahead of us—together—Emily Ladd."

His words were full of hope and peace. There was no tangible reason why the old guilt should creep in, but it did. Nagging doubts filtered into Emily's mind as she recalled all that had brought them back together. Six months ago, she had considered leaving Ryan to marry Michael. She'd made the decision to stay, but now Ryan was dead. The accident had been a shock initially, and eventually, a relief. But still, there was the guilt.

"Are you all right?" Michael was quick to notice the distress in her expression.

Emily reminded herself not to lose sight of her happiness. Surely these feelings would work themselves out.

"I'm wonderful," she said and truly meant it once she pushed the guilt away. "I'll see you tomorrow."

Michael winked again and slipped away.

Emily was arranging the roses in water when Penny came through the door with Amee and Alexa.

"You're pretty tricky, Penny." Emily grinned.

Penny shrugged. "It was Michael's idea." After a lengthy silence she added, "So, what now?"

Emily glanced up, concerned by the tone in her friend's voice. "Is something wrong?"

"No, I was just . . . wondering what your plans will be now. I mean . . . you and Michael are engaged. I still can hardly believe it."

"That makes two of us," Emily laughed. "And to realize he's joined the Church after all these years." Her voice cracked slightly. "I wonder why I am so blessed."

"I wouldn't wonder about that." Penny smiled serenely.

"Well," Emily sighed, "right now my life is a complicated mess, and it will be interesting to see how Michael adjusts, being thrown into a slice of apple-pie American life. I hope he doesn't change his mind," she added almost lightly. "Of course we haven't discussed any plans yet. I imagine it won't be too long before he'll have to go back to Australia." She glanced hesitantly at Penny. "He did say he wouldn't go back without me."

"Oh, no." Penny's voice fell as she perceived a reality. "I don't know if I can bear having you move to Australia."

Emily shrugged her shoulders. "It is his home. As I said, we've not discussed details, but I know he is heavily involved in his family's business. He needs to be there."

Penny managed a smile, but they both knew this would not be easy in light of their decade-long friendship. She rose reluctantly. "I should go and get dinner started. How is Allison doing, by the way?"

"She doesn't say much. I'm concerned about how she's going to take all of this. She was a sensitive nine-year-old to begin with, but losing her father has not been easy. I've asked her if she likes Michael, but she doesn't answer."

"That sounds like Allison," Penny said as she moved to the door.

"Thank you, Penny," Emily called. Then she inhaled the sweet fragrance of the roses once more before she started dinner.

The evening passed slowly until Michael called at bedtime; they talked until Emily was exhausted. After a lengthy attempt to convey through prayer her gratitude for what Michael had done for her life, Emily crawled into bed. For the first time in months, she didn't have to wonder where she was going to find the strength to make it through another day.

Emily's strength showed up in person, right in the middle of morning rush hour. Allison answered the door with an indifferent, "Hi. Mom's in the kitchen."

"Hurry up, Allison," Emily called, unaware of Michael's presence. His knock at the door had been lost in the fit Amee had thrown while being been dragged out of playing in the sugar bowl. "You'll have to walk to school alone if you're not ready in a minute."

Allison went to the table to sort papers and put them into her backpack. "I don't care. I don't want to walk with them anyway.

Yesterday all they did was talk about . . ." She glanced warily toward Michael, and Emily's eyes followed.

"When did you sneak in?" she smiled.

"Hours ago," he stated. Allison looked up hesitantly. The tension was evident.

Emily turned her attention back to Allison. "What were they talking about, Allie?"

She looked again at Michael with an expression that indicated they were in mixed company. "Well, you know," she said to Emily.

"Oh, no." Emily stopped feeding Alexa long enough to react fully. "Not that."

"They think it's so funny, and it makes me mad," Allison insisted.

Michael concentrated quietly and attempted to perceive the implications. If he wasn't totally certain of the topic, he could at least appreciate the situation.

"If you don't want to talk about it," he said as Allison looked up in surprise, "you need to just say so, without getting angry."

"I did," Allison retorted, "and they called me a nerd." Emily sighed with disgust. "At least you have the peace of mind to know you tried," Michael consoled immediately, "and if you're trying to do the right thing, you know in your heart that you understand something the other girls don't, and your life will be happier because of it, even if it's not so easy now." He felt blank stares directed at him and wondered if he had spoken out of line.

Emily was awed at Michael's ability to express something that she had found difficult, and she sensed that Allison was surprised to hear such an observation from a male figure in the home. Ryan, for all his wanting Allison to be happy, would have told her that she needed to learn to live with it, but would not have given her any advice on how to do it.

Allison zipped her backpack and grabbed her sweater. "I'd better hurry, or they'll leave without me." She hesitated and looked Michael over as if he were some kind of alien, giving a subtle glare that seemed to say, *You're not my father and I don't want you here.* While he was trying to think of something to say that might ease the tension, Allison kissed Emily and the babies and hurried out the door.

"I don't think she likes me." Michael sat on a bar stool and leaned his elbows on the counter.

"Don't expect everything to fall into place overnight," Emily replied in a tone that made Michael wonder if she was implying something beyond Allison's guarded behavior.

Not wanting to delve into that, Michael went back to the original topic. "Were they talking about what I think they were?"

Emily concentrated on feeding the baby. "I was sixteen before my friends began discussing such things, and I thought I was young to be exposed to it. You would think a nine-year-old could have some time to grow up before she had to know the physical technicalities of where she came from."

"Where do these kids hear it?" he asked.

"That's a good question, Michael. These are children from good Mormon homes."

"Maybe it's the good Mormon homes that get hit the hardest from the opposition. Isn't that where Satan knows he can do the most damage?"

"Good point."

"I hope I didn't speak out of line," he said to reassure himself. "You're going to have to help me know where I should stand with her."

"I think you did just fine. It will take time, but it's nice to feel like I'm not teaching her alone."

"It's a tough world out there. We'll just have to do our best to give her the strength to know how to face it—which is better than trying to protect her from it."

Emily smiled at him, liking the way he'd used *we*. "It's nice to have you here, Michael." Their eyes met and she felt a rush of butterflies. She could still hardly believe it.

He grinned and resisted the urge to kiss her. "It's nice to be here."

"So," she asked, "what are your plans today?"

"I was about to ask you the same thing."

"Did you have any breakfast?"

"Yes, thank you. I'm certain you have better things to do with your time than fix me breakfast."

"I could likely manage once in a while," she smiled.

Michael leaned over the counter and said mischievously, "Let's go to the mall."

Emily smiled. "That sounds fun, but I'm not sure if Penny can watch the babies. I think she is—"

"I meant *all* of us. You do have a . . . what do you call it over here?"

"I'd tell you if I knew what you were talking about."

"A . . ." He snapped his fingers, trying to think of the word, "a pusher."

"A pusher?" Emily laughed. "Michael, that's an illegal drug dealer."

"I know!" he admitted in frustration. "I've spent enough time here to figure out most of the differences, but I've never dealt with babies before."

"Do you mean a stroller?"

"That's it!" He pointed at her in exaggerated delight.

"Yes, I have one." She smiled.

"Then let's go. They'll love it."

"I should do the dishes and—"

"We'll do that later. Just feed the baby and let's go."

Emily thoroughly enjoyed the excursion, mostly because of the opportunity to observe Michael in a way she would have never thought possible. He insisted on pushing the stroller, as if it were a privilege, and he stopped often to show the babies something, speaking to them as if they were adults. He occasionally asked Emily to interpret Amee's vocabulary, but he was certain that Alexa said "water" when they stopped to watch the fountain.

"It was coincidence," Emily insisted.

"She said it," he retorted adamantly, and a while later, when they paused at a different fountain, Alexa pointed upward and uttered, "Wawa." Michael grinned smugly at Emily and took the babies out of the stroller to let them touch the water in the little pool. "It's cold," he said to Amee, who giggled.

"It's code, Mommy," she said proudly.

Michael bought the babies each a big lollipop, then personally cleaned up the sticky mess when they'd had their fill. At lunch, Amee repeatedly tried to climb on the table, spilled water, and rearranged Michael's dishes several times. Alexa crumbled crackers on the floor and began to fuss before they were finished eating. But Michael just gave the waitress an extra tip and carried Alexa with him to pay the bill.

"Your baby is adorable," the cashier said to him.

"Thanks," he replied, casually disguising the thrill he felt. "She looks like me, don't you think?"

Emily nudged him in the ribs, but the cashier said, "Yes, I think she does."

"Sorry," he said on their way to the car, "I couldn't resist."

Emily smiled up at him. "You do well with them, Michael."

"They're easy to love," he said, looking at Alexa as he carried her and pushed the stroller with the other hand.

"Just wait. One of these days, they'll have you so infuriated you'll want to scream."

"I can't wait," he grinned.

"You know," Emily put her hand on Michael's arm, "you're the only father they will ever know."

"Does that bother you?" he asked carefully.

"It's a little . . . sad on Ryan's behalf, but . . ." She looked up at him again. "I know they could not want for a better father."

Michael put his arm around Emily's shoulder and she took over pushing the stroller. "You keep saying things like that, and you'll never get rid of me."

"That's the idea."

In the car, Michael spoke quietly. "Emily, I don't want to put you on the spot, but . . . well, how long does one wait before he carries a beautiful young widow and her children off to Australia?" Emily hesitated and he added, "A year? Two? Five?"

"Don't be ridiculous," she chuckled.

"Well?"

"I don't know. I have to think about it, but—"

"Think about it," he interrupted. "We'll talk later. I just want to have a vague idea, so I'll know how to plan."

"Let's just say no longer than absolutely necessary." He looked at her, and mutual anticipation fluttered through them. "Of course there are things to deal with and take care of, but I want to get on with our lives."

He smiled. "That's all I wanted to know."

Emily could hardly believe this was happening—and so quickly. It was incredible to sit back and realize that eleven years apart had not diminished the depth or intensity of their relationship. It seemed in many ways that they were able to pick up where they had left off. Impulsively she reached over to take his hand, and his expression alone filled her with peace.

Emily thought of her parents and wished, as she often did, that they were still around to share her life. They had both respected and cared for Michael, and she knew they had been aware of the struggles in her marriage to Ryan. But both of Emily's parents had passed away in the years since college, and she could only hope that they were aware of the joy she was finding now. She felt certain they would be pleased.

With the babies down for naps, Michael insisted he was going to wash the dishes. Emily was trying to think of a way to talk him out of it when the doorbell rang.

"Saved by the bell," he grinned, and Emily laughed to herself as she went to answer it. Having a handsome man wash her dishes was not something she would take for granted.

Emily was taken off guard by the woman standing on the porch. Middle-aged and thin, with prematurely graying hair, she was dressed humbly and clutched a big purse in front of her as if she was terrified. When she didn't speak, Emily asked, "May I help you?"

"Mrs. Hall?" she said with a shaky voice.

"Yes," Emily answered cautiously. Could this be someone Ryan had worked with? She certainly didn't look the part.

"My name is Ruth Carper." The woman held out a trembling hand. "Please forgive my nerves. This is terribly difficult for me, but I had to come and talk to you."

Emily took the offered hand and shook it briefly. Her heart quickened a little as she began to sense this woman's purpose was intense, but she wasn't prepared for Mrs. Carper's announcement.

"Mrs. Hall," she said, drawing back her shoulders with fortitude, "my daughter was driving the car that killed your husband."

Emily was stunned into silence. She didn't realize Michael was behind her until he said kindly, "Come in, Mrs. Carper. You should probably sit down."

Mrs. Carper hesitantly moved inside and lowered herself to the edge of the couch. Emily sat close by, nodding gratefully toward Michael. She tried to convince herself that she had dealt with all of this well enough to handle it, but she couldn't deny the knot forming in her stomach as the memories came rushing back.

"I know I'm probably the last person on earth you want to talk to, Mrs. Hall," she began, "but I just cannot get on with life until I tell you that . . . I mean . . . I want you to know that . . . you see, Melinda was only seventeen. I'd struggled with her ever since her father left." She chuckled with no trace of humor. "I was glad to see him go, really, but raising the children alone has taught me that I'm not a very competent parent." Mrs. Carper glanced down at her trembling hands. Her voice cracked. "I knew Melinda was drinking some, but I didn't know how to stop it. I've always tried to do the right thing and go to church and all, but I . . ."

Emily wanted so badly to speak and console this woman, but emotion knotted painfully in her throat—not only from this disconcerting reminder of Ryan's death, but also with compassion for this sweet mother. She turned to Michael with a silent plea and was relieved when he picked up on it.

"There are many wayward children in the world, Mrs. Carper, who come from fine parents. I'm certain you've done your best."

Mrs. Carper managed a smile. "Thank you, but . . ." her voice cracked again, "I never thought she would be killed before she had a chance to come around." At this the woman visibly fell apart. She fumbled for tissues in her big purse while Michael and Emily exchanged helpless glances.

"I'm sorry," she continued. "I swore to myself I would do this without getting upset, but . . ." Mrs. Carper's eyes went to Emily and a silent bond seemed to connect them. "Mrs. Hall, the heartache of losing my daughter was bad enough, but when I realized she had killed someone else—a young father with children, no less—I just wanted to die."

That did it. The tears streamed without restraint down Emily's face as disjointed memories bombarded her: the hospital, the funeral, the way Ryan had held her the night before he died.

"I've had no peace these past months," Mrs. Carper continued, "wondering if you were making ends meet."

Mrs. Carper again fumbled in her purse and pulled out a check which she pushed abruptly toward Emily. "Here, I want you to have this. I know it's not much, but it's all I have."

Emily finally found her voice. "I can't take your money, Mrs. Carper," she insisted gently. "I can assure you that my needs are being met."

"No," Mrs. Carper choked back a sob and shook her head vehemently, "you must take it. Don't you understand? If you don't, I'll never feel any peace. I have to do something to try to make it right. I can't bring him back to life, Mrs. Hall, but I want to help you."

"I appreciate your concern." Emily wiped her tears and took the woman's hand. "Truly I do. I'm glad you came to talk to me. But I won't take your money. You have children who need this more than I do."

A look of intense frustration came over Mrs. Carper's face. Emily glanced again at Michael. It was evident that he shared her confusion.

After an awkward silence, Mrs. Carper stated her case again. "My daughter's loss has been difficult for me; but somehow I know if you'll allow me to help you, things will be better for both of us. Please."

"Mrs. Carper," Emily began, "as I said, I appreciate your concern, but—"

Michael stepped forward and took the outstretched check. "Thank you, Mrs. Carper. Your kindness has surely blessed us."

Distracted from her fresh sorrow, Emily gaped in disbelief. But Michael wouldn't even look at her. Mrs. Carper was visibly relieved as she came to her feet.

"I'm truly sorry for the loss of your husband, Mrs. Hall," she said calmly. "I pray for you every day."

"Thank you," was all Emily could manage to say. Inwardly, she was fuming. How could Michael do that? But what could she say without embarrassing all of them?

"Your prayers have been felt, Mrs. Carper," Michael said gently, "I can assure you. And I'm certain that God doesn't judge too harshly when our loved ones are taken in the midst of their earthly mistakes. Surely he knows the difficulties of Melinda's life and takes them into consideration."

Mrs. Carper looked up at Michael as if he were some kind of saint. Emily wanted to slap him.

"Thank you," she smiled more easily now. "Are you . . . related to Mrs. Hall?"

"Not yet," he smiled. "I'm her fiancé."

"Oh, that's wonderful." Mrs. Carper truly beamed now. "Then you'll see that she's taken care of from here on."

"I will," he assured her.

"Thank you for coming," Emily said politely.

Once Mrs. Carper was gone, Emily let loose. "How could you possibly take that poor woman's money? Have you gone crazy or—"

"Calm down," he chuckled and took hold of her shoulders. "If I didn't have the check, I wouldn't know where to find her."

Emily waited in disbelief for him to explain.

"Don't you see, Emily? She needed to give of herself. She would have never accepted your refusing it."

"You're not going to cash it, are you?"

"Yes, I am," he stated. "And then I'm going to send her a cashier's check—anonymously, of course—for ten times this amount. Unless you have a problem with that."

Emily sat down and sighed. She felt awful for jumping to conclusions. "I'm sorry, Michael. I should have seen it, but—"

"I dare say her visit was as difficult for you as it was for her."

"I don't think so." Emily shook her head while tears welled up again, as if to declare that she was lying. She met Michael's eyes. "I can't comprehend losing a child like that, and suffering with the guilt of knowing the damage caused to others. It took a great deal of courage for her to come here."

Michael nodded in agreement and studied the check in his hand. "One hundred and twelve dollars," he said aloud. "It's as if she scraped together every dollar she had."

"It's like the widow's mite," Emily added.

"Well said."

"I love you, Michael."

He smiled. "Even though I take money from poor women and—"

"What you're doing is a great thing."

"Nah," he said humbly, "I've got ample of something she is in need of. It's no big deal."

"It's a big deal to me."

Michael cleared his throat and looked suddenly embarrassed. "I've got dishes to wash, Mrs. Hall. I haven't got time to be chatting all day."

Emily watched him walk to the kitchen, marveling at his goodness and the way it blessed her life. Then, almost against her will, her mind became absorbed with Ryan as the untimely tragedy of his death came rushing back. Pressing a hand to her chest, she felt an almost tangible emptiness as she tried to comprehend the part he had played in her life, and the reality that he was now gone. She forced herself to work on the laundry, hoping to push the memories away, but it made little difference. She returned to the kitchen to find Michael rinsing out the sink. Stopping to watch him, she suddenly felt confused and afraid. She ached to be a part of Michael's life completely, but wondered if she was moving too fast.

"What's wrong?" he asked while he dried his hands and tossed the towel onto the counter.

Emily forced a smile and shook her head. She didn't trust her voice, fearing it would betray her.

"You're thinking about Ryan," he guessed, and she turned away guiltily. When fresh emotion overtook her, she hurried toward the hall. But Michael took hold of her arm to stop her.

"Go ahead and cry, Emily," he said, his face close to hers. "Cry all you want; scream if you must. But don't shut me out. I know you loved him. I know it's hard. But you can talk to me. Tell me how much you miss him. Tell me how it hurts. I can take that far better than I can take your silence."

As if his permission was all she needed, Emily took hold of his shirt and pressed her face to his shoulder, where she sobbed helplessly. Michael held her and whispered words of comfort, trying not to feel upset by the evidence that his fiancée still held some very deep feelings for another man—a man Michael didn't even like.

When she managed to calm down somewhat, he took hold of her chin and forced himself to ask a question that he had no desire to ask. "Emily, are we moving too fast? Would it be better if I weren't here, or—"

"No," she sobbed, "I mean . . . I don't know . . . I mean . . . " Her eyes connected with his, and there was no questioning her sincerity as she said firmly, "I want you here, Michael; I need you. Please . . . be patient with me."

Michael smiled sadly and kissed her brow. "It's okay, darlin'. Just keep talking to me, and we'll be fine."

Emily hugged him tightly and decided she felt better. She slipped away to compose herself, then went back to the laundry as if nothing were out of the ordinary. Michael left to do an errand and returned to find Emily folding clothes on the front room floor. He still sensed a subtle tension, but felt it was best ignored for the moment.

"You did that the last time I was here."

"I do this every day," she said with mock horror. "And no, you can't help."

"Got any more photo albums?"

"I'm not sure what you've already looked at. They're in the cedar chest."

Michael sat quietly on the floor, absorbing more of the life he was attempting to work himself into. When he'd had his fill of photographs, he turned his attention to the genealogy. Penny dropped by with a cheerful, "Am I intruding?"

"No," Michael said, "we were in need of a chaperone anyway. Amee is asleep."

Penny chuckled and sat to help Emily fold.

"How come you let her help and you won't let me?" Michael demanded.

"Why is everyone so anxious to do my housework?"

"It's fun to do somebody else's housework." Penny gave her classic reply.

"What's your excuse?" Emily asked Michael.

With complete seriousness he said, "If we do the work together, we'll have more time to play."

He turned to put the books back in the chest and curiously picked up an object wrapped in tissue paper. Emily wasn't paying attention so he carefully unwrapped it, then wished he hadn't when she looked over just as the little glass temple came into view.

Emily stopped with a half-folded towel spread over her legs. To see Michael holding this keepsake of her wedding, regarding it with a kind of fascination, seemed almost eerie. He looked at her with a question in his eyes and she answered tonelessly, "It's from the top of the wedding cake."

Michael didn't miss the sadness in her eyes, but he didn't know how to console it.

"If you'd have married me," he said matter-of-factly while he wrapped it back up, "you wouldn't have gotten one of these."

"Oh, there's much better stuff down at the bottom," Penny announced. Emily gave her a familiar glare that she ignored.

Michael looked at Emily, mischief glowing in his eyes. "Go ahead," she said. "I don't care." Though her tone indicated the opposite, Michael carefully removed the contents of the chest while Penny and Emily gave him a running commentary on their value. He wondered if what he'd find at the bottom would help Emily face her memories with Ryan, but as he pulled back the double layer of blue tissue, it only took a moment to realize that what was there had nothing to do with Ryan. He looked to Emily, who stated quietly, "I had you put away there for ten and a half years."

"Well, I'm glad you let me out," he quipped. "It was getting rather uncomfortable." Penny giggled, and the three embarked on an excursion of memories and stories that had them all laughing. Michael was relieved to see the solemnity fade from Emily's eyes.

When he came across her old passport and visa, he came abruptly to his feet. "That reminds me," he said and went to find the phone book. He looked up a number and dialed, then quietly scribbled notes but said nothing. Emily looked at him questioningly and he explained, "It's a recording." Her expression relaxed, and she rose to begin carting the folded laundry to various rooms.

"Must have been fascinating," Penny said when he hung up the phone.

"What's fascinating?" Emily asked as she returned to get another armload.

"We can have passports in two to three weeks, and then we'll have to send for visas, which will likely take another two or three weeks. Here's a list of what we'll need." He tossed the notebook on the table. Emily and Penny exchanged uneasy glances. Michael turned in time to catch them and added, "We'd better get one for you too, Penny. You will be visiting often, I assume."

"Oh, yes," she agreed, keeping her sarcasm light, "I'll just jump on a plane every once in a while and drop by."

"That could be arranged," he said as if it were no big deal.

Michael returned to the contents of the chest, intrigued with the things Emily had kept as keepsakes of the months they had dated in college. A few minutes later, Emily knelt beside him to help replace them, minus the tissue paper divider.

"Hey," he whispered, "you let me know if I get overzealous here. You're the one at the center of this. You've got to choose the pace."

Emily glanced at Penny, who was out of hearing range. "We're fine."

"What?" Michael said more loudly. "No more smothering me in the bottom of that chest?"

"No," Emily said proudly and handed him the crumpled paper.

"I think she prefers you here," Penny interjected. "She needs you."

"Ah," he grinned at Emily, "she just needs my money."

"I could live without your money a lot easier than I could live without you."

"Just checking." He smiled and closed the chest.

"If I were going to marry for money, I'd have married you a long time ago."

"That's a good point," he added as Emily picked up the last armload of towels and headed for the kitchen. Michael followed.

"However," she said lightly, "the money helps. At least I didn't have to beg for mercy."

"You wouldn't have had to anyway. All it would have taken is a simple 'I need ten thousand dollars, Michael,' and I'd have had it wired here in a day, no questions asked. Even if I had married Jenny, I would have gladly supported you until the girls got a little older and you could go back to school."

"You're a good man, Michael." She turned and he took her hand. "But I must say that I prefer it this way. I'd like to think that your support will be of personal benefit to you."

"More than you can imagine." They looked at each other for a long moment, and Emily felt him squeeze her hand in a way that expressed all of the hope in his eyes.

"So, what's on the agenda now?" she asked to distract herself from the quiver evolving in her stomach.

Amee made a noise to indicate she was awake. "I'll get her," Penny called from the other room.

"I was in the mood to cook something," Michael stated. "What would you like for dinner?"

"I don't know. You decide. I'll go to the store as soon as Alexa wakes up and get whatever you need. I do have a little money."

"Is that what you call that three digit figure with a one at the front of it I saw on your savings statement prior to my deposits?"

"Don't be obnoxious, Michael."

"I will if I want to, just as long as you keep what you've got and . . . I don't know, buy yourself a sweater or something." He impulsively opened the fridge to assess what was available of the basics. After a quick glance he turned back to Emily, who shrugged her shoulders. He opened the freezer and found nothing but ice cubes. He slammed it shut and proceeded to open and close cupboard doors until he was certain it was as bad as it appeared.

"What," he asked, leaning against the counter and folding his arms, "have you been living on?"

"I haven't had a chance to get to the store," she said, not wanting to admit that she found it difficult to spend his money.

"There isn't even a can of soup in this house."

All the pain Emily had felt over the past weeks concerning that very thing, rose and hit her in the throat. She moved toward the front room before he could see it surface. Michael almost felt angry as he realized that was the second time this afternoon she'd walked out on him. He moved quickly to catch her by the arm and forced her to face him, oblivious to Penny sitting on the floor with Amee, who was building a tower out of blocks.

"I asked you a question," he insisted. "Ryan might have let you walk out of a room without facing an issue, but I won't have it. If you were that destitute, I want to know why you didn't write to me a month ago and get some help."

"It's not as easy as all that, Michael. I couldn't just—"

"Why not?" he interrupted.

"You have never been without money, Michael. You have no right to judge what has been going on here."

"All right, so maybe I don't," he agreed. Penny attempted to slither away, but Michael stopped her. "You sit down and stay right where you are. I want a witness here." Penny dutifully sat and looked on in amazement as he continued.

"We have established that I am a spoiled, rich boy. So be it. I have no right to judge the situation here. So be it. But I have a right to do something about it, and I will. From this moment forward, money is not an issue between us. I don't care if it's another five years before we are married, I consider myself the provider for this family. If we're going to argue about money, we can argue about whether to spend it at K-Mart or Shopko. But I will see that the needs of this family are met, and I will not tolerate anything less than your full support of my taking that responsibility. We will consult each other in all financial decisions, and once we are married I will have you as my equal beneficiary in all things. Until that time, there will be no going without anything under this roof. Do I make myself clear?"

Emily said nothing.

"I think it was pretty clear," Penny stated.

"Who asked you?" Emily snapped.

"He did." Penny pointed at Michael, who was moving toward the door.

"Where are you going?" Emily insisted, almost panicked.

"I'm going to the grocery store, with or without your permission, Mrs. Hall."

"Wait. Let me go. I need to get . . ."

"What?"

"Diapers and . . . other things."

"What things?"

"Personal things."

"Like what?" he asked in exasperation.

Not feeling the embarrassment of a new relationship that Emily felt, Penny stated simply, "She means feminine things."

"Oh, hush!" Emily demanded. "I can go shopping for myself."

"I'm a grown man with a sister, Emily. I think I can manage. Is there anything else you need?"

"A little of everything, I'd say," Penny observed. Emily scowled at her.

"Fine," Michael said and left them alone.

"Thanks a lot," Emily said tersely.

"Didn't you hear what he said?" Penny retorted, coming to her feet. "I have a hard time believing that you, of all people, are having such a problem with humility."

"Humiliation is more like it."

"Just open your heart and accept the blessings, Emily. You prayed for help and you're getting it. Lighten up!" Emily was speechless.

Michael stuck his head back in the door as if he'd forgotten something. His words to Penny had no hint of the anger he'd conveyed a minute ago. "You busy tonight, Penny?"

"No. Did you need a babysitter?"

"No, I need guinea pigs. How many mouths do you think you can produce who would be willing to try my cooking?"

"If you mean my husband and five children, they love food. It's their hobby."

"Good. We'll see you at seven." He pointed a finger at Emily and winked. "I'll see you a little sooner than that."

"I guess he told me," Penny quipped, moving toward the door. "And I think he told you, too."

"It would seem that way," Emily admitted, then she smiled. "I'll see you at seven, Penny."

"Should I bring something?"

"Just all those guinea pigs. I'm certain he'll have it under control."

"Between you and me," Penny asked, halfway out the door, "can the man cook?"

Emily's eyes filled with nostalgia. "He's superb. 'Chef' was just below 'writer' on his list of things he wanted to be when he grew up. He used to cook dinner once a week for me and my roommates. It was the highlight of our lives."

"Oooh," Penny lifted her brows quickly, "this could be fun."

"Where Penny?" Amee asked from the back of the couch where she looked out the window.

"Penny went home," Emily informed.

"Where Mikow?"

"Michael's gone crazy."

"No," Amee giggled, "Mikow go to stow."

Emily laughed and hugged her. "A two year old could get into a lot of trouble being so smart."

"Amee pwitty," the child announced.

"Yes, Amee is beautiful." Emily gingerly touched the nearly-healed stitches above her eye. "How is Amee's owee today?"

"Amee got a owee. Amee faw down."

Alexa cried from the other room and Amee jumped off her mother's lap.

"What baby do? Baby cry? Baby wake?"

Emily followed Amee to get the baby while she contemplated her argument with Michael. She was surprised that she felt no anxiety. Arguments in the past had always left her with sick knots in her stomach, while a tension hovered over the house for hours, or even days. Issues were rarely resolved, only forgotten in order to go on living, until they came up again with renewed intensity. Emily knew that Ryan had not intended to make it that way, but it had been nonetheless.

Yet here, in a matter of minutes, the anger had been released and it was over. She found another big difference, as well. When Michael argued with her, he was usually trying to convince her that she was too hard on herself, that she didn't give herself enough credit. His anger came from wanting her to be happy, to be provided for, to buy herself something. Emily actually emerged from arguments with

Michael feeling better about herself instead of degraded.

With Alexa's diaper changed, Emily took the babies to the kitchen to see what she might be able to find for a snack. She straightened what little was in the fridge and cupboards, knowing Michael would return with groceries. Her mind went to Ryan, and she couldn't deny the ache she felt at his absence. Still, with Michael's commitment to support the family, and the evidence of their solid relationship before her, Emily realized it would be futile to try and hold back for the sake of propriety or some sense of abstract dedication to her dead husband. She had needed Michael enough six months ago to contemplate leaving her husband. Surely, then, her desire to get on with her life now was something Ryan would understand. And surely the occasional stab of pain and confusion would go away with time.

She thought of Michael, and a recently familiar flutter engulfed her. Delighted by the sensation, Emily rubbed her arms in an attempt to be rid of a sudden rush of goose bumps. Then she glanced at the clock, hoping he wouldn't be too long.

CHAPTER TWO

"Hi, Mom, I'm home." Allison swung the door closed behind her.

"Hi yourself. How was school, sweetie?"

"Fine," she answered as usual.

"Any problems?"

"No. What's for dinner? We're not going to have macaroni and cheese, are we?"

"No, actually Michael went to the store. He's going to cook dinner." Allison looked skeptical; but then her father had never "cooked" anything more than a peanut butter sandwich. "He's really a good cook, and he likes to do it. I won't complain. Whatever he makes will be better than macaroni and cheese." Allison still looked dubious. "Penny's family is coming over for dinner. Why don't you get your reading done now, then you can enjoy the rest of the evening. Do you have homework?"

"A little. I'll go do it." Allison glumly went to her room, and Emily followed.

"Is everything all right, Allie?" she asked gently.

"Yeah."

"Are you excited about the party tomorrow?"

"Yeah," she admitted, brightening a bit. "I thought I'd wear my new clothes—the ones Michael bought me."

"That's a good idea." Emily paused. "By the way, what do you think of Michael?"

Allison looked up anxiously. "He's nice."

"Does it make you feel uncomfortable to have him around?"

"No," she said sincerely, "I just miss Dad."

"I miss him, too, Allison. That's one reason I enjoy having Michael here. I don't feel so lonely."

Emily expected some concern in response to her statement, but Allison surprised her. "He has a lot of money, doesn't he?"

"Yes, he does," she admitted, "and I believe he wants very much to help us out that way. But that's not the reason I want him here."

"You like him, don't you?" Allison seemed dismayed.

Emily decided on honesty. "I like him very much, Allison. This might be difficult for you to understand, but Michael and I were very close long before I married your father. I married your father because I loved him, and I knew he was the right man for me at the time. But now that he is gone, I have been very lonely, just like you have, and I am grateful for Michael's friendship. Michael doesn't want to take your father's place. He just enjoys being with us because he's lonely, too. He's older than your father was and he's never had a family, except for his mother and his sister. His father died when he was quite young. I think he likes to be here with us. I think it makes him happy, just like it made him happy to buy us those things last week."

Allison contemplated this for several moments, then said, "I think I'll get my homework done."

Emily tried to smile, wishing she had a clue to what her daughter was feeling. "All right. I'll go check on the babies."

A short while later, Michael came through the back door unannounced, arms loaded with groceries that he deposited on the table. He stopped for a moment and just looked at Emily. She smiled timidly, wondering if he still had trouble believing this was real, just as she did.

"Hello, my love," he said, then turned and went out to the car for more groceries. Emily watched in amazement as he returned again and again, when each time she thought it would be the last. He covered the counters, the bar, the table and much of the kitchen floor with bagged goods. The babies began investigating the contents of the crinkly sacks while Michael loaded the fridge, humming a familiar melody as he did.

He looked up at Emily, who was gaping in disbelief. "Well, don't just stand there. I don't know where most of this stuff goes."

Emily began to unload sacks, finding everything she could imagine. There was soap, toilet paper, toothpaste, cleaning products, shampoo, dish and laundry detergent, fabric softener, hand lotion, and yes, a small cache of feminine items that she was in desperate need of. Emily found cans of soup and fruit and vegetables, flour and sugar (regular, powdered, and brown), and boxes of cereal and crackers and snacks.

The babies began making a mess of the purchases and Emily called to Allison, who came running. "Do you think you could keep your sisters occupied while we put this stuff away?" she asked. Allison's eyes went wide with wonder at the scene before her, but she said nothing as she eased the babies away with practiced expertise.

Emily opened the freezer to put in some frozen juice and found packages of beef and chicken and pork; frozen waffles and vegetables; popsicles and ice cream. In the fridge were four gallons of milk, margarine, butter, eggs, and cold-cuts. Fresh vegetables filled the crisper drawer. She found three types of cheese, sour cream, cream cheese, and two kinds of jam. Turning around, she nearly stumbled over the three bags of Huggies.

"I hope those are the right size," he said absently. "I figured she felt like a medium-sized baby to me."

"They're perfect," she said. "I usually buy a cheaper brand, but these are better because . . ."

"They have these cute little pictures on them," he answered quite seriously.

"Michael," Emily sighed, exhausted from just trying to take it all in, "I can't believe this. I don't think I've ever had so much food in my house at one time in my whole life."

"Well, it's about time you did. Obviously you didn't have any food storage."

"Not enough to last very long."

"Well," he smiled up at her from where he was systematically arranging cans in a lower cupboard, "when we get to Australia, you won't have to worry about that. We have this little system set up, you see. It began with my great-grandfather, Jess Davies. He spent many years struggling just to make ends meet, and he nearly lost his land several times. After he finally got on his feet, and soon thereafter inherited the Byrnehouse fortune, he decided that he would never let his family be left in a position of need. Back then the station was hours by horseback to the nearest town, which now is a much shorter drive by car, as you remember."

"It was long enough."

"Well, yes, that's my point. Being isolated as they were, Jess set up a system of storing and rotating food. In the years since, we have added other features of self-sufficiency. We have power sources of wind and sun, and enough fuel stored to heat all the buildings for two years. The food supplies are rotated continually, but there is enough to feed fifty people for two years."

"Fifty?" Emily gasped.

"It's not so unreasonable." He moved to another cupboard. "We average twenty to twenty-five residents in the boys' home, plus the faculty. We have stable hands and other employees affiliated with the breeding and training. Then of course the family, and a few that help around the house. On the average, we're regularly feeding more like sixty or so. But we know we could survive for at least a year if the need arose."

"But you would never be totally stranded with all those horses."

"No, I suppose we wouldn't. But a city could be depleted quickly if . . . well, I'm not living for doomsday, but I like having a sense of security."

"So do I," Emily admitted readily, looking around her at the evidence of the windows of heaven.

"I can't cook with all that stuff in here," Michael said lightly, indicating the items that went to the laundry room and bathroom. Emily called Allison in and loaded her arms for a trip to the bathroom. She sent Michael to the basement with the laundry products, since the soap was a heavier package than she had ever purchased before. He returned to find her putting things in final order, then she turned the kitchen over to him while Allison returned to her homework.

"Can I help?" Emily asked. "No," he answered with a firm smile. "Why don't you go play with your babies or read a book or something. I dare say you've spent far too much time in the kitchen the last ten years."

"I don't usually mind," she said. "Besides, I don't think I could find anything to compare with the last book I read. It was written by this handsome Australian . . . "

"I can't cook and write at the same time," he grinned. "It's a nice day. Go for a walk or something, and let me cook."

Emily took his advice and loaded the babies into the stroller. She walked through the neighborhood, stopping to visit with an elderly sister who was grooming marigolds in her yard. Emily found she was enjoying the early autumn scenery, feeling it in a way she hadn't been able to with the oppression of financial strain that had weighed upon her.

Allison finished her homework and went to the kitchen to find Michael with a dishtowel tucked into the front of his jeans while he pressed a graham-cracker crust into a pie plate.

"Hi," Michael said. "Did you have any more enlightening conversations with your friends today?"

"They just talked about the party tomorrow," she said idly.

"Ashley's big day, eh?"

"She'll be eleven."

"And you'll be ten soon, I bet."

"Next month."

"And what do you want to do for *your* birthday?" Michael asked casually, while he observed her every expression and voice intonation.

"I don't know. Mom usually lets me have some friends over for games and stuff."

"Ten is a pretty special number, though," he said. "Maybe you should do something different this year."

"Like what?"

"I don't know, but we'll think about it. Maybe you'd like to go somewhere you've never been, or do something you've never done. Can you think of anything like that?"

"I always wanted to see the Grand Canyon."

"That sounds interesting. Would you like to go there?"

"No," she said tersely. Michael was surprised in light of her last statement.

"Why not?"

"Dad was going to take us there. I don't want to see it if he won't be there."

"I guess I can understand that."

"How old were you when your dad died?" Allison asked, and Michael had to stop what he was doing for a moment. "Mom told me your dad died when you were a kid."

"I was eleven," he answered.

"Did he die in a car accident?"

"No, he got cancer when I was eight, and was very ill after that. He finally died three years later. It's not very fun, is it?"

"No." Allison looked thoughtful.

"Want to talk about it?"

"No."

"Well, if you ever decide you want to, let me know. I remember well what it felt like. My dad and I spent a lot of time together with the horses. When he got sick I felt so lonely, and when he died I just felt empty inside. But I had my mother and my sister, and I still had the horses."

Allison said nothing.

"Do you like horses, Allison?"

"I don't know. I've only seen them on T.V."

"That sounds like your mother." He smiled, certain that Emily at this age must have looked much the same. "She'd never touched a horse until I took her to Australia." He finished what he was doing with the crusts and looked until he found the mixer. "I taught her to ride."

"She never told me about that," Allison said.

"That doesn't surprise me."

"Did she like it?"

"I guess you'd have to ask her. She seemed to."

"Do you have very many horses?"

"A few."

"Can I help?" Allison nodded toward his cooking project.

"Sure. You can pour this milk in here and mix this. Careful not to splatter it."

Allison did the chore efficiently, and Michael could tell she had helped in the kitchen before. When the noise of the mixer was finished, Allison asked, "What do you do with your horses? Are they just for fun, to ride and stuff?"

Michael smiled. "Oh, they're a lot of fun, but they're also a very big business. My family has been in the horse business since the 1870s. We breed and train them, for racing and other such things."

"What's 'breed'?" she asked like she might have questioned the presence of clouds in the sky.

Michael smiled. "That's making baby horses." Allison gave an understanding nod and Michael put dessert in the fridge to chill. "Maybe you would like to learn to ride a horse for your tenth birthday," Michael suggested while he began cutting vegetables.

"Maybe," she said noncommittally.

"Here," Michael pushed a bowl and a clean head of lettuce across the bar, "could I get you to tear that into little pieces for a salad?"

"Okay, but why don't you just cut it?"

"It makes a nicer salad, and it stays fresh longer," he explained. She said nothing more, but Michael observed her unobtrusively, trying to comprehend the reality that he would be acting as this child's father for the rest of his life. He happened to look up and see her stop her work briefly while a grimace came over her face.

"Is something wrong?" he asked.

"No." She looked surprised that he'd noticed. "I'm all right."

Michael took it at face value and continued to work in peaceable silence until Emily came in, carrying Alexa and holding Amee's hand.

"How do you rate?" Emily said to Allison. "He wouldn't let me help."

"You're not as cute," Michael said to Emily, winking when Allison wasn't looking.

"I think I'll go rest for a while," Allison said and left.

Emily showed concern as she set the babies free to play. "How's it going?"

"Fine. Allison and I had a little chat."

"Any progress?"

"At least she speaks to me," was all he said.

"Michael, I've been thinking, and . . ."

"Yes?" he prodded when she hesitated.

"Well, I guess there is nothing here except my friendship with Penny and some other minor associations. I want to put it behind me. You said we could have our passports and visas in a month or so. I want to leave just as soon as possible. There's a lot to do, but . . . well, what do you think?"

Michael stopped and leaned his palms on the counter. "I told you it was up to you."

"But I don't know anything about your plans or obligations or—"

"My plans and obligations at this time depend on you. Anything else is flexible." He paused deliberately. "I'm not going back to Australia until I take you with me."

Emily gave a visible sigh.

"But," he continued thoughtfully, feeling it was something he needed to say, "I've seen some pretty strong emotions toward Ryan." Emily looked down guiltily. "Are you certain you're ready to put it behind you?"

Michael waited while she thought about it—far too long, in his opinion. The reality at moments was a little unnerving.

"Michael," she said quietly, "I admit, there are moments when I feel a bit . . . torn, perhaps. But . . . I need you. I was almost willing to leave him six months ago to marry you; surely there should be no problem with marrying you now. There are some things to deal with, but I see no reason why we can't face them together."

Michael nodded, feeling peace in what she'd said. After losing her twice, he was almost afraid to leave the country without her.

"Do you want to get married here or in Australia?" she asked matter-of-factly.

Michael smiled. He'd had no idea what to expect from her. He figured the healing after a death was relative to a person's individual needs, and he was willing to respect that. But for himself it had already been too long. He'd wanted to marry her eleven years ago. What she said narrowed it down to a matter of weeks, and the thought filled him with incomparable joy—a joy he never would have felt had he married her long ago, when it would have been easy.

With purpose he came around the bar. He took her hand, then decided it wasn't enough and reached further to hold her arm. Emily held her breath and looked up into his eyes as his arm came around her waist. For a long moment he just studied her face. She heard pulsebeats in her ears as her arms moved by their own will around his back to hold him closer. A thousand thoughts tumbled through her mind, but life seemed to fall perfectly into place as he bent to kiss her.

He kissed her meekly at first, then drew back slightly to check her response. Tentatively he brought his fingertips to her face, marveling at its softness, when it looked as fragile as porcelain. He idly brushed a thumb over her lips as if to test them, then he pulled her impossibly closer and pressed his mouth there in its place.

Years flew while time stood motionless. Michael tried to remember how long it had been since he'd kissed her like this. But then, he had never kissed her like this. In college he had tried so hard to hold back, fearing he might offend her or be tempted to get carried away. Just last spring, when he had begged her to leave Ryan, it had been tainted with guilt and agony. But now it was different. He kissed her undaunted, over and over. Eleven years of aching and longing passed into her and back again.

Michael was relieved to feel no evidence that she might be holding back or still caught up in feelings for Ryan. He pushed a hand into her hair, threading his fingers into it, marveling at the reality. It all felt so familiar, and yet so new. With his eyes closed, he could believe they were college sweethearts and nothing more. But this was not the girl who had meekly and innocently accepted his affection then. This was a woman with the experience of marriage and real life behind her. He found himself wondering what she knew that he didn't, and the adrenalin rose like a thermometer in the hot Australian sun. He reminded himself of their values, and swore he would do nothing prior to their marriage that might bring pain into their lives. Instead he concentrated on the future before them, a life so full he couldn't begin to comprehend it. There were no words to describe all he felt now. He could only kiss her and hope she felt it, too.

While Emily considered herself reasonably knowledgeable in matters of affection, she couldn't recall ever being kissed in a way that so completely consumed her. Everything emotional and spiritual whirled together in delicate combination with the taut awareness of her every nerve. Could she be so blessed, to spend the future with this man who fulfilled her every need? Their kiss seemed to go on and on until she breathlessly eased her lips away, fearing she could bear no more without crossing boundaries she knew they couldn't—yet.

"I love you, Michael," she whispered, burrowing her face into his neck, inhaling the scent of his shaving lotion that was so much a part of him. The stubble on his face scratched her tender skin, reminding her of how good it felt to have a man in her life again. Michael lifted her chin and kissed her again. "If it's all the same to you," he said softly, touching her face, her hair, as if for the first time, "I want to marry you in the spot where three generations before me have been married."

"Australia would be fine," she replied breathily.

Michael kissed her again. "And in a year, I'll take you to the temple."

"That would be wonderful." Emily kissed him in return.

"We'll leave here soon, my love. As soon as we can."

"There's so much to do." She pushed a hand into his hair and another over his shoulder. "I've got to get started right away."

"I'll help you." He kissed her brow, her eyelids. "We'll work together."

"It feels so good, Michael." She lifted her lips to his.

"So right."

"We've waited so long."

Michael kissed her again, drawing it out until he finally forced himself away with a reluctant, "I fear our dinner will burn, Mrs. Hall."

Emily giggled and stepped back, setting both hands to her flushed face.

Michael bent forward to kiss her once more, then he couldn't resist pulling her into his arms to just hold her. "You know," he spoke softly near her ear, "when I stop to think that I'm actually a Mormon, and I can share all of it with you, I can still hardly believe it."

Emily looked up at him, a smile of peace warming the corners of her mouth. "It is wonderful."

His eyes sparkled. "And when I think that you and I can go to the temple together, and be sealed—forever—I can hardly comprehend the . . ." Michael stopped when her eyes went wide with a look nothing short of terror. "What?" he insisted quietly. She tried to move out of his reach but he wouldn't let her. "What did I say?" His voice became sharp. His eyes reflected the panic she tried to conceal but couldn't.

"I . . ." Emily forced the one syllable out, but it was all her voice would give.

"What?" he demanded, holding her tighter as if it might force the words out of her.

"I . . . just . . ." Emily stammered helplessly as tears rose in her eyes and her heart beat painfully. How could she tell him? How could she possibly bring herself to say it?

"Emily!" Michael's frustration merged into anger.

"I just . . . assumed . . . that you . . . knew . . . I mean . . . maybe I took for granted that . . . you did or . . ." The tears spilled and she wiped at them helplessly, wishing he would let her go. He stared at her with a dazed kind of fear etched into his face, and she realized he wouldn't relinquish his hold until he got an explanation. She took a deep breath and made another attempt.

"I'm sorry, Michael. I just . . . never thought about it. I mean . . . when I agreed to marry you . . . I didn't know you'd been . . . baptized . . . and . . ." The emotion overtook Emily and she hung her head and cried, unable to look at him.

"What on earth are you talking about?" he demanded, his patience gone. He shook her gently and she forced herself to look up. "Just say it!"

Emily took a deep breath and swallowed hard. "We can't be sealed, Michael."

His eyes narrowed and his brow furrowed tightly. The deep instinct that told him they were meant to be together forever made him certain she was wrong. He chuckled and shook his head, not willing to believe it. "Why not?" he asked, almost daring her to prove it.

Emily took a step back, relieved at least that he had relaxed his grip. "I am already sealed to one man, Michael. I can't be sealed to another." She choked back a sob and grabbed a dishtowel to wipe her tears. "You took all those religion classes; surely you knew that—"

"In the next life," he stated with confidence, "a man can have more than one wife. That's why the—"

"But not the other way around," she interrupted. He looked stunned. She bit her lip then clarified, "A woman cannot have more than one husband."

Michael tried to ignore the way his heart fell to the pit of his stomach. He stuffed his hands into his pockets and looked at the floor, hoping she wouldn't see the anguish in his expression.

"I see," he said with a cold voice that defied all he felt inside. He didn't want to admit to the confusion welling up in him. But when he looked up at Emily he knew he had to.

"I'm a little . . . confused here, Emily. Everything felt so right, but now I . . ."

Emily held her breath when he faltered. "What are you saying?" she croaked. He hesitated still and she had to ask, "If you're trying to tell me that you're having doubts about marrying me, then—"

"Oh, no." His eyes went wide and he rushed forward to take her arms into his hands. "That's not it at all, and don't think for a minute that it is."

Emily sighed visibly, at the same time praying that she would know what to say. She found she was having trouble herself with the reality, but her concern was for Michael. His membership in the Church was new and fragile. Their relationship was the same in many respects. But at least she didn't have to wonder if he loved her. The conviction in his eyes as he went on made that evident.

"It's just that I . . . I became a part of this church because it all felt so right. But I'm having trouble with this, Emily. Am I supposed to be content to have you in this life alone? I have a hard time believing that God would—"

"Why did you join the Church, Michael?" Her tone was severe.

"Because I knew it was true," he said without hesitation.

"Is it any less true now than it was when you received that witness from the Spirit?"

Michael sighed. "No."

"Do you believe that we, in our mortal state, could possibly comprehend why God does things the way he does?"

"No," he answered again.

Emily touched his face and looked into his eyes. "Michael, I don't believe it's a coincidence that you and I are here together again after all these years. I can't say that I understand all of this. I haven't even had a chance to really think about it in relation to myself. But I do know that God is just and fair. We have a lifetime to prove ourselves worthy of sharing eternity. We will receive the rewards we live for. Surely God would not deny us the right to be together if we live for that blessing."

Michael contemplated it a moment, then pulled her into his arms as if he feared he might lose her. What she'd said made sense, and it felt right, but he couldn't deny the twinge of confusion still smoldering inside him. He told himself it would take time to accept this and understand it. And time was something they had plenty of. He would not let it mar the happiness he was finding with her after all these years.

"We should tell Allison," he said, wanting a distraction.

"What?" She looked up at him, disoriented.

"That we're getting married." He smiled, but she sensed the tension still hovering in his eyes.

"With all there is to do, she's got to know."

"Do you want to tell her yourself, or—"

"I want you with me. Let's tell her now."

"Just a minute." Michael hesitantly let her go to check the progress of dinner, then he followed Emily down the hall where she knocked quietly at Allison's door.

"Allison." Emily peered in to find her lying on her bed. "Michael and I want to tell you something. Can we come in?"

Allison sat up and made no protest. Emily led Michael by the hand into the room. Emily sat beside Allison on the bed and took her hand. Michael squatted down in front of them.

"Allison, you know I talked to you earlier about how long Michael and I have been friends." Allison nodded. "And you know how difficult it has been for us since your father died."

Allison looked warily at Michael as if she sensed something was coming that she didn't want to hear. "Sweetie," Emily continued,

"Michael has asked me to marry him. He wants to take us to Australia to live with him. He'll take good care of us. I believe we can all be happy there."

Emily allowed her daughter time to absorb this information. She put her other hand into Michael's while they waited for a reaction. Allison looked deeply at her mother and asked, "Is it because of the money?"

Emily glanced to Michael in search of support.

"Allison," he said gently. "I care very much for your mother. Whether or not she made the decision to marry me, I would make certain that you have the money you need to live comfortably."

Emily took over. "The reasons I want to marry Michael have nothing to do with money, Allison. What he has to offer in that respect will make our lives easier, and I am grateful for that, but there is only one real reason that I am going to marry Michael. It's because I love him. I love him very much."

"As much as Daddy?" she asked, defying her quiet nature.

Again Emily glanced to Michael. His eyes were full of understanding, but tinged with a subtle doubt. Emily wondered what to say, but quickly decided that the truth was her only option. Allison was an intelligent girl. She had observed much in her young life, and there was no good trying to deceive her.

"At least as much as Daddy," Emily said gently. Allison's brow furrowed and she continued quickly. "I loved your father very much, Allison, but you know that there were things between us that caused difficulties. Those things had nothing to do with you. You and your sisters are the most wonderful things that ever happened to me. Your father was changing before he died, Allison, but whether he had changed or not, I would have always loved him, if only because you are a part of him. I love Michael, too. I love him because he is a good man and he makes me happy."

Allison looked again at Michael in silent contemplation.

"Your father loved you very much, Allison." Michael quietly took Allison's hand and was relieved when she didn't reject his effort. "I don't want to take his place. I just want to take care of you, and your mother, and Amee and Alexa, too. I think if we live together like a family, we can all be happy. What do you think?"

"I guess so," she said tonelessly.

"Would you like to go to Australia, Allison?" Michael added.

"I don't know." She turned to Emily. "Mom, I think I have a stomach ache."

The timing made Emily wonder if it was just an excuse to be left alone, or perhaps a reaction of nerves. She said with empathy, "Does it hurt badly?"

"Kind of."

"You lie down some more and maybe it will go away. I'll check on you again before dinner. If you need anything, let me know."

Allison nodded and lay back down. Michael followed Emily into the hall, where he stopped her with his hand on her arm.

"You all right?" he whispered. She nodded firmly but Michael could see the concern. "She'll not want for anything, Emily; most especially love and guidance."

Emily put her arms around Michael and hugged him tightly, hoping he knew how much that meant to her.

CHAPTER THREE

"What I wouldn't give to know what she's thinking," Emily said as she pulled dishes out of the cupboard and Michael slid a pan into the oven.

"I'm not sure she's terribly fond of me," Michael replied. "But I suppose it's to be expected under the circumstances. All we can do is tread carefully and be patient."

The babies started to scream in a struggle over a toy, and Emily hurried off to referee.

Penny's family arrived a few minutes after seven. Emily was setting dishes out on the bar to serve the meal buffet style, since there wasn't enough room for everyone to sit around the table. Penny's children, except for Heather, who was with friends, gathered around the babies as they always did, which left Emily free.

Penny brought her husband into the kitchen for introductions and inhaled deeply. "It smells . . . Italian."

"I love Italian," Bret commented. Michael grinned as he stirred the contents of a large pot.

"Michael," Penny said, "this is my husband, Bret Millner. Bret, this is Michael Hamilton."

Michael wiped his hand on the dishtowel hanging in front of him and reached out to accept the handshake. "It's a pleasure to meet you, Bret. I understand your family is to credit for keeping Emily sane these days."

"Boy, that's an understatement," Emily added.

"Ah," Bret said sheepishly, "we're just there. Penny does all the doing." Bret put his hands in his pockets and leaned against the counter. It was obvious he felt comfortable in this house. Michael wondered if Bret and Ryan had been close in any way. "I read your books, Michael," he said. "I managed to get hold of them after Emily loaned them to Penny. I must say I really enjoyed them."

"Thank you," Michael said humbly. "Let's hope you enjoy my cooking as much."

"So, you're from Australia," Bret said, as it was impossible to hear Michael speak and not be aware of the fact.

"The great 'Down Under'," Michael quipped.

"I hear it has some incredible country."

"That it does. You should drop by sometime and see it."

"Let's do that," Bret said to Penny. "We'll farm the kids out and just hop a plane."

"Were you going to buy the tickets with your good looks and charm?" Penny retorted.

"Sure," Bret grinned.

Michael exchanged a warm glance with Emily and decided to bring up something that he was certain they were already aware of. "You could come down for the wedding."

"Are you making the announcement official?" Penny asked.

Emily smiled at Michael, ignoring the subtle tension still hanging in the air around them. "I suppose we are."

"That's nice," Bret said. "We've all been hoping Emily wouldn't be alone too long."

"We?" Emily questioned.

"Everybody. It's one of the best topics of gossip in the ward these days."

"I see," Emily said, only slightly irritated. She knew that by gossip he really meant concern, but she wasn't certain she liked being the topic of casual conversation.

"Have you set a date?" Penny asked, then she spoke more directly to Michael. "Can we help with something here? We're good at standing around like a couple of dead trees."

"He doesn't like help," Emily observed.

"She's right. I'm pretty independent in the kitchen. You stand there like trees and keep me company, and I'll have this ready in a few minutes."

"You were saying." Bret nodded toward Penny.

It took her a moment to remember. "Oh. Have you set a date to get married?"

"I guess we'll do that when we get to Australia," Michael stated. "Emily and the children have to get passports and visas, which can be a little unpredictable. If everything goes well, we could have them in a month, but we can't count on it."

"A month?" Penny sounded panicked. Emily gave her an empathetic smile. "And you're really getting married there?"

"I said you could come," Michael insisted.

"Very funny," Penny retorted and Michael grinned.

"In the meantime," Emily said, "we have a lot to do." A new thought occurred to her. "Michael, exactly how does one go about moving to Australia? It's not exactly like moving to the next town."

Michael continued to work as he spoke. He'd already carefully thought this through. "You pack up everything of sentimental or personal value that cannot be replaced, and we have it shipped over, except for the bare necessities you need for the journey. Anything else stays. The house is already fully furnished and equipped, and we can buy anything you might need once we get there."

"You mean like a new wardrobe?" Penny asked. Emily glared at her.

Michael chuckled. "I'd rather buy her a new wardrobe than ship the old one. But it's up to Emily what she wants to take with her."

"That means I have to go through this house with a fine-tooth comb, get everything sorted and in order so I know exactly what is what." She sighed. "This is not going to be fun. I've got ten years of accumulated clutter in this house."

"I think it sounds great," Penny said with enthusiasm.

Bret added to Michael, "Clutter is her hobby."

"She told me earlier that food was yours," Michael grinned slyly and Bret chuckled.

"I have a question, Michael," Emily said. "What exactly do we do with everything that stays?"

"Oh, that's easy," Penny volunteered enthusiastically. "We have a big yard sale, and what we don't sell after worthy effort, we take to D.I."

"I refuse to sit on my lawn and sell my belongings," Emily insisted.

"I'll do it after you go," Penny offered, as if it were a bright side to losing her best friend.

"Sounds good to me," Michael stated.

"But where are you going to put it all?" Bret asked Penny. "Not in my garage."

"We'll pay rent on the house long enough for Penny to do her business," Michael said. "Whatever you make on it can compensate your efforts. How's that?"

"I don't care what I make on it," Penny said. "It'll just be fun."

"I care what you make on it," Bret said. "It might make up for all the money you spent at yard sales this summer."

"Now, Bret," she said with a patronizing smile, "you know you love all the bargains I come home with."

Bret put his hands up in resignation. "I'm not even going to touch that one."

Emily chuckled and said to Michael, who was obviously amused, "They argue like this all the time. That's how you know they like each other."

"I'll have to remember that." He lifted his brows comically. "I think this is ready . . . finally. Send in the troops and we'll serve it up."

Penny gathered the children while Emily helped Michael set out the food.

"Where's Allison?" Penny asked.

"She's lying down," Emily replied. "Would you mind checking on her?"

Allison came to the dining room looking slightly peaked. Michael and Emily exchanged a concerned glance. After Bret offered a blessing, in which he included a request on behalf of Michael and Emily starting a new life together, the meal was served in orderly chaos. Compliments were dished out as abundantly as the spaghetti with perfectly seasoned sauce, thick with sausage and beef and mushrooms. There was colorful green salad with croutons and four choices of dressing, and perfectly toasted garlic bread, hot from the oven. For dessert, Michael served cheesecakes that he apologized were from a package mix, topped with blueberry filling that he apologized was from a can.

"Give me more warning next time," he said, "and I'll really feed you."

Emily realized halfway through the meal that Allison was absent. She found her lying down. "Does it still hurt?" she asked gently, checking for fever but feeling no unusual warmth. Allison nodded. "Show me where," she added and Allison indicated with a grimace when Emily touched it. "Do you feel sick, or does it just hurt?"

"I threw up."

"Why didn't you tell me before?"

"It just happened."

Emily sighed. "You've probably got the stomach flu, Allie."

"Does that mean I can't go to Ashley's party?"

"I guess we'll have to see how you feel tomorrow. Hopefully it's just one of those quick ones that will be over without much trouble. You rest, and I'll check on you in a little while."

Emily went back to finish her meal and found the house unusually quiet. She went to the yard where everyone was sitting on the lawn, eating in the shade of the maple tree. Amee walked around stealing food from anyone who would give her a chance, and Alexa crawled back and forth on the grass, giggling as if it were a great adventure while the children urged her on in amusement. Michael observed the scene with a contentment that deepened when Emily sat beside him. It was easy to momentarily forget that she was mourning for another man—a man she was sealed to.

Emily exchanged a warm glance with Michael, and butterflies flitted into her stomach when she thought of him kissing her earlier in the kitchen. She cleared her throat and looked away, turning her thoughts back to Allison.

"What's wrong?" he asked, noting her expression.

"I think Allison has the flu."

"It's getting worse, I take it."

"She says she threw up, but I can't feel any fever. I hate to say this, but I hope she's not making it up. She's never done anything like that before, but—"

"But you just told her you're getting married and leaving the country. Yes, I see your point. But nerves can cause very real physical symptoms. Chances are she does feel ill."

"It's probably just the flu. I'm sure she'll be fine." Emily moved quickly to pull Alexa from nearly attacking Bret's dinner. "It seems they're enjoying your food," she commented to Michael, sitting beside him again with Alexa on her lap.

"Where's yours?" he asked.

"It's inside. I'll get it in a minute."

Michael immediately set his plate aside and took Alexa. "Go eat your dinner, Emily. I can handle the little beast." Alexa grinned up at him. "Yeah," he said to the baby, providing her with a bite-size piece of bread, "we'll get along just fine. You'd better get used to my cooking now, princess. You're going to grow up on it."

"That's a nice thought," Emily smiled.

"Go get your dinner," he ordered. And she did, unable to help recalling all the meals she had reheated for herself because she had been busy with the babies while Ryan went ahead and ate.

When dessert was finished, Penny put into action a well-practiced assembly line of dishwashers, ranging from eight-year-old Danny to fourteen-year-old Scott, and a couple in between. The kitchen was left spotless under Michael's supervision. He finished by cleaning the sink.

"What are you doing?" Penny asked. It already looked clean to her.

"Can't leave the sink dirty," he said, not bothering to tell her the point he had to make from a college days issue.

The Millner children went their separate ways to play with friends or do homework. The adults sat in the front room to visit while the babies played on the floor.

"So, where you staying?" Bret asked Michael.

"I've got a hotel room in Provo," he answered.

"Are you going back to Australia soon or . . ." Penny began to ask.

"I told Emily I'm not going back until I take her with me."

"Well, you can't stay in a hotel fifteen minutes away for more than a month," Penny protested. "That's silly."

"It's not a problem," Michael insisted. "Really."

"Don't think I'm offering to put you up," Penny retorted, "because I have absolutely no place to put you. But I would think if you're going to spend your days here, there's got to be someplace closer that you can stay."

"I know," Bret pointed at Penny. "We'll call Sister Swann."

"It's perfect," Penny squealed.

Michael looked skeptically toward Emily. She seemed to know what they were talking about, but he wasn't sure if this was necessary. "Really," he insisted, "I'm fine where I am. The money isn't a problem, and the drive is not so bad."

"But, Michael," Penny argued, "you can't know the pleasure you might give Sister Swann if you were to stay there. I know she'd want you without even asking her. She and her husband are always putting people up. It's like a boarding house."

"Not just any people," Bret corrected. "Foreigners."

"That's right. Her hobby is foreigners."

"How quaint," Michael said dryly. "I really think all of you should come to Australia. Then you can be the foreigners."

"Being a foreigner is marvelous," Emily interjected. "When I was there I couldn't open my mouth without people getting really friendly, wanting to know where I was from and all."

"Okay, so being a foreigner is not so bad," Michael admitted, "but I'm not certain I want to be part of somebody's hobby."

"It's not as bad as all that," Penny pressed. "Over the years they've had several foreign exchange students on and off, and somehow they get these connections to have temporary foreign visitors for all kinds of reasons. I think she'd enjoy having you stay. I'm going to talk to her."

"There's no need for that, Penny. Honestly, I'm fine. I don't want to put anybody out. I'm just fine."

Penny made a nondescript noise and the subject was changed to Australia. Michael answered questions about his homeland, keeping the interest in the conversation high. Emily listened and occasionally added a comment, feeling a deep sense of contentment. She gathered nightclothes for the babies and began to undress Alexa. The usual struggle ensued, as the baby would rather do anything than hold still long enough to be dressed. While Michael talked he took Alexa and proceeded with the chore, albeit a bit awkwardly. Emily said nothing. She just grabbed Amee and began to work on her, realizing as she often did, why bedtime was so exhausting.

"Where's a napkin?" Michael asked, interrupting his oratory on an experience at the Melbourne Cup.

"A what?" Emily asked.

"A napkin."

"What do you need a napkin for?"

Michael's eyes narrowed. "Oh, I forgot. It's a . . . what do you call it . . . a . . . you know, those things I bought with the cute little pictures on that . . ."

"Diapers?" Emily wrinkled her nose.

"That's it!" He beamed. "Give me a diaper."

"I'm confused," Penny said.

"In Australia, it's a napkin," Michael said. "I've spent enough time in the states that I've got most of the differences down, but occasionally I embarrass myself."

"If we do go over there," Penny said to Bret, "don't embarrass yourself by asking for a diaper in a restaurant."

"It couldn't be any worse than some of the things I said my first year or two in college," Michael chuckled, then turned to Emily. "I need a diaper, love."

"I can do it," she protested.

"So can I."

"Have you ever put a diaper on a baby in your entire life?" she questioned.

"It's about time I learned, isn't it?"

"Here." Emily gave in and watched with amused interest.

The conversation came to a halt as Michael went carefully through the diapering process, holding Alexa down at the same time. As if it were an important business issue, he commented, "I never comprehended there was such a technology to diapering. This is like saddling a horse on the move."

"You'd know about that," Emily chuckled.

Michael held Alexa up to proudly show the results, and Penny applauded. "Now let's see you get those pajamas on her. I've tended the child."

"I'm not the kind of man to turn down a challenge," he said soberly and proceeded with the task. When Alexa finally broke free, she crawled away with a giggle, snug in faded pink pajamas. Michael gave a quick, triumphant grin toward Penny, who applauded again.

"Does that qualify me to be a stepfather?" he asked Emily.

"No, but it helps."

It was Bret who said, "Ryan wouldn't change a diaper unless it was desperate and there was absolutely no one else he could talk into doing it."

Penny gave him a terse glance and he shrugged his shoulders. They both missed the long glance Emily gave Michael that said more than words how much she appreciated his attitude.

With the Millners departed and the babies in bed, Emily went to check on Allison and found her sleeping. She returned to the front room to find Michael standing by the window, silhouetted against the glow of a single lamp, his eyes distant, almost sad.

"Are you okay?" she asked gently.

Michael wanted to tell her he was fine, but he couldn't bring himself to lie. Without looking at her he answered, "I'm just . . . disappointed."

"About the sealing." There was no need to guess.

"It just seems so *unfair*." The words erupted in a burst, tinged with anger.

Emily tried for several moments to think of something to say— anything that might console him. When she came up empty, all she could do was sink onto the couch with a deep sigh.

"I'm sorry, Michael," she finally said when the silence became unbearable.

"Sorry?" he echoed, turning away from the window. "What on earth are you apologizing for?"

Emily pushed her hair back with a trembling hand. "If I had left him . . ." Her voice was almost a whisper. ". . . it would have been different."

Michael gave an emotional cough. "*That* is totally irrelevant to any of this. Not only is it in the past, we both know you had to stay. We did the right thing."

"If we did the right thing," she met his eyes and the irony was almost tangible, "then why should we be punished for it? Shouldn't I be blessed . . . for being obedient . . . for sticking it out?" Her voice turned husky with emotion. "I want to be with you forever, Michael."

"Maybe that's not the way it's meant to be," he stated almost coldly.

Emily couldn't find the words to tell him that she didn't believe that. But how could she approach the matter with conviction when a part of her still felt torn?

"I suppose it's an issue of faith," she finally said. "We have to trust in God and know that everything will be all right in the end."

"I suppose that's all we can do."

Their eyes met and for a moment Emily thought he was going to cry. He looked away abruptly and blinked several times. Emily stood beside him and touched his face. "Michael, we have our whole lives ahead of us. We must be grateful for that."

"Yes," he agreed, his eyes softening with his voice, "you're right." He took a deep breath and eased her into his arms. "Oh, Emily, I'm sorry. I am truly blessed to have you back in my life. Don't ever let me forget that."

Emily looked up at him and smiled serenely. "It's the other way around, my love."

"I suppose I should go," Michael said as he forced himself to take a step back.

"I don't want you to," she said, "but I guess you're right."

"We're Mormons, Emily. We have to be good." He smiled down at her. "Did you catch that? I said *we*."

"I caught it." She smiled back. "But you were always good."

"I tried, but we Mormons know better than to be alone together without babies to chaperone."

He looked at her deeply and Emily felt a flutter inside that made the prospect of marrying him all the more inviting. She thought back to his standards when they had been dating in college, and she admired him for sticking strongly to values that had nothing to do with religion. He simply had a respect for what was proper.

"All right," he cleared his throat tensely, "I'm leaving. If you didn't stand there looking so pretty, making me feel so . . . " he grinned, "well, you know."

"Do I?" she asked coyly. He'd always been so guarded on such things that she had to wonder.

"You'd better believe it," he said ardently, and her respect for him deepened as he implied that it took a good bit of willpower to stick to those values. It also added to the security of her future to know that he felt for her as she did for him, in spite of his disappointment.

"Thanks for dinner, Michael." She followed him to the door. "And everything else."

"Thanks for being my fiancée and leaving everything behind to become a foreigner." He kissed her brow and touched her face. "I'll see you in the morning."

"Come for breakfast. I think I can find something to cook."

"I'll see you early," he promised.

Emily got ready for bed, then sat to read the Book of Mormon for a few minutes. Habitually she checked the children again before turning in. She tucked a blanket over each of the babies, knowing it was futile with all the wiggling they did. She expected to find Allison asleep, but immediately heard a moan as she pushed open the door. Following the illumination of the hall light, she knelt by Allison's bed.

"What is it, sweetie? Does it still hurt?"

"It's worse," Allison whimpered.

Emily felt certain now it wasn't imaginary, but she had known many a stomach flu to cause great pain.

"Do you want me to lie here by you?" she asked and Allison nodded. Emily left the hall light on and crawled into bed to hold Allison close. As her daughter relaxed, Emily gradually fell asleep. Some time later, she was awakened by a more vehement whimper. Recalling that she'd forgotten her evening prayer, Emily squeezed her eyes shut and silently filled her mind with private conversation with her Father in Heaven. The moment she thought the *amen*, Allison's exclamation of pain put Emily on her feet to turn on the light.

"Allison, show me where it hurts."

Allison showed her and Emily pressed gently, only to have her cry out in anguish. Panic hit Emily in the throat. This was not stomach flu. She didn't know what it was, but she knew what it wasn't. Trying to think what to do, all she could feel was confusion. With Allison's hand in hers, she knelt by the bedside and prayed again, this time aloud.

Emily rose from her knees with only one recognizable thought. Call Michael. Frantically she rummaged through the phone book to find the hotel's number, which she punched out quickly.

"Michael Hamilton's room, please."

"What?" he answered. Being aroused in the night already made him suspect it was urgent.

"Michael." Emily felt relief in the connection alone. She glanced at the clock. Two-forty.

"Emily! What is it?" He fumbled for the light and threw his legs over the edge of the bed.

"It's Allison. She's still having pain. It's not like her to complain this way. I don't think it's the flu. I'm afraid something is terribly wrong."

"Then we should get it checked out," he said with calm concern. "Do you want me to meet you at the hospital? Does it seem urgent?"

"I don't think so, but then . . . I don't know! I don't want to go alone."

"I'll be right there. You be ready to leave."

He hung up the phone and flew into action while Emily called Penny and quickly explained. She arrived to stay with the babies only a minute before Michael pulled up and ran into the house. He found Emily on the sofa with Allison draped over her lap, whimpering and holding her middle.

"Any worse?" he asked.

"Maybe."

Michael scooped Allison into his arms. "Come on, baby. We're going to make it well."

Emily followed him out the door. Penny locked it behind them and made herself comfortable on the couch.

"You drive." Emily got into the passenger side of the rented car. Michael gently situated Allison on her lap. Emily whispered soothing words to Allison and rocked her while Michael drove through deserted streets.

"Where are you going?" she asked, looking up to see where they were.

"To the hospital."

"Orem has a hospital. It's closer." She evaluated their location. "Well, not any more."

Michael shrugged and continued to drive. Emily felt knots in her stomach as he pulled in near the emergency entrance of Utah Valley Regional Medical Center. He carried Allison through the automatic glass doors. Emily followed, wishing she could block out the image of Ryan's barely-living form being wheeled through these very doors.

They talked to a nurse. They waited. They saw a doctor who poked and prodded and ordered an abdominal X-ray. They continued to wait while Allison became steadily more uncomfortable.

The doctor finally returned to inform them, "It looks like classic appendicitis. We can't know for certain without further tests, but from what I see, we'd be better off to just get in there and remove it."

Emily grabbed Michael's hand, but tried to control her expression. All she could think of was her little girl undergoing surgery.

"An appendectomy is fairly risk free," the doctor continued. "Let's take care of the formalities and get on with it."

When the surgery was underway, Michael returned from the men's room to find Emily staring with distant eyes.

"Where are you?" he asked, taking her hand.

Emily sighed. She was at least glad they were able to wait somewhere besides the emergency area. "I was just thinking that . . . I'm glad Allison didn't know where she was."

"What do you mean?"

"Ryan died just down the hall from where she was examined."

"Emily, I'm sorry. I didn't even think about—"

"I was standing by those doors we came in, when the ambulance arrived and . . ." Michael put his arm around her and she buried her face against his shoulder. "He looked so horrible," she sobbed quietly. "There was so much blood, and . . ."

Her words became lost in her tears. Michael brushed his lips over her brow in a feeble attempt to offer comfort. Seeing and feeling her emotion once again, he wondered if they were moving too fast. But at least she was being open with it, which was far better than trying to hide it from him. It felt strange, despite the years of her marriage, to sit here and comprehend the life she had shared with Ryan Hall. Despite the evidence of unhappiness he had seen in her six months ago, and her apparent eagerness to marry him now, he still knew that Ryan's loss was heartbreaking for her. Though there had been difficulties, Ryan was the center of her life for more than a decade, the governing force behind all she had done. He was the father of her children. She had eaten with him, slept with him, shared the ins and outs of everyday living with him.

Michael's thoughts brought out a familiar ache that had been a common companion to him these many years. He would never forget the tangible pain he'd felt as he sleeplessly cried silent tears on Ryan and Emily's wedding day. The pain had varied in degrees over the years, and he had learned to live with it, but it had never left him. While his friends and associates were starting families, Michael was writing books and dating women that either disgusted him by their lack of values, or frustrated him by their lack of depth. He had only wanted Emily.

The moment he looked up to see her that day in the mall had been as incredible to him as the parting of the Red Sea. He now believed that their unexpected meeting was somehow part of an intricate plan that he didn't understand, but he was grateful to be a part of. There were aspects of it that left him baffled and frustrated; but it was, as Emily said, an issue of faith. He had to remember how far they had come.

Emily sniffled and eased away. "Don't you ever get tired of watching me cry?" she asked.

"No," he said easily.

She straightened herself and looked at the clock. "You must have been inspired to get that medical insurance."

"I doubt an appendectomy will be terribly expensive."

"Maybe not for you. I shudder to think where this would have put me if you hadn't shown up when you did."

"It's those ministering angels," he stated, smiling pleasantly. Her expression told him she didn't understand. "When I was ordained to the priesthood," he explained, "they told me that I would have ministering angels to assist me in blessing the lives of others."

"Michael," she sat forward to look at him more fully, "you didn't tell me."

He chuckled. "I was ordained the day after I was baptized. Of course, I won't be an elder until next August, but it's a privilege I look forward to."

Emily felt warmed. "I can see the change in you, Michael. You were always a good man, but there is an essence of . . . peace about you. And faith. You were always so logical, and now I can see the faith putting balance there."

"Really?" He grinned like a child. "The changes felt so natural, I guess I didn't recognize them."

"I'm glad you didn't do it for me, Michael."

He eased her head to his shoulder, holding her close.

Emily sighed. "My poor Allison. She looked so frightened. I hope everything will go all right."

"Everything will be perfect," he said. "You've got to have faith." He smiled down at her. "You look tired."

"Why should I be any more tired than you?"

"Because you work harder than I do. I've seen what you do to take care of those children. You're always moving. It's no wonder you're so skinny."

"You're flattering me, Michael."

"No, I'm not." He brushed a kiss over her brow. "I'm—"

"Emily." A woman's voice interrupted and she straightened abruptly, though Michael kept his arm around her. "Penny called me a while ago." Launa Wright sat by Emily and took her hand. "I couldn't believe it when she told me you'd called from the hospital. Poor, dear Allison."

"I couldn't believe it myself," Emily said. Launa's eyes moved to Michael as Emily's moved behind Launa to her husband. "Bishop," she said, and Michael came immediately to his feet. Emily followed. "Michael, this is Bishop Wright and his wife, Launa." Michael extended an eager hand. "This is a very old friend of mine, Michael

Hamilton."

"It's nice to meet you, Mr. Hamilton," the bishop said with full acceptance. Emily wondered if he recalled the name from their interviews last spring.

"The pleasure is mine," Michael said, "but I'm not sure I like the way she put that." He smiled at Emily. "I think I would prefer to be a long-time friend than a very old one."

"So technical," Emily quipped.

"You're not American," Launa said, a look of curiosity coming into her eyes. She was obviously intrigued by this foreigner associating with the young widow in the ward.

"Not usually," Michael answered. "I went to college at BYU for several years, and I'm in and out of the country occasionally for other things. My family claims I sound Americanized."

"So, how is Allison?" the bishop asked as they were all seated.

"She's in surgery. They say it's routine and she'll be fine."

"But it does add to the stress," Bishop Wright said with compassion, and Emily nodded in agreement.

"We've got to stop meeting like this." Launa put a gentle hand on Emily's arm.

"If I have to be here, it's nice to know you won't leave me alone." Emily added to Michael, "They showed up just a few minutes after Ryan died." Michael nodded his understanding.

After an uncomfortable silence, Launa said, "I would assume if you went to BYU, that it was there you became friends."

"That's right," Michael said.

"You know, with the university right here, I guess we forget that it brings in members from all over the world."

"Actually," Michael tried not to sound tense, "I came to BYU because I wanted to attend a reputable college that had values. I always wanted to come to the U.S. to go to school, but I didn't want to put up with what I've heard runs rampant at many of them. My reasons for coming here had nothing to do with the Church."

There was a vague disappointment evident in Launa's eyes. The bishop showed no reaction.

"But he got straight A's in all of his religion classes," Emily said proudly. "He knows the Book of Mormon like the back of his hand."

"I wouldn't go so far as to say that," Michael said sheepishly.

"So, what brings you to the U.S. now?" the bishop asked.

Michael wondered how the situation would be perceived, but he had no intention of being anything less than honest. "Emily and I have kept in touch through letters. When several went unanswered, I was going to call her, but I felt prompted to come."

"And he saved me," Emily smiled.

"She's just trying to flatter me so you'll think I'm a nice guy," Michael said to ease the embarrassment.

"He *is* a nice guy," Emily argued, then decided to get to the point. If Penny knew, it would be all over the ward by tomorrow anyway. "Michael and I are going to be married."

Launa gaped in surprise, but the bishop only smiled. "So soon?" Launa asked, then looked embarrassed. "I mean . . . well."

"Michael and I have known each other for a long time," Emily explained. "We both know it's right."

"That's good then," the bishop said.

"Where will you be married?" Launa asked carefully. Emily knew it was a typical way of politely asking if the marriage would be in the temple. She was relieved when Michael answered for her. "We're getting married in Australia," he announced, "in the same place that my forefathers have been married, three generations back."

"How fascinating." Launa did well at hiding her disappointment on Emily's behalf, but Emily still sensed it. She hoped the rest of the story would come out in a natural way. But then she had agreed to marry Michael before she knew he'd been baptized. She knew she'd be happy either way. His membership simply made a good situation better. She squeezed his hand and didn't care what anybody else thought.

CHAPTER FOUR

"And where is that?" Launa Wright pressed curiously.

"In our family home; the upstairs hall, to be exact. The house was built by my great-grandfather in the 1870s. He was married in the upstairs hall in 1890, and my grandparents were married there in 1912."

"And what do you do for a living, Mr. Hamilton?" Launa asked. Emily threw an amused glance toward Michael. This was much like the visit he'd paid to her parents in Idaho when he'd asked permission to take her to Australia.

Michael wasn't disturbed. In truth, he felt confidence in being able to assure these people that Emily and her children would be well cared for. "I'm involved in a number of things," he said humbly. "My family runs a boys' home, and also works with horses. The one brings in enough to support the other. As for myself, I'm a writer."

"Really?" Launa sounded intrigued. "What do you write?"

"Just bedtime stories for big people," he said as if it were nothing.

"I enjoy reading fiction," Launa said. "I'd like to read your work. Have you been published?"

Michael chuckled humbly and looked down. Ask him about Australia or horses and he'd love it, but Emily knew he wasn't one to talk about himself. She gracefully took over. "He's had two novels published and a contract for more. They're both best-sellers."

"What are they called?" the bishop asked.

"*Crazy's Day* and—" Emily began.

"*Verity!*" Launa finished, pointing at Michael with an expression of enlightenment. "You're J. Michael Hamilton."

"That's me."

"Well, copies of your books have been passed around the ward regularly."

"They have?" Emily wondered how she'd have felt to have one loaned to her by a friend.

"You've done well for yourself, then," Launa said.

"I get by," Michael replied, and Emily discreetly nudged him with her elbow. He smiled at her.

"When are you planning to be married?" the bishop asked.

"Just as soon as we can get passports and visas," Emily said quickly.

"Does that take long?"

"A month or so if it goes smoothly," Michael provided.

"Is there anything we can do to help in the meantime?" the bishop asked.

Emily looked to Michael, who shrugged. "Not that I can think of," she said. "Michael has everything under control." She decided to add, so there would be no questions that could promote gossip, "He arrived in no time to bring us here when I called the hotel."

"Don't hesitate to let us know if we can help." The bishop came to his feet.

Michael did the same and shook his hand again. "Thank you for coming, Bishop."

"Might we see you at church Sunday?" the bishop added.

"I was planning on it," Michael said. "That is a general requirement of membership in this church, isn't it?"

Emily relieved their puzzled expressions. "Michael is a convert."

"Oh," Launa beamed.

"BYU got to you?" the bishop asked lightly.

"Actually, I'd say it was more like Emily got to me."

"How long have you been a member?" Launa asked.

Michael chuckled. "Three and a half weeks. No, wait. Four weeks today."

"That's why he's still glowing." Emily rose and put her arms around his waist.

"Then we hope you'll do us the honor of glowing at church so we can all absorb it a little." The bishop grinned.

"I'll be there," Michael said. "I can't promise any glowing."

"Thanks again," Emily said as they walked away.

Michael sat back down. "I finally met someone as curious as my mother."

"I don't know," Emily mused as she took his hand. "The running would be pretty even."

"Yeah," he gave a conspiring grin, "just wait until you get to Australia, then we'll see who gets interrogated."

"I just hope I measure up."

"If you measure up to me, nothing else matters. But if you must know, in my mother's eyes you could do no wrong. There was a time or two when I expressed some anger toward you, and she put me in my place as quick as gunshot."

Emily's eyes widened. "Do you think you can survive living with the two of us?" she asked slyly.

"I can think of no greater pleasure."

"If it weren't for your brother-in-law and nephew, you'd be surrounded by women."

"You've got a point there." He kissed her cheek. "We'll just have to have a son, or maybe two."

"Or three."

"Don't get carried away."

"Or we could have a few more girls."

"My father was the youngest of six children. The other five were girls. That's why I'm the last Hamilton in my line."

"Then I hope we have a son."

Michael squeezed her hand, wishing he knew how to express what such a prospect meant to him.

After a lengthy silence, Emily felt a sudden need to bring up something that had disturbed her since last spring when they'd said good-bye.

"Michael," she said quietly, "there's something I want to talk to you about."

His eyes narrowed at the severity of her tone. "Go on."

"In the spring, when you came to the house and . . ." She paused when Michael's eyes widened, surprised by the topic. "You said some things that made me stop and think. Looking back, I couldn't believe I had been such a fool."

"I'm lost," he admitted.

Emily looked down to her hands, where they fidgeted with the buttons on Michael's shirt cuff. "All those years, I had no idea how I had hurt you. I mean . . . I knew that my leaving would be difficult, but I never realized how it all appeared to you. I just want you to know that I . . ." She met his eyes courageously. "I never intended to deceive you . . . or lead you on . . . or . . ."

Michael pressed his fingers over her lips to stop her. "Hush. I should have never said those things to you. I was the one in the dark. I know you were just doing what—"

"No, wait, Michael," she interrupted. "There's something I have to say. Just hear me out. Okay?"

Michael nodded reluctantly.

"From where we sit now, I wouldn't change any of it. I only did what I felt was best, but looking back, I realize that I had not been fair with you, and you had a right to be angry." She wiped her sweating palms on her jeans then clasped her fingers together. "I suppose that I . . . well, maybe I had some deep hope that you would join the Church and I could have everything I wanted."

Emily looked up at Michael and was surprised to see moisture glistening in his eyes. "Michael, I just want to say that I'm sorry. I'm sorry for all the hurt and trouble I brought into your life, and I'll be eternally grateful that I've been given the opportunity to make it up to you. I'll be a good wife to you, Michael. I'll do my best to fit in and—"

"Emily." He pulled her close to him, holding her tightly, nuzzling his face into her hair. "Enough said. It's in the past."

"I love you, Michael," she whispered against his throat.

"And I love you," he replied, urging her head to his shoulder where he toyed idly with her hair, marveling at the miracles in his life—miracles that made the disappointments seem insignificant.

The surgeon soon appeared to report that all had gone well. Emily sat with Allison while Michael went to do some errands, feeling it might be better for them to be alone for a while. He returned to find Allison sleeping and Emily watching T.V. in the hospital room.

"What a welcome distraction," she said, but left the T.V. on so Allison wouldn't be awakened by their talking.

"How is she?"

"Fine, but she has some fever. The doctor said it's likely nothing, but she'll probably have to stay until Monday or Tuesday. I talked to Penny; she said that Allison's Primary teacher and one of the Primary counselors each wanted to spend some time here with her so I can have a break."

"I stopped at the house and checked on the babies. Penny said everything was fine."

"People are so good to me," Emily concluded.

"You deserve it."

"How did your errands go?" She disregarded the compliment.

"Good. I'll pick up applications for the passports on Monday."

Allison began to stir and Emily moved closer to her bedside. "What time is it?" she asked groggily.

"It's nearly noon, why?"

"I guess I won't be going to Ashley's party."

"No, sweetie," Emily said gently, "I'm afraid not, but we'll make certain she gets your gift."

"Can you take it over before the party starts?" she implored.

"What time does the great social occasion begin?" Michael asked, and Allison turned to see they weren't alone.

"Two," Emily answered.

"Give me the address and I'll get it there," Michael offered. "Then your mom can stay here with you."

"Okay," Allison agreed.

"You sure you don't mind?" Emily asked, finding a paper and pencil.

"It's no problem."

Allison repeated the memorized address to her mother and said to Michael, "I have it all ready. It's on my dresser."

"It's as good as done." Michael kissed Emily's cheek and squeezed Allison's hand. "You get better now, kid, and when the doctor says it's okay, I'll fix you anything you want to eat."

"Can you barbecue hamburgers?" she asked.

"Better than Burger King," he replied, and Allison smiled feebly.

"Can I get you anything?" he asked Emily.

"A good book, maybe," she said, mostly teasing.

"I'll see you later," he said, and at half past two he knocked lightly then peeked his head through the door. "Are you awake, Allison?" he asked.

"Yeah," she said, turning her attention from the T.V. that barely interested her.

"Are you up to visitors?" he added. Emily wondered if he had brought the babies.

"Sure," Allison said without enthusiasm.

Michael opened the door wide. Seven girls and a dozen helium balloons filed into the room. Allison's face lit up like the sun while Emily looked on in amazement. Michael tied the balloons to the bed and leaned against the door to observe them chattering away. Emily brushed past the girls to join him.

"You're a genius, Michael."

"Nah," he said humbly, "I just told them Allison was in the hospital and she felt bad that she couldn't be there. Ashley's mother said it was too bad they couldn't all go to see her, so I offered to drive. We just happened across this place that sold balloons on the way."

"Yeah, I bet it just jumped out in front of you."

"This is for you." Michael handed Emily a large manila envelope.

"What is it?"

"I hope it's something that measures up to the last book you read." She looked puzzled. "It's the first five chapters of the book I'm working on, but this one is different. I mentioned it in my letters."

"I can't wait. Thank you."

After a lengthy visit, Michael took the girls back to Ashley's house, then went again to check on Penny. He watched the babies while Penny went home to feed her family. After eating leftover spaghetti, he experimented with expressions and noises that brought out the most giggles. Alexa showed a preference for peek-a-boo with wide eyes and breathy noises. Amee liked growling sounds and wrinkled noses.

Michael answered a knock at the door to find an attractive, middle-aged woman holding a loaf of homemade bread and a jar of jam. He quickly grabbed Alexa as she crawled for the open door, then he waited for this woman to say something expected, like "Is Emily here?" or "How is Allison?" Or maybe "Who are you?" But she squinted her eyes carefully and looked him up and down as if he were an alien. Then her face filled with exaggerated enlightenment and she stated, in thick English cockney, "You must be the Aussie."

"I've been called that a time or two," he admitted, his voice betraying she was right.

"It's a pleasure to meet you," she added, seeming to want to shake his hand, but finding hers full. "I've just come with a little compassionate service."

"Come in," he offered, still trying to get used to her.

"Thank you," she said like a prudish maid and bustled past him into the kitchen as if she'd been there a hundred times. With her offerings deposited on the counter, she turned back to Michael, who was pulling Amee away from the door while he still held Alexa. He closed it to keep them from escaping, then turned to his visitor.

"I'm Lucinda Swann." She offered a hand, her voice changing to a southern drawl. Michael's eyes widened as he shook her hand. "And I understand," the drawl continued just as naturally as the cockney had, "that you are in need of a boarding house."

"Oh, I'm fine," he said, piecing it together now. "I have a room in Provo that is—"

"Perfect—except in the case of appendicitis attacks or any other misfortune that might require you to be close to your betrothed."

"News travels fast." He scowled slightly.

"Yes," she returned to cockney, "it does, at least when Penny Millner wants to get something accomplished. Now, I have this perfectly lovely room. It's complete with a bed. You'd have to share a bathroom with my son. He's eighteen. He works late and sleeps late. I doubt you'll cross paths very often. Under the circumstances, your curfew will be ten-thirty, but milk and cookies are provided regularly. Breakfast is optional."

Michael had to ponder a moment over whether or not the woman was sane. Either way, he was amused. He couldn't help feeling that it would be better to be closer to Emily, and he had to admit that he hated hotels. If he had room for doubt on any account, it was quickly dispelled when she picked Amee up with perfect familiarity and said, in a normal American tone, "Now, seriously, Mr. Hamilton. Penny's told me all about the situation, and I think you're just what little Emily needs. But I see no reason for you to be staying in one of those tacky hotels when you could stay in the same room as Germans, Russians, Brazilians, and . . . well, a few others, all come and gone."

Michael chuckled. "Penny did say you had a hobby of foreigners. I wasn't certain whether or not to believe her."

"Did she say that?" Sister Swann said in perfect, proper British. "That was rude! I can't imagine whatever gave her that idea." Her voice returned to normal and her smile was kind. "Say you'll stay with us. My husband is really a nice man, despite what they say about him. No, I'm just kidding. He really is. He humors me. You've got to give the man credit there. We'd just love to have you. You can come and go as you like, as long as you're in by ten-thirty so Emily can get some sleep and I'll know you're minding your manners." She clicked her tongue. "Young people these days."

Michael was beginning to pick up on the switching in and out of character when she said, "I don't think we've ever had an Australian before. I did see 'Crocodile Dundee,' and my granddaughter has a stuffed Koala bear."

"That should qualify you," he chuckled.

"Then you'll stay?" she beamed.

"I don't see why not," he admitted. "You do make the offer sound . . . intriguing."

She gave a genuine laugh. "Good," she declared in proper British. "When might I tell the butler to expect you?"

"Some time tomorrow," he said. "I'll wrap things up at the hotel tonight."

"Very good. Tell Miss Emily to call me in the morning and we'll see to the details."

"I'll do that." He took Amee from her as she moved to the door. "And thank you for the compassionate service. It looks delicious."

"There's more where that came from." She smiled and uttered

elaborate good-byes on her way to the car.

Penny came in before Michael closed the door. "I see you met Sister Swann."

"All three of her," Michael stated, and Penny laughed at the analogy. "Is she always so . . . colorful?"

"Only when she really likes someone. Honestly, the first time she called me for ward business, I didn't know her from the man in the moon, and she starts in with this phony accent and calls herself some false name like Lucretia Longbottom, or Melvina Balch, or something. She has a whole list of them. But not to worry, Michael. I can assure you she's perfectly sane and wonderful. She just enjoys life. You'll like her."

"I'm certain I will."

"Now," Penny announced, "why don't you go to the hospital and make certain Emily gets some dinner. I'll get the babies to bed, then Heather is going to stay with them so I can go over. I'll bring Emily home and you can go to your hotel from there. Tomorrow we'll get you moved to Orem."

"Yes, ma'am." He gave her a comical salute.

"Get out of here," she laughed.

"Don't eat all the bread and jam," he called back after giving the babies each a kiss and a hug.

Michael took Emily a hamburger and a chocolate malt that she ate while Allison slept. He reported Sister Swann's visit and Penny's plans, then yawned a good-night.

Once settled in his hotel room, Michael got comfortable with the phone, waiting for the connection to go through.

"Hello, Mother," he said with exaggerated jubilance.

"Michael! I've been wondering when I'd hear from you. Is it yesterday there?"

"Yes," he chuckled. Every phone call began this way, back from college days. "It's yesterday here, and it's tomorrow there. How are you?"

"Everything is fine. How about you? Did you see Emily?"

"Yes." He drew the word out to evoke anticipation.

"And?"

"Well," he became more serious, "it's a long story. You aren't baking pies or anything, are you?"

"Not without you here to eat them."

"Just checking."

"Get on with it, Michael. I've been dying of curiosity since you left here in such a frantic hurry. You said you felt like she needed you. Did she?"

"I'd say that's an understatement."

"I'm not going to prod it out of you," she scolded when he didn't go on.

"All right," he chuckled, "she needed my money."

"At least you're good for something," LeNay Hamilton said with slight irritation. Michael was well aware that his mother had not been totally pleased with the effect Emily had had on his life, in spite of the fact that she was extremely fond of Emily. But he hoped what he had to tell her would make a difference.

"Yes, I am," he said proudly, "but I'll tell you that later. I'll start at the beginning. I found Emily in financial devastation, so I helped her out a little. No big deal."

"Why wasn't she writing?"

"It seems she's been under a lot of stress."

"So, where is she now?"

"At the hospital."

"What's wrong?" LeNay questioned.

"Emily's fine. Her oldest daughter had her appendix removed this morning."

"Is she all right?"

"Oh yes, she's fine."

Michael was silent and LeNay said with exasperation, "Michael, I'm still waiting for this long story. You can write them, but you sure like to torment me by not telling them."

"Tease," he corrected, "not torment."

"At least you're in a good mood. Is that an indication of good news?"

"Good and bad," he said soberly.

"For whom?"

"For all of us."

"She's changed her mind," LeNay guessed. "She's decided to

leave him."

"Mother," Michael said with an emotion in his voice that caught her attention, "I don't know if you'll understand what this means, but I think you will. I have been able to see as much as anybody that my obsession with Emily has been unreasonable. But I always felt there was something more—something I didn't understand. I believe now that God somehow instilled those feelings in me, to keep me hanging on until now."

"She *is* going to leave him," LeNay guessed with more certainty.

"She doesn't have to, Mother." Michael hesitated and found it difficult to say, without fully understanding why. "He was killed in June."

Silence. Michael waited. "How?" she finally asked.

"A car accident," he reported dryly. "But the strange thing is . . . well, you know I told you that she'd said in her letters they were doing better. Apparently she was feeling a great deal of hope. She's pretty upset over it. I think it's been difficult for her."

"I can imagine," she replied softly. "Is she all right?"

"She's doing better now than when I got here. Honestly, Mother, I could not believe the financial ruin I found her in. I don't have a clue what she'd have done if I hadn't shown up. Any job she could have gotten wouldn't have begun to touch it."

"Then your prompting must have been for good reason."

Her statement gave a hint of acceptance to Michael's new religion, and he smiled. "Yes, I believe it was."

"How are the children, other than the appendix?"

"Of course the babies are too young to know the difference. They seem fine."

"How old are they now?"

"Amee turned two in June. Alexa is barely one."

"And the other is . . ."

"Allison," he prompted. "She's not doing so good. This whole thing seems to have left her rather upset. I suppose it will take time."

"You would know about that," LeNay said gently.

"Yes, but circumstances vary. I can't begin to know what Allison feels, but I'm going to try and figure it out."

"I take it, then, that you didn't call to tell me you're coming home soon."

"No," he said almost proudly.

"What are your plans, Michael?"

"Right now, I was planning on going to bed."

"In the middle of the afternoon?" She feigned innocence, but he knew she was well aware of the time difference.

"Yes," he went along. "If you must know, I was up half the night at the hospital."

"It would seem you're giving more support than financial," she speculated.

"I'm trying."

"So, what now?"

"I'm going to marry her."

"You don't waste any time."

"It's not like I just met her last week, Mother. I don't need to tell you how I feel about her."

"And how does she feel about you?"

"She loves me enough to be willing to leave everything and go to Australia."

"Michael, are you saying that—"

"I'm saying that I am not coming home until I bring her with me. I'm not taking any chances of losing her again."

"You've already proposed, then."

"Yes, and she accepted." He added what he considered an important point. "Before she knew I had joined the Church."

"She does love you."

"So how do you feel about instant family, Mother?"

LeNay finally made a noise of pleasure. "You're serious about this?"

"You'd better believe it. I don't know how long it will be. We're waiting on passports and visas, but she seems eager to put the past behind her. I think there are difficulties in the situation that a fresh start would ease."

"I can understand that. How long do you think it will be?"

"I'm guessing a month or so, but it's unpredictable. We'll be getting married there."

"I hoped you would say that."

"I hope you don't mind preparing things a bit. I want them to feel welcome."

"Mind?" she laughed. "This could be the most fun I've had in years."

"I hoped you would say that," he chuckled.

They discussed the arrangement of rooms and technicalities for quite some time, then she asked, "What exactly are you doing to occupy your time?"

Michael knew it was a polite way of asking if he was being a good boy. "I'm spending my nights at the hotel," he said emphatically, "and during the days, well, so far I've just tried to help out. I'm doing a little cooking, and I am proud to say that I successfully changed a napkin."

"Your father would be disgusted. He never touched one. But I'm proud of you."

"Well, a man who doesn't go to work has got to do something to look useful."

"You work plenty hard when you're home," she insisted.

"Yes, but I'm not going to stop changing napkins, if it's all the same to you. I know I don't have to tell you this, but there's something wonderful in helping to care for these children. I love them already. They could drive us all a little crazy, but I love them."

"Spoken like a true parent." She chuckled. "I'm proud of you, Michael. She's a good woman. I think you deserve each other. I must say, I've never seen fate work two people together quite so . . . poignantly."

"That's what I thought."

"Thanks for calling, Michael. I miss you."

"I miss you, too. How is Katherine?"

"The same," she answered. "Robert is around less and less. I'm concerned."

"Give her my love."

"I will, and tell Emily I'm looking forward to seeing her again. Make sure she knows they are welcome. I'll be getting the house ready."

"Good. I'll call next week and keep you posted."

"You do that."

"Oh," he added, "I'll give you Emily's number, in case you need it."

"Good idea," she said and he repeated it before he hung up the phone and called to make certain Emily had gotten home all right. He smiled just to hear her voice.

"Hello, beautiful," he said almost roguishly.

"Hello." Her voice smiled.

"I just talked to my mother."

"How is she?"

"Fine. She said to tell you she's looking forward to seeing you again."

"You told her everything, then."

"I told her what she needed to know. She sounded pleased about our plans. I think she'll enjoy the children."

"I hope you're right."

"There is no need to worry, I can assure you."

"I read your chapters. I love it, even more than the others. I didn't realize you were such a romantic."

"Am I?"

"You are to me."

"That's all that matters."

"I love you, Michael Hamilton."

"And I love you."

"Thank you for being here."

"Thank you for letting me be here. I don't think I've ever been happier."

"Maybe that has something to do with being a Mormon."

"That's part of it, I'm certain. But the rest is more a . . . " He paused before saying with humble sincerity, "It feels good to be needed, Emily, to have purpose. I've missed that."

"Since you put it that way, it's nice to need you."

"What time is church?"

"It starts at noon, but—"

"You need to be with Allison," he guessed.

"Actually, I don't. Allison's Primary teacher got permission to take the class to the hospital, so they'll be taking Primary to Allison."

"That's nice. I guess that means I don't have to go to church alone."

Emily chuckled. "After one Sunday with Amee and Alexa, you'll wish you could."

"I don't think so. Now, get some sleep while you can. I'll come by early and we'll take the babies to see Allison before meetings."

"All right," she agreed enthusiastically.

"I love you, Emily Ladd," he said quietly, and Emily went to sleep with the words echoing through her mind.

CHAPTER FIVE

Michael arrived at Emily's early to share a breakfast of Cheerios and sliced bananas with his new family. He played with the babies until Emily was ready to go. She emerged from the bathroom with the declaration, "I don't know how to act. I can actually do my hair and makeup without seventeen interruptions."

"The results are marvelous." Michael smiled warmly, belying the intensity of what just seeing her did to him.

Emily smiled in return and handed him the diaper bag. "What's that?" he asked, referring to the other bag she carried.

"I'm teaching today," she stated and hurried Amee toward the door while he picked up Alexa.

Michael was familiar with Emily's church calling through her letters, but he couldn't help being interested. "Do you think anyone would notice if I came to Relief Society?" he asked while he buckled the baby into her seat.

"Yes," she smiled at him over the top of the car, "I think they'd notice."

"Too bad." He walked around to open the door for her, pausing to give her a quick kiss before she got in.

"But it would help immensely if you took Alexa during the meeting, then I wouldn't have to ask somebody else. I feel like such a burden sometimes."

"I doubt you're that to anyone, but I would be happy to take Alexa."

Allison enjoyed their visit and seemed in good spirits when they left her. At ten minutes to twelve, they walked through the meeting-house door, and Emily felt a twinge of nerves.

"What's wrong?" Michael asked. She was amazed at his discernment of her emotions, when Ryan would hardly notice if she was crying.

"It just seems . . . strange," she whispered. "I dare say we'll be the biggest topic of conversation today."

"Oooh," he said with mischief in his voice, "I don't think I've ever been gossiped about before."

"It's not gossip. People are just concerned and curious."

"As they should be," he quipped dramatically. "It's not every day the beautiful, young widow gets engaged to a foreign bachelor."

"I doubt it will be news by now." She led the way into the chapel. "Between Penny and Bret, and Lucinda Swann, it's likely traveled far already."

Michael chuckled. "Let them talk." He leaned toward her and whispered, "Let me kiss you, and we'll really give them something to talk about it."

Emily giggled and tried not to blush. She noticed a few curious glances, but the chapel was mostly empty. "I don't think I've been to church this early in years," she said. "By the time I get myself and the babies ready, I'm always late."

A question came to Michael's mind that he hesitated to ask, but he figured it was better to keep such things in the open. "What did Ryan do?"

"The last several weeks, I was grateful just to let him get ready and go to church."

"And before that?"

Her reply was toneless. "He watched T.V. while I got the children ready and took them to church."

"How did you manage through the meetings with two babies?"

"The same way I've managed these past few months. People help some, but it's still difficult. Allison's always helpful. Actually," Emily smiled, "Allison likes any excuse to take one of the babies into the foyer."

"Good morning." Bret leaned over the bench, offering a hand to Michael.

"For a few more minutes." Michael glanced at his watch.

"Hey," he said to Emily, "you didn't tell me this guy had just joined the Church."

"I figured Penny would."

"Well, she did . . . eventually." He nodded to Michael. "I guess that means we won't have to send the missionaries over."

"I could feed them," Michael offered.

"It's good to have you here," Bret added. "How's Allison?"

"Doing better," Emily reported. "She'll be coming home the day after tomorrow."

"Let us know if there's anything we can do."

In the next few minutes the chapel filled considerably. Michael noticed Bret seated on the stand and Emily explained, "He's second counselor in the bishopric."

Michael nodded, and a moment later they were approached by a balding man in his late thirties who offered his hand with a boisterous, "I don't think we've had the pleasure."

Emily made the introductions. "This is my fiancé, Michael Hamilton. Michael, this is Lee Reynolds, the elders quorum president."

"It's a pleasure to meet you, Brother Hamilton." Michael opened his mouth to reply, but Lee went on. "With our minimal youth, it's the quorum's turn to do the sacrament. Could we ask you to help bless it?"

"Oh," Michael shifted slightly, caught off guard, "I'm not an elder yet. I just—"

"You are a priest?" Lee questioned quietly.

"Yes, but . . ." Michael's heart began to pound.

"That's all we need."

Michael looked to Emily as if for approval. She gave an encouraging nod and he turned back to Lee. "I can certainly try, but I've never done it before."

Lee put a hand to Michael's shoulder as he came to his feet, and they walked together toward the front. Emily situated Amee with some story books and Alexa with some quiet toys, hoping they'd be good long enough for her to appreciate the sacrament. She caught Michael's eye as the meeting commenced, and she could feel his emotion. She knew without any exchange of words that he considered this a privilege.

The babies were miraculously well behaved, and Emily turned her mind to gratitude for all that had come to her life in the past weeks. Emotion filled her eyes with moisture as Michael's distinctive voice filled the chapel with a blessing on the water. She looked up when it was finished to find her emotion mirrored in his expression. He caught her eyes again and she smiled. He looked so distinguished, and he nearly glowed from the Spirit. In a word, he was the most handsome Mormon she'd ever known.

When the sacrament was finished, Michael returned to sit beside Emily, putting his arm on the bench behind her. "You did beautifully," she smiled up at him. "How was it?"

"Wonderful," he said fervently, and their eyes met with something tangible that had been absent before now, even in the blissful relationship they had shared in college. Emily felt their unity in a spiritual sense, deepening all else they shared that had remained through the years of separation. She squeezed his hand and he pulled Alexa onto his lap.

Halfway through the meeting, Amee began to scream because Alexa tried to pull the bow out of her hair. Michael was quick to take Amee out, well aware of the curious glances he got on the way. He caught sight of Penny, seated near the back with her children, and she smiled as he passed. After Amee got her fill at the drinking fountain and ran some of her wiggles out, he took her back in and managed to keep her occupied through the remainder of the meeting.

On their way to take Amee to the nursery, they were stopped several times for introductions and congratulations. Emily wondered what people were thinking of the quick engagement, but when Michael smiled at her she realized she didn't care. In her heart she knew it was right, and she explained it to others with a simple, "We dated in college and kept in touch through letters now and then." The general response was positive, and Emily felt warmed by the acceptance of her peers, who seemed only to want her happiness.

Emily was caught off guard as the Sunday School teacher stood and said, "Sister Hall, would you like to introduce your guest to us?"

Michael smiled to see the slight blush that rose in her cheeks. Without standing she said, "This is my fiancé, Michael Hamilton."

"How nice." The teacher pretended to be surprised. "It's good to have you with us, Brother Hamilton. Maybe you could tell us a little more about him, Emily."

Emily sighed, but decided she'd rather say it now and spare herself having to repeat it another dozen times before church was over. "Michael is from Australia. He has two degrees from BYU, and he's a writer," she smiled at him, "among other things."

"You forgot the best part," Michael said.

"You tell them!"

"I'm happy to say I was baptized four weeks ago."

A pleasurable rumble went through the group and the teacher commented, "How does the Church differ in Australia?"

Michael shrugged his shoulders. "Same church." A few gentle chuckles could be heard. "The biggest difference is that it's very spread out, except in the cities. Where I live, it takes more than an hour to get to church, and part of that is by plane."

Emily turned to him, eyes wide. Of course she had gone to church with him during her stay in Australia. But she had forgotten. Her heart began to pound as she did a reality check on the changes forthcoming in her life. Michael noticed, but now was not the time to discuss it.

"Well," the teacher repeated with sincerity, "we're happy to have you with us. Can we expect to see you in our ward for a good, long time?"

"Actually," Michael glanced at Emily warily, "we'll be moving to Australia in a month or so. We'll be getting married there."

This brought a rumble of disappointment from the class, but the teacher said, "Well, we'll just have to enjoy you while you're here."

He then proceeded with the lesson, and Emily enjoyed it once she stopped thinking about traveling an hour to get to church. Michael gave a comment that added to the uplifting discussion, and Emily was reminded of that first time she'd heard his voice.

Alexa began to show signs of crankiness before class ended, but Michael took her and the diaper bag without hesitation, saying quietly, "Good luck. You can give me the lesson later."

Emily found it easier to teach Relief Society today than at any time since Ryan's death. She had been given the choice of being released, but she found fulfillment and spiritual nourishment from the opportunity, and had stuck to it, despite the emotion that she was rarely able to conceal.

Ten minutes into her lesson, the door at the back of the room opened and Michael slipped quietly inside, Alexa sleeping on his shoulder. He gave her a nod of encouragement, and she realized quickly that no one was aware of his presence except her. His silent support meant much to her. He slipped out before the closing prayer and returned with Amee in tow as Emily gathered her materials. While Michael became occupied with some friendly ward members who asked him questions and fussed over the babies, Emily was approached by Sister Taylor, a middle-aged woman who lived across the street and one house down.

"Isn't it nice," she said with a smile that didn't seem totally natural, "for you to find such a fine young man, only three months after your husband's death." Emily gave a weak smile, not liking the way she'd emphasized that word: only. "And my, but you got engaged quickly, dear."

Emily gave the standard answer. "We met in college, and we've kept in touch through letters more recently."

Sister Taylor's smile seemed to become even more counterfeit. "Is that since he stopped by last spring?"

Emily's eyes widened as she tried to remember exactly what had passed between her and Michael as they'd said good-bye on the sidewalk. Reminding herself that she had no reason to justify anything to this woman, she simply said, "Yes. We ran into each other one day at the mall, and he stopped by to meet my husband before he went back to Australia."

"How nice," she said and seemed to mean it. "I wish the two of you the best." She tipped her head. "And I hear he's rather well off. Isn't that convenient, especially after the way you've struggled."

"He's a wonderful man, Sister Taylor," Emily said, inwardly bristling at the defensive edge in her voice.

"Yes," she patted Emily's hand, "I'm certain he is, even if he's a foreigner." Sister Taylor walked away; Emily just stared after her until Michael approached and handed over Alexa, freshly awake.

"Something wrong?" he asked lightly.

Emily looked up at him, momentarily wishing he wasn't quite so perceptive. "Let's go home, Michael, and I'll fix some dinner."

He picked up Amee and followed her to the car, pausing for a few more introductions in the parking lot. They were silent until he opened the house door with a key. "Somebody said something," he guessed. Emily ignored him and took Amee into the bedroom to put her down for a nap. She quickly changed into comfortable jeans and her Australian T-shirt, then went to the kitchen to start dinner.

"What are you doing?" she asked Michael, who was looking deeply into the freezer. She didn't wait for him to answer. "I'm cooking dinner today. I've learned a thing or two in the past ten years, so go take a nap or something."

"Fine. You cook, but you can talk while you're at it." He folded his arms and leaned against the counter. "You enjoyed church, didn't you? I mean, you weren't embarrassed to be seen with a foreigner, were you?"

"I was delighted to be seen with a particular foreigner, and yes, I enjoyed church. All except the last two minutes."

"Somebody said something," he guessed again.

"You could put it that way," she said while she began to mix a meatloaf.

"What happened?" he pressed.

Emily repeated the gist of the conversation, becoming steadily more upset.

"Where does this woman live?" he asked as she put the meatloaf in the microwave and began to heat potatoes prepared earlier.

"Across the street and one house east," she stated. "I can just imagine what she got out of those five minutes we stood outside together last spring. Why couldn't she have been doing her laundry, or in the bathroom, or . . . anything! Why did she have to be looking out her window right at that moment?"

"Just lucky, I guess," he mused, then attempted to offer an objective point of view. "And what happened out there that was so horrible? If she's implying anything at all, she's doing it from assumptions."

"Assumptions and implications are exactly where real gossip gets started. And unless your memory fails you, those few minutes we spent out there were full of food for implication."

"We talked!" he protested. "And I held your hand for a minute or two."

"I was crying!" she retorted. "You kissed my hand. I kissed your cheek. And don't tell me that what we were feeling wasn't conveyed in our expressions."

Michael sighed. "Perhaps your sensitivity on the subject is making you defensive. Maybe she wasn't implying anything." Emily glared at him. "I was just suggesting a possibility."

"I know this woman, Michael. She's been a good neighbor in many ways, but I know how she works, because she's a lot like Ryan. She can smile and politely tell someone they're not fit to walk the face of the earth. If she would outright accuse me of something I could defend myself, but she might as well have told me I should be wearing a scarlet letter, and I—"

"Emily! Don't be absurd! From what I see, the woman's insinuations might have been out of line, but there is no reason for you to take them so seriously."

Emily stopped cutting potatoes and looked up. "Michael, what one woman thinks is not going to weaken my testimony. Nothing could do that. Not even having to travel an hour to get to church." He smiled slightly. "But the woman talks, and I have no desire to spend my final weeks in this ward enduring tainted whispers about our relationship."

"You have nothing to be ashamed of, Emily."

"Don't I?" she chuckled dryly. "I nearly left him, Michael. Imagine what they'd have said about that." She raised her voice to mimic the gossips. "Emily Hall left her husband and ran away with some foreigner. And Ryan was always such a nice man. What did he ever do to deserve such a thing?" Her tone returned to normal. "My husband was outwardly charming and friendly, Michael. Most people didn't have a clue to anything beyond his inactivity in the Church. You should have heard what the people he worked with said about him."

"Why don't you tell me," Michael said gently, realizing there were many facets to what disturbed Emily. Sister Taylor's subtle implications had only brought her emotion to the surface.

Emily vigorously continued with her cooking.

"Emily," Michael said firmly, "I am talking to you." She stopped and squeezed her eyes shut. The expression alone told Michael something was terribly wrong. "Emily, you're suppressing something, and I want you to talk about—"

"Well, I don't!" she declared, turning to face him fully. "I do not want to talk about it, Michael. My husband has been dead only a matter of weeks. There is still far too much that hurts, and I do not want to talk about it right now."

Michael watched her a long moment and felt compassion take over. With purpose he took her hands.

"What are you doing? I'm not finished cooking yet, and—"

"As soon as we eat, I want you to go to the hospital and visit your daughter. Relax. Read something Sundayish. I'll call Penny if I need anything."

Emily turned away to put dinner on, wondering why he was so good to her. The meal passed in tense silence, excepting Michael's sincere, "This is great, Emily."

When they were finished, Michael immediately said, "Go see Allison."

"But, Michael, I—"

"Either go see Allison right now, or start talking," he insisted. Emily picked up her purse and left before she had time to think about it. In the car she cried. She wondered what had happened to bring out these feelings she found so difficult to face. The intensity could almost make her doubt her own sanity. But she reminded herself of her blessings, prayed inwardly for strength, and smiled when she entered Allison's room.

Five minutes after Emily left, Michael answered the door to Launa Wright.

"Hello, is Emily—"

"She went to the hospital." He stooped to pick up Alexa, who was trying to crawl out the door.

"Well, I was wondering if we could help with the babies this afternoon. I figured she would want to go to the hospital, and . . . my children love to play with the babies, and I thought it would be a good activity for them to . . . you know what I mean. After all, they practically lived with us just before the funeral."

"That would be fine, I'm sure," he said, wanting to be gracious, "but Amee is asleep, and I can manage if—"

"Come now, Brother Hamilton. Let me take Alexa for a while, and we'll come back for Amee. My family will love it."

Michael provided the diaper bag they had taken to church and Launa left with Alexa, who was apparently familiar with the woman. He returned to the kitchen to finish cleaning up the dinner mess, and impulsively decided to bake something.

When brownies were in the oven and the dishes washed, Penny called with a jubilant, "How's it going, Daddy? I see Emily is not at home. Are you surviving?"

"If you must know, Sister Wright took Alexa, and Amee is asleep. I'm baking."

"Oooh." Penny made a noise to indicate she was impressed. "I think we should come over for a sample."

"Feel free."

"I was just teasing," she insisted. "I called to see if you need anything."

"I think I'm fine," he said. "Thank you anyway, and you are welcome to sample."

"If you're fine, why do you sound like your dog just died?"

Michael chuckled. "Interesting analogy."

"Anything I can do?"

"Not unless you can tell me what I'm doing that's keeping Emily regularly infuriated with me."

"I can't tell you that," Penny said kindly, "but I can tell you that her life has been a roller coaster since . . . well, since she ran into you last spring. The highs have been very high, and the lows very low. And I think you have a lot to do with that. I'm no expert, but I think she just needs some time to adjust and get settled."

Michael absorbed Penny's observation. He already knew Emily needed time, and he understood why, but for some reason he was having a difficult time remembering that. "Of course," he said. "Perhaps this is a lesson in patience for me."

"Just be careful you don't pray for it, Michael," she said lightly.

"I'm sorry?"

"Oh," she laughed, "it's just a little joke around here. If you pray for patience, the Lord will send you ample ways to learn it."

"I see," he chuckled. "I guess we converts have much to learn."

"We all do, Michael. And the more you learn, the more you realize you don't know anything. Knowledge only brings more humility, and the more you get to know someone like Emily, the more you realize she's one in ten million."

"That's what she said about you."

"Really?" Penny giggled. "Isn't that funny?"

"Thank you, Penny."

"What did I do?"

"I don't know, but it worked. The brownies will be done in ten minutes."

"Call if you need us," she said and hung up the phone.

Michael read while the brownies cooled, stopping often to contemplate his need for patience. He knew Emily had much to face and deal with, and she would be happier once she did, but he realized it was not for him to determine the pace or the manner in which she faced it. He decided that what he needed was more divine guidance, and determined to turn his prayers in that direction. And while he was at it, he could pray for help in accepting the fact that Emily could not be sealed to him.

As he was cutting brownies and setting them out on a plate, Michael's mind went back to what had happened at church. An idea came that made him grin, and he picked up the phone.

"Penny," he said when she answered, "could I bribe you to stay with Amee for ten minutes? I have a quick errand. There are warm brownies in the deal."

"I'll be right over."

She arrived a minute later with Bret. "Where you going?" Bret asked, noting the plate of brownies Michael carried past them.

"Visiting," Michael answered, lifting his brows quickly. "Amee's still asleep. Enjoy. There's milk in the fridge."

Michael knocked at the door next to the mailbox bearing the name Taylor. The woman in question opened the door, looking briefly startled.

"Hello," he drawled the word carefully, "I don't believe we've met. I'm Michael Hamilton, Emily Hall's fiancé, and—"

"Oh, of course," she interrupted.

"Well, Emily was telling me how good you've been to keep an eye on her these past months, and I was just doing a little baking while she was at the hospital, and—"

"How is little Allison?" she interrupted again.

"Fine. She'll be home soon. As I was saying, I thought you might like some of these. I'm really not such a bad cook, and—"

"Oh, they look delicious." She took the plate. "Won't you come in for a minute?"

"Thank you." He stepped inside and she offered him a seat. "I can't stay long, but I wanted to be a good neighbor and thank you for watching out for Emily. It really is kind of you to show such an interest."

"Oh," Sister Taylor patted his hand, "she is such a dear little thing. And she's been through such a difficult time these last several months, what with her husband getting killed and all. It was such a horrible—"

"Who's there, Mabel?" Mr. Taylor sauntered into the room.

"This is Michael Hamilton," she stated. "Emily's fiancé. He brought us a little treat. Isn't that nice?"

"It's about time we got somethin' home-baked," he said, not totally serious.

Sister Taylor turned back to Michael. "As I was saying, the accident was such a horrible thing."

"Yes," Michael agreed, "I understand it's been difficult for her. She loved him very much. It's hard to face such a thing when—"

"Yes, I know. And with those young children and all. Well, it's good she has you to help out." Sister Taylor lowered her voice and motioned for him to come closer. "Just between you and me, I don't think he treated her very good." Michael looked perfectly surprised. "It was nothing obvious, but you hear things, you know, and—"

"Mabel," her husband scolded, "I don't think the man came to hear gossip."

"I was not gossiping," she insisted.

"What would you call it?"

"I just want him to know how we appreciate his being there for Emily. That's all." She smiled. "Such a nice young man."

Michael cleared his throat and came to his feet. "It's been a pleasure talking to you, Sister Taylor." He nodded toward her husband, "Brother Taylor."

"Take care now," the man replied, "and come over any time."

"Thank you." Michael moved toward the door.

"And thank you for the little treat." She added to her husband, "Such a nice young man."

Michael walked back across the street, unable to keep from smiling. If Sister Taylor was the malicious gossip of the ward, he didn't see much reason to be concerned.

CHAPTER SIX

Emily returned from the hospital to share brownies and milk with Michael while the babies were still at the Wrights. She was amused and comforted by Michael's visit to the Taylor home, and felt added peace when Michael sat her down and they read together from the latest *Ensign*.

Long afterward they sat in tranquil silence, each lost in thoughts that were much the same. Though Emily hated to break the mood, she felt sure she'd get no better opportunity to bring up something that she knew had to be faced.

"Michael," her voice was barely a whisper. He looked at her and smiled. "About the sealing . . ." She hesitated when a definite sadness rose in his eyes. "I know it's difficult to—"

"Emily," he interrupted gently, "I love you and we're together. If there is nothing to be done about it, we'll just have to accept it and enjoy life in spite of it. I'm not going to let it bother me, and you shouldn't either."

"But it does bother you," she said. It was not a question.

Michael glanced away. "Yes," he admitted reluctantly, "it does, but . . ." He turned to look at her, his eyes moist. "I've lived without you too long, Emily, to waste away the time we have by worrying about it when it's out of my hands."

Emily nodded, knowing he was right. It was too sensitive an issue to want to dig any deeper. She only hoped that by the time they were married they could both feel peace concerning it. She reminded herself to be patient and have faith.

"I love you, Michael," she said, and he bent to kiss her.

"I love you, too." He almost laughed when he said it, as if he couldn't contain his joy.

The babies were returned at bedtime, and Michael helped get them in their pajamas before he left.

"Going so soon?" she asked quietly.

"I saw Sister Swann at church and promised I'd get there early to settle in. She was quite insistent, and since I checked out of my hotel this morning, it might be a good idea."

"Good point." Emily tried not to sound disappointed. "I guess I'll see you tomorrow. I'm going to the hospital early. Allison's getting rather restless. I promised her."

"I'll find you." He kissed her quickly.

Brother and Sister Swann met Michael and his two pieces of luggage at the door. Introductions were made and he was shown through the large home, enjoying the feel of it. He liked the room and left his bags there, after which he was escorted to the dining room for hot chocolate and cookies. Michael felt a growing warmth as the three engaged in conversation that took them past midnight. When he finally declared he had to get some sleep, the very sane and enjoyable Lucinda Swann said to her husband, as if Michael weren't present, "Isn't it nice to have someone we can understand?"

"Understand?" Michael questioned.

"You speak English," she declared with enthusiasm, "and more than two words of it. Of course, it is Australian English, as opposed to American English, or British English, and then there is Irish English, and—"

"Lucinda," Brother Swann said, "let the man go to bed. Tomorrow we'll see if we can find an English-to-Australian dictionary, and maybe you can learn the language."

Michael laughed. "Or you could rent 'Crocodile Dundee' and watch it again."

"What a brilliant idea," Lucinda declared quite seriously. "I think we'll do that."

"Good-night," Michael smiled, "and thank you."

"It's our pleasure," Brother Swann replied.

"And the cookies were delicious," Michael added.

"I'll send your compliments along to the cook," Lucinda added in proper British. Michael chuckled and went to bed.

The next morning after breakfast, Michael drove past Emily's house and saw that the car was already gone. He made a quick stop then went to the hospital to present the bored Allison with a shopping bag. She hesitated briefly, but Emily nodded her approval. "You bought me a present?" Allison questioned.

"Sure," he said. "I was in the hospital once when I had my tonsils out. I was bored senseless."

Allison eagerly pulled out a color book and crayons, paper dolls, a sticker book, and she nearly squealed to find a new Barbie with clothes and accessories in the bottom of the bag. "Thank you, Michael," she said and spread the items over the bed in front of her.

"You're not going to yell at me for spoiling her a little, are you?" Michael said quietly to Emily.

"No," she smiled, "I'm not."

"Good," he said with exaggerated relief. "We're making progress."

Michael visited for a while, then returned to the house to see how the babies were faring in Penny's care. "They're fine, as you can see," she insisted. "Go find something to do."

"Why don't *you* go find something to do?" he retorted.

"Because I'm babysitting."

"Penny," he stated, "let me get specific. I am embarking on a whole new aspect of my life. Fatherhood. I have nothing better I could possibly do with my day than to spend it here. Call it a self-appointed challenge." He lowered his voice. "I'd just like to see if I can do it, okay?"

"You're sure?"

He nodded and Penny laughed.

"It's not funny."

"It might be before the day is through." She laughed again.

"I'm not totally ignorant," he said in his defense.

"Yes, I know, but . . . well, Amee and Alexa can be a handful."

"Penny, I have accomplished many things in my life. Let's just say a day with Amee and Alexa will be the ultimate."

Penny moved toward the door. "You know my number. Call if you need me."

"I will. I promise."

"Oh, by the way . . . " She added a long list of instructions and cautions.

"Thank you, Penny. Good-bye."

"And call 911 for emergency if—"

"Good-bye, Penny."

She waved comically and left him alone.

"So," he turned to Amee, the mischief in her eyes putting him on guard, "what's first, my love?" She giggled and ran down the hall.

The first hour went well. Michael got down on the floor and played with the babies, trying to see the world from the perspective of a crawler and a toddler. When Amee brought stories to read, Michael put on his glasses and did his best to recite them in histrionic tones that kept Alexa's interest as well. Amee screamed when Alexa tried to get the books and eat them, and Michael finally put them away. He pushed his glasses back on his head to be able to see what they were getting into, until Amee held her finger up to show him something.

"Wook a dat," she insisted.

"What?"

She held her finger closer. "Wook a dat!"

Michael examined the finger closely and thought it looked pretty normal. "I can't see anything," he stated.

"Wook a dat!" Amee got downright impatient.

"I can't see anything!" he repeated.

In a perfect twenty-one-year-old tone, she looked up at him and ordered, "Put you gwasses on, Mikow."

Michael laughed himself into a heavy sigh and decided it was time for lunch. He sat Amee at the bar and Alexa in the highchair. While Amee played more than ate, Michael attempted to spoon-feed Alexa. When they finally got to the bottom of the bowl, he looked at her and declared, "It's just a hunch, but I don't think we were supposed to make that big of a mess, little lady." He decided spoon-feeding was a skill one had to acquire through much practice. "I think a bath would be in order," he added and carefully hauled Alexa to the bathroom.

Amee climbed down and followed. "Amee take a baf!" she said

eagerly.

Michael felt sure he couldn't safely handle both of them in the tub at the same time, but he managed to keep Amee occupied with bath toys on the floor. It dawned on him that this chore was not nearly as easy as Emily made it look. Washing and rinsing the baby's hair nearly did him in.

By the time Michael had Alexa dressed, Amee was bawling for a bath, and he had no choice but to repeat the process. By the time he got them down for naps, every room they had been in looked hurricane-struck, and he was as tired as if he'd been training horses all morning.

He hurried through picking up toys, wiping up the bathroom, putting the wet towels and soiled clothes in to wash, and finding the kitchen. When that was done, he allowed himself to sit down and eat his lunch. It was after two o'clock, and he was barely finished when Amee woke up. Five minutes later, Alexa did the same.

Michael changed one's diaper and escorted the other to the potty, then Amee brought more story books for him to read while Alexa fussed for some unknown reason. Cheerios in the highchair finally solved Alexa's problem, but Amee was no longer interested in the books. They built towers with blocks and trains with Legos, then Alexa joined the action and Amee screamed and beat on her sister to keep her out of the toys. After Michael broke up the fight and soothed the hurt, he occupied Alexa with a basket of odd baby toys, and Amee climbed on his lap with an insistent, "Doodasoosie."

"I'm sorry?" Michael said.

"Doodasoosie," she repeated, bouncing up and down impatiently.

"Doodasoosie?" he repeated and she beamed, as if he'd figured it out.

"Doodasoosie. Doodasoosie!"

For twenty minutes Michael attempted to figure out what the strange word meant, or distract her from wanting it, whatever it was. Her tone became more demanding, and he finally broke down and called Penny.

"All right," he said, "I've reached the end of my rope!"

Penny laughed. "I'll be right over."

"No, everything's fine."

"They're alive?" she asked with exaggerated amazement.

"Yes," he replied with mock disgust, "they're alive."

"And healthy?"

"Yes!"

"And the house?"

"Is presentable."

"Wow. So what's the problem?"

"Please, tell me what on earth 'doodasoosie' means."

"Come again?"

"'Doodasoosie.' Amee has said it a hundred times. I'm apparently supposed to get something, or do something, but for the life of me I can't—"

"What does she do when she says it?"

"She bounces up and down and—"

"Oh." Penny's voice filled with enlightenment. "If you'd say it in English, maybe I could understand it."

"Funny. Very funny."

"Well," Penny justified, "baby talk with an Australian accent does have an interesting twist."

"Just tell me what it means."

"Soosie is horsie," she stated. "I would assume that 'doodasoosie' is 'do the horsie.'"

"I know how to do that," Michael said eagerly. "Thanks, Penny. You're a gem. Slightly obnoxious," he teased, "but a gem, nevertheless."

"Anytime."

Michael filled Amee's request and bounced her on his knee while she giggled hysterically. Alexa seemed interested so he did a more gentle version for her, then mastered doing them both at the same time. When he couldn't take any more, he lay on his back on the floor and they started crawling back and forth over him, giggling with perfect baby charm.

The back door opened and Emily called, "Penny, have you seen Michael? His car is here, and—"

"Michael's right here," he called back.

She appeared in the hallway and leaned against the wall, folding her arms with an amused smile. The babies hardly noticed her presence as they continued their game.

"Where's Penny?" Emily asked.

"I sent her home right after I left the hospital."

"You've been here all day?"

"Yeah," he said proudly.

"Alone?"

"No. I've been with Amee and Alexa. We successfully survived lunch, baths, and naps. Amee's hair is a sight, though. I'm no good with those little elastics you put in it."

Emily chuckled. "How are you?"

"You want the truth?" he laughed and she nodded firmly. "I'm absolutely exhausted."

Emily chuckled again. He could never know what that meant to her. On the rare occasions when Ryan had watched the kids, she'd come home to find the house a catastrophe, and his attitude told her it was nothing, as if the stress she felt in caring for them was imagined.

"Does this get me any closer to qualifying as a stepfather?" he asked quite seriously.

"I'd say you're doing pretty good, Jess Michael Hamilton. Getting closer all the time."

"Well, my mother taught me many things. She said she didn't want me to go to college and not be able to take care of myself. And she also said she didn't want any wife of mine to think I wasn't capable of helping around the house. I've often been grateful for what she taught me, but never so much as today." He laughed and attempted to sit up. "Although she never bothered with the fine art of spoon-feeding and bathing babies. I think I need a little more practice."

"I'll give you plenty of opportunities," Emily smiled, finding an unfamiliar peace. For the first time since she'd begun her family, she didn't feel the responsibility of caring for the children by herself. Tearing herself away from the cozy scene, Emily admitted, "I need to do some laundry."

"I put a load in to wash," he announced.

"Thank you." She headed toward the stairs. "And when are you going to start bringing your laundry around? You're not part of the family until you do."

"Since you put it that way . . ." The rest of his sentence was lost in Amee's giggles.

The phone rang while Emily was in the basement, and Michael went to answer it.

"Michael!" his mother's voice exclaimed. "I didn't expect you to answer the phone."

"Well, there's no one else handy to answer it."

"Is it yesterday there?" she asked.

"Yes, Mother."

"How are you?"

"I'm great. How are you?"

"Good as ever. What are you doing?"

"If I told you, you wouldn't believe me."

"Tell me anyway."

"I've spent the day babysitting, if you must know."

"And you survived?" she laughed.

"Keep it up, Mother. Is that why you called—to tease me about my newly-acquired skills?"

"Actually, no." Her voice sobered so quickly that Michael felt nerves twitch at the back of his neck. "There's something I need to ask you, and something I need to tell you."

"All right, ask."

"Murphy wants to know if you'll be here for the Cup. And if not, he wants to know what the bet should be on Private Collection."

"I don't know if I'll be there or not, but tell him not to count on it. Tell him I'm not betting, but my advice is that he put the usual on Private Collection, and the same on Sweet Repose to show."

"You think she can do it?"

"I know she can. Simon's the best jockey we've had in ten years. He rides Sweet Repose like they were born in the same room."

"I'll tell him, but I don't think Murphy shares your confidence."

"You tell Murphy he can plan on eating some words." Michael laughed, then his tone softened. "Now tell me why you really called."

"It's Katherine," she stated.

"What's happened?" His voice was edged with panic.

"Apparently Robert's threatening divorce." Michael sat down. "And Katherine is falling apart over it."

"I can't blame her." Michael groaned in frustration. "Is there anything we can do?"

"I don't think so, but I wanted you to know so you won't come home to a shock."

"Do you think if I talked to her it would—"

"It's not Katherine that needs the talking to, Michael. What can we do?"

"Pray," he offered.

"I have been."

"So have I."

"Then that's all we can do."

Alexa began to cry in the distance. Michael stretched the cord to get her, but Emily got there first.

"Sounds like you're busy," LeNay said.

"I'm fine."

"There's nothing else, really. You take care of yourself and that family of yours. Let me know when I can expect you."

"I'll call when we've got the tickets, and a few times before. Thanks for calling, Mother."

Michael hung up the phone and stared at it until Emily said, "What's wrong?"

"Nothing we can do anything about," he said. "My sister is having some marriage difficulties, that's all."

"That's all?" Emily said dubiously. "I'd say little can be more torturous."

Michael was hoping she'd expound on that and vent some tension that he felt sure she was feeling, but she hurried down the hall with the laundry and nothing more was said.

The day after Allison came home from the hospital, Sister Taylor called early to wish Emily a happy birthday. The first surprise was in getting such a wish from Sister Taylor, and the second was the realization that it *was* her birthday. She had to look at the calendar to make sure. It wasn't until after she'd hung up that she began to wonder how Sister Taylor knew. Six phone calls later, Emily began to wonder what was going on. She called Penny, who swore complete innocence, but when Michael walked through the door, he was met with a hard glare.

"What?" he demanded.

"Why do you suppose everybody in the neighborhood is calling to wish me a happy birthday?"

With perfect innocence, Michael said, "Is it your birthday?"

"Don't you dare try to deny it, Michael Hamilton. I know you're behind this somehow."

"I have no idea what you're talking about," he insisted. But he chuckled and his eyes sparkled, and she knew he was lying.

Emily made a noise of disgust and went to do laundry. A minute later Michael called down the stairs, "Someone here to see you, darlin'."

Emily came upstairs to be greeted by a sister in the ward, bearing a plate of cookies and a birthday card. Emily tried to be gracious, but she felt embarrassed. "Excuse me," she said as the woman was leaving, "but how did you know it was my birthday?"

"Uh . . ." her eyes went wide, ". . . just a hunch."

When the door closed, Emily glared at Michael, who grinned like a Cheshire cat.

The day continued with visits and phone calls, until Emily was nearly ready to beat Michael with a rolling pin. Every time it happened, he just laughed. Allison observed the entire thing from the couch, seeming amused if nothing else.

"How old are you, Mom?" she inquired innocently.

"Too old," Emily retorted.

"She's thirty-three," Michael informed her, only to be frowned at. "And she's nearly three years younger than I am."

"When's your birthday?" Allison asked.

"December." Emily grinned with mischief. "And just you wait, Michael Hamilton."

"I don't know what you're talking about." Michael chuckled. "What did I do?"

"That's what I'd like to know."

"People just love you, that's all. I have nothing to do with it. By the way, Penny's family is coming over for dinner . . . and cake and ice cream."

"Michael, did you—"

"And a few other people might drop by. I don't know. Penny was in charge of the guest list."

"Michael!"

"I'm going to cook your favorite," he said slyly.

"You mean . . . Chinese . . . with all those little wontons in the soup, and stir-fried chicken, and—"

"All of it," he declared.

"But who else is coming over?" she asked in exasperation. "It's so embarrassing."

"People love you!" he grinned. "You're so cute and sweet. You deserve to be embarrassed once in a while."

"Ooooh," she growled at him and went to the kitchen for the rolling pin, if only for a good threat.

Michael just laughed and begged Allison to save him before the phone rang and he answered it with a quick, "Saved by the bell."

He handed the phone to Emily, who graciously received another birthday wish, this time from Launa Wright. "Wait a minute, Launa. Before you go, I have to know . . . how did you know it was my birthday?"

"Well, who wouldn't?" she replied. "What, with that sign in front of your house, and . . . oops, I don't think I was supposed to say that."

"On the contrary, Launa. I am deeply indebted. Thank you."

Emily hung up the phone and turned to Michael, rolling pin poised. "What sign?"

"Sign?" he squeaked with wide eyes.

Emily moved toward the door. Michael tried to stop her, but she brandished the rolling pin and he moved aside.

"You have to leave it up, Emily. I refuse to let you take it down until after dark." He followed her out, mumbling a string of justifications. "You know I never got even with you after what you did when I turned twenty-four. Better late than never, I always say."

"Michael!" she shouted and couldn't help laughing at the banner spread across the house, with bright orange letters that read: "Don't tell anybody, but today is Emily's birthday."

"I wasn't that mean on your birthday!" she insisted.

"Huh!" he snorted. "You filled my Blazer with balloons, you tied a hundred of them to my front porch, and you told somebody in every one of my classes that it was my birthday so they'd sing to me. Now, that was embarrassing."

"I thought it was fun," she smiled.

"I had big plans to get even," he said, his tone softening, "but you were engaged by then." Emily looked down. "Still, like I said, better late than never. That could apply to marrying you as well, I suppose." She looked up and he grinned. "Now we're even—or at least we will be, once the day is over."

Emily had to hug him. She couldn't remember Ryan ever doing anything for her birthday that had shown thought or planning. Her mother had always sent a package; but since her death, it was only Penny and her visiting teachers that made her realize she even had a birthday.

"You aren't really going to hit me with that rolling pin, are you?" he asked, close to her ear.

"Not yet," she smiled and hugged him again. "Do you think Sister Taylor is watching?"

"I hope so." He grinned and kissed her.

Emily embarked on this new year of her life with bright hope for the future. Allison recovered quickly and was soon back at school, while Michael supervised getting everything ready for the passports. He marked a big red "X" on the calendar over the day it was all turned in.

Michael found a new sense of fulfillment as he embarked on another week of sharing Emily's world. For the first time in his life, he felt legitimately part of a family that meant more than life to him, and a religion that *was* life to him.

Emily watched life settle quickly into a routine that brought music and laughter into a home that had, for the most part, been tainted with continual tension. She was surprised, though she decided she shouldn't have been, to see Michael make a conscious effort to bring the family together with daily prayer and scripture study, and family home evening became the highlight of every week. Though Allison remained quiet and generally unreadable, she seemed to react positively to the influence brought into the home by Michael and Emily's love for each other, the children, and the gospel.

Emily began a thorough project of sorting and organizing, beginning with storage boxes and clutter stashed in the unfinished basement, and moving through each room of the house in slow, steady progress.

Michael helped with the babies and did most of the cooking, writing some in a notebook when he had free time. He made certain they took time out regularly for recreation, even if it was just a walk to the park where Allison and Amee played on the swings. Once a week Michael took Emily out without the children, and to compensate for the babysitting, once a week Michael had Penny's family over for dinner.

The day the passports arrived in the mail, Ryan's mother called. Michael answered the phone.

CHAPTER SEVEN

"Who is this?" Mrs. Hall snipped.

"The butler," Michael replied. "Who is this?"

"This is Mrs. Hall," she stated indignantly. Michael grimaced in self-recrimination.

"Mrs. Hall," his voice lightened, "what a pleasure to meet you. You're looking fine this afternoon."

"Why, thank you," she said, then made a noise of disgust as she apparently figured out that she couldn't be seen. "Who is this?" she repeated.

"Did you want to speak to Emily?" he asked, thinking it might be better if she handled this. "I think she's close by. I'll get her." He didn't give the older woman a chance to protest before he ran to get Emily. "It's Ryan's mother," he whispered with his hand over the receiver. "I made a fool of myself. I'm going to let you get me out of this mess. Thank you."

"Hello," Emily said while Michael sat close by to observe and listen, chewing his thumbnail. "No," she smiled, "he is not the butler. He was just joking. He likes to do that. Well, he's an old friend of mine, from college. No, he's not living here. He's staying with a couple in the ward. He just comes by during the days some to help me out. Well," Emily drew the word out in hesitation, "he's mostly doing the cooking while I pack." Emily covered the mouthpiece and whispered to Michael, "I hope she doesn't go into heart failure when I hit her with this." Michael smiled tersely.

The conversation continued. "Yes, I did say I was packing, because we're moving. I meant to tell you. I've just been so busy I haven't thought to call. Well, we'll probably be gone in a month or two. I know the house is yours now, since you co-signed the mortgage note with Ryan; I'm certain you can rent it out easily enough. It's a popular area. No, I'm not moving because I'm angry with you. I know Ryan's death has been hard on you. It's been hard on all of us. Yes, Allison is doing better. She's still having trouble with her friends, but she is doing better in school. I think a change will do her good. I think a change would do me good, as well. That's part of the reason we're moving. The other part is . . . well, I'm getting married again." Emily paused, then winced, then was silent for several moments as she was obviously getting a lecture. Michael shook his head and took Emily's hand to offer support.

"Listen to me," she said quietly, then with more insistence. "Listen to me a minute. I loved Ryan very much, despite what you might think. And I am not jumping into something thoughtlessly or prematurely. The man I am marrying was a close friend of mine from college. We knew each other well. Until this year, we hadn't seen each other since before Ryan and I were married. No, he's never been married. Yes, he's very good with the children." *Better than your son ever was*, Emily thought to herself.

"I don't think I need your permission to get married again," Emily continued, finding it more difficult to maintain self-control. She sighed as the ultimately dreaded question had to be answered. "Australia. No, I am not joking. We are moving to Australia. Michael is Australian." Emily smiled as she repeated, "Yes, that's why he talks funny, but then, he thinks I talk funny. Are you sure you can afford this call?" she finally asked, unable to bear this any longer. "Yes, I'll have Allison call you later. I'm sure she would love to talk to you. Actually, yes, if you'd like, I'll have Allison call you every week from Australia. Yes, I think we can afford it." She paused and sighed. "Yes, if you must know, he is rich. I promise I'll have her call. Good-bye."

"I don't think she likes me," Michael remarked.

"She never liked me."

"Why?" Michael couldn't imagine anyone not liking Emily.

"That's what I always wondered."

"Where is Allison, by the way?"

"She's at Ashley's."

"Is that good or bad?"

"That depends on the day of the week. When Ashley is on, Allison is great. When Ashley is off, Allison is depressed."

"Allison deserves a better friend than that."

"I think getting her away from Ashley could be one of the best things that will ever happen to her."

"Friends are not in abundance where we're going."

"I know."

"Katherine's daughter, Stacy, is nearly twelve, but beyond that, there are no children."

"Who does Stacy play with?"

"She and Wade both have friends in town. We go back and forth regularly."

"I guess we'll just have to worry about that when we get there. What about school?"

Michael sighed. It was evident he didn't want to tell her. "We've always had tutors at the house; the same ones that teach at the boys' home. The closest school is an hour away, but if Allison wants to go to school, we'll find a way to work it out."

"I guess we'll worry about that when we get there, too."

Emily went to referee the babies while Michael started dinner. An hour later, Allison rushed jubilantly through the door to report an enjoyable afternoon with Ashley. She asked Michael what was for dinner, then asked if she could help him.

"Sure," he said. "You shred this cheese."

"When you gonna make hamburgers again?" she asked.

"I could possibly arrange that tomorrow."

"Allison, you're home." Emily came in to find the cheese almost shredded. "Grandma wants you to call her, but . . ." Emily glanced at Michael and bit her lip. "She's kind of upset about us going to Australia. I don't want you to let anything she says bother you. We'll talk about it later."

"Okay," Allison said and dialed the number from the list by the phone. Michael and Emily hovered near, but all they got from their end was a string of "I don't knows" and "I guesses." Allison wasn't yet trained in the art of reflecting conversation for the sake of concerned eavesdroppers.

After a lengthy, mostly one-sided call, Allison hung up the phone and went to her room. Emily followed and tried to talk to her, but got no worthwhile response. Allison picked at her dinner, and despite Michael's jokes about the cooking being bad, she didn't crack a smile.

As she stood to leave the table, Allison said quietly, "Mom, can we go to the cemetery?" Emily glanced warily toward Michael, who showed no expression.

"I suppose we can," Emily said. "Michael, would you mind staying with the baby while—"

"Yes, I would mind," he retorted. Before Emily could question his attitude he added, "After we put the food away, we will *all* go to the cemetery."

"Can we afford to buy some flowers?" Allison asked timidly.

"Yes, Allie," Michael said with compassion in his voice, "we can buy any kind of flowers you want."

When Allison had left the room, Emily said, "You don't have to go, Michael."

"Do you want me to be a part of this family, or not?"

"Of course I do, but—"

"Emily, I think that Ryan's memory is something we *all* need to face up to."

Emily said nothing as she helped clear the table. They barely made it to the florist before it closed, and it was almost dusk when they walked together between the rows of graves, Allison in the lead. She stopped and looked down at the stone a moment before she carefully set the flowers beside it and arranged them.

Michael held Alexa while Emily and Allison shared a quiet moment. He looked down at the name engraved in the shiny, unweathered stone, and tried to comprehend the reality. He'd only met Ryan Hall once, and it was not a pleasant memory. But he reminded himself that Emily and Allison loved Ryan, and that was something he had to learn to live with.

Emily sighed and turned to look around, her gaze coming to rest on Michael, who was watching her closely. "It's peaceful here," she said.

"Yes, it is," Michael agreed.

"Thank you for coming." She smiled, and he was at least glad to see that she could come here and not be overcome with emotion.

"I'll take you anywhere, Emily, as long as we can go together." She smiled again, and Allison, who had not said a word, started back toward the car. The drive home was silent. While the babies played quietly, Emily helped Michael wash the dishes. She found it an intriguing distraction to her concerns when he made a game of finding her hand beneath the bubbles in the water. She giggled when he caught it and wouldn't let go. He laughed when she put suds on his nose. Then, with little warning, he pulled her close and kissed her with a gentle fervency that slowly intensified as she lifted her wet arms around his shoulders.

"Michael," she murmured as he spread kisses across her cheek and to her ear. She wanted him to go on and on. As long as he held her this way, all they had yet to do, all the difficulties still ahead, seemed insignificant. He captured her lips again with his, and she wanted to drown in the sensation.

"Mom?" An appalled little shriek shattered the moment, and Emily turned abruptly to see Allison gaping in disbelief. Emily might as well have dyed her hair purple for the way Allison stared in shock.

"It's all right," Michael whispered so only Emily could hear. He relaxed his hold and she eased out of his arms, but she was completely lost on how to console her daughter's obvious distress. After a long, strained silence, Emily was relieved when Michael spoke up.

"If you're upset, Allison, then let's talk about it."

Allison said nothing, but the glare she gave Michael plainly told him the situation was not good.

Deciding it was about time this family learned to communicate, Emily asked outright, "Do you think there's a reason why I shouldn't kiss Michael?"

Emily could see by Allison's eyes that her mind was working, though she retained her defiant stare. After a long moment she said, "You never kissed Dad like that."

Emily didn't look at Michael, but she felt the tension radiating from him as he folded his arms and leaned against the counter. She wondered briefly how to handle this, then she decided Allison's feelings were more important at the moment. She could deal with Michael later.

"How do you know?" Emily retorted with a confidence that increased when Allison immediately looked befuddled. "Just because you never saw it, doesn't mean it never happened. Your father and I loved each other, but he's gone now. Michael and I love each other, too. It's good for two people to express affection, Allison. One day you might understand that, but until you do, you're just going to have to trust me."

Allison huffed away to her room, leaving no indication of how she really felt. Emily sighed and pressed her forehead into her hand.

"I should be more careful," Michael said tonelessly.

"We should both be more careful." Emily glanced at him, then looked timidly at the floor. "But not because of Allison." She hoped he understood the implication, since she had no desire to explain how his affection made her long for what simply had to wait. She felt sure he would ask her to clarify that, and was relieved when Alexa cried from the other room.

With the children in bed and the dishes done, Emily found Michael standing in the front room, concentrating on her wedding portrait.

"I've been meaning to take it down," she said quietly.

"Don't rush on my account," he replied, but it didn't seem totally sincere.

"Is something wrong?" she asked.

"Nothing new," he admitted, still gazing at the portrait, if only to avoid her eyes.

Emily watched him a moment, feeling a distinct tension. She wondered if it had anything to do with what had happened earlier in the kitchen. "I'm not as skilled at prodding things out of people as you are, so if you've got something to say, you'd better just say it."

"I must confess, there's something I've had trouble dealing with." He still didn't look at her.

"And what is that?" she asked, wondering if she wanted to know. Between Ryan's mother and Allison, she had all the stress she could handle.

Michael's eyes turned to meet hers, filled with a stifled torment.

"*Did* he kiss you that way, Emily?"

Emily hardly knew how to answer, but he was obviously expecting her to. "Michael, he was my husband. I . . ." She stammered into silence.

Michael took hold of her upper arms and pulled her so close that the heat of his eyes nearly melted her. "I know he was your husband, Emily," he whispered vehemently. "I know he fathered your children and shared your bed for ten years. But what I want to know is, did he kiss you the way I kiss you? Did he hold you the way I always wanted to? Did he rub your feet and tickle your knees and run his fingers through your hair? Did he lie with you in the dark and whisper in your ear that you were the most beautiful woman ever created?"

Emily stared up at him in disbelief, feeling like a rag doll that might collapse if he let her go. His words were tinged with anger, but the evidence of his motivation shone through brilliantly. Was it possible that a man could love her so much?

She wanted to tell him the truth—that Ryan's passion had rarely been more than a display of his need for gratification. She wanted to tell him there was no comparison. But how could she explain that one man's embrace depleted and drained her, while the other's replenished and rejuvenated? How could she tell him that his kiss sparked something to life in her that she had never known existed?

She was fighting to find the words when his mouth covered hers as if to demonstrate the accuracy of her thoughts. She clung to him and responded with every fiber of her being, hoping he could feel the answers to his questions coming back to him. When he pulled back slightly, a smile teasing at the corners of his mouth, she felt certain he knew. But she added for good measure, "Need I say more?" Then she kissed him again.

"I think I'd better leave," he whispered, forcing himself away from their embrace.

"One day . . ." she said. Michael nodded his understanding and left for the night. Emily gently touched her lips and muttered a prayer of gratitude for the opportunity she had been given to come back to life.

The following morning when the phone rang, Emily felt hesitant to pick it up. A man's voice said, "Is this where I can reach Michael Hamilton?" His accent was Australian.

"Yes, but he's not here right now. Can I take a message?"

"Yes, thank you. This is Douglas. Tell him to ring me up. He knows the number."

"I'll tell him. He should be back within the hour."

She'd barely hung up when the phone rang again. By the time Michael returned, Emily was in tears.

"What's the matter?" he questioned, but she became almost hysterical. She could hardly think clearly, let alone put the words together with any clarity.

Michael forced her to sit down and breathe deeply until she could speak. "Ryan's mother called." She caught her breath sharply with intermittent whimpers. "She says that . . . that . . . she won't let . . . let me take the children . . . out of the . . . country."

Michael's answer was quick and calm. "She can't do it. This is not a divorce, and even if it were, she would have no say in this. They are your children, Emily. She can't do it, but I'll call a lawyer if it will make you feel better."

"And what if she can?"

"Then we'll stay here." There was no hesitation or regret in his statement.

"But Australia is . . . your home, and . . . "

"Emily, my home is with you. We will be together, wherever we have to be."

"Oh, Michael." She threw her arms around him and wept. "Sometimes I think she's just trying to hurt me somehow to compensate for the hurt she feels over losing her son."

"One day she'll figure out that it didn't help."

Emily wiped her eyes and decided she felt better. "How long do you think it will be before the visas come?"

"Two weeks at the soonest. But it could be longer. How is the packing coming along?"

"Come see." She took his hand and led him to the basement. "So far," she pointed to a corner where a box and a few odd objects were sitting, "that is what I want to have shipped, along with my cedar chest and its contents. But I haven't gone through our clothes yet. And that," she pointed to a huge collection of boxes, "is staying for the great sale."

"I'm glad it's not the other way around," he chuckled, then went to investigate a familiar object among the "go to Australia" items. The artist's easel leaning in the corner was covered with an old sheet that he pulled away. After a studied gaze, he turned to Emily with emotion showing in his eyes. Her gift with oils had always intrigued him. "When did you do this?"

"I started it when Allison began school. I got it out again last spring."

Michael looked at it closer, wishing he had his glasses. "You didn't do this from memory. It's too accurate."

"No," she admitted, "it's from a photograph. I think I tried to convince myself I was doing it just because it was beautiful. I know now that deep inside, it always meant something to me."

"It's incredible," he said breathily. "The color, the realism. I could almost swear I was standing on my front lawn at home, looking out at the . . ."

"'The epitome of Australian beauty,'" she quoted; that was the way he'd put it when he'd shown it to her in person. "'Land earned by blood and sweat for future generations to honor.' Yes," she said, her tone changing, "I remember well your sentiment for the land you were raised on. I tried to put into it the sense of vastness that the photograph didn't capture."

"I think you succeeded."

"I'm going to call it *Listen to the Land*."

"Perfect," Michael said after he thought about it.

"Oh," Emily remembered. "You got a call." He looked surprised. "You're supposed to call Douglas."

"Oh, great," he said with sarcasm.

"What?" Emily sounded panicked.

"Oh, it's nothing serious, it's just . . . well, he's my editor. He wouldn't call unless it was to remind me of deadlines. I'd better call him and get it over with."

Emily stayed in the basement to do laundry, then went upstairs with a basket of clean linens to find Michael sitting at the kitchen table, tapping his fingers thoughtfully.

"What?" she queried.

"It's time to reevaluate. Your beloved has to go back to work."

"Oh, you can't leave now, when—"

"I didn't say I was leaving." He took her hand and smiled up at her. "I said I had to go to work. I already called my mother and told her to send the working copies of my diskettes. All I need to do is get my hands on a computer. I suppose I could go buy a used one and just add it to Penny's garage sale, or perhaps . . . "

Emily set the laundry down and motioned with her finger for him to follow her. Michael realized they were going into her bedroom—the one room in the house he'd never ventured into. He hesitated a moment, then peered around the door to see what she had led him to.

"Ask and ye shall receive," she stated histrionically. "Top of the line, all updated, IBM compatible, with every word processing feature you could dream of."

"I guess that solves my problem, but . . ." He looked at Emily closely, trying to perceive this. "Did Ryan . . . work with computers?"

"Yes."

"Then he must have needed this to do his work," Michael stated to assure himself.

"It came in handy occasionally, but for the most part, he just wanted it."

"Emily," Michael's voice picked up an edge, "are you trying to tell me that—"

"Don't say it, Michael. I know what you're thinking because I thought it myself. It wasn't fair, and it wasn't right, but it's in the past. We can be grateful we have it today. You start writing, and I'll start cooking."

Michael put his anger in check. "No," he said, "you keep organizing. I'll stock up on frozen dinners and check out the fast food scene. How much do you have left to go through?"

"Too much."

"Then you'd better get going. I'll keep things under control until my materials arrive in a day or two."

Allison came home from school in an unusually melancholy mood. Michael barbecued hamburgers for dinner, but she hardly touched hers.

"All right, let's have it," Michael said, deciding the child could not live with bottled-up emotions all her life. "If something is bothering you, Allison, you have got to speak up. We are a family, and whatever problems any of us have, we must face them together. We can't do that if one of us won't talk about the problems." Allison looked wary. "Is it Ashley?" he prodded. She shook her head. "School?" he guessed again without success. "Is it me?" he had to ask. Allison gave no response. "All right. We've narrowed it down. It's me. What about me? Don't you like my cooking?"

"I like it better than all those dumb casseroles Mom used to make."

Michael smiled. At least she was talking. "Those dumb casseroles were all your mother could afford to make," he said in Emily's defense. "Food costs money, Allie. Some food costs more. If you like my cooking, then what's the problem?" No response. "Still mad at me for kissing your mother?" he asked, and didn't miss the faint blush that rose in Emily's cheeks.

"I guess you can kiss her if you want to," Allison said tonelessly.

"So, if that's not bothering you, what is?" Michael pressed, feeling a degree of progress. At least he had her permission to kiss his fiancée. He gave her a minute to think, but still got no response. "You're as bad as your mother. She doesn't like to talk either. But she can tell you that it's no good trying to keep it from me. Tell her, Emily."

"He's right, sweetie. You might as well just say what's bothering you and we'll talk about it. He'll make you sit there until you do, but once you let it out, you'll feel better."

Emily nearly regretted all the prodding when Allison said without looking up, "Mom, when you go to Australia, I want to go live with Grandma."

Michael looked quickly to Emily. The pain was evident. After all she had suffered, all they had been through, something worse always managed to come up.

CHAPTER EIGHT

After an hour of making Allison talk, Emily finally managed to get the children to bed, then she nearly collapsed on the couch.

"I can't leave her, Michael. I know how much your home means to you, but I will not sacrifice my daughter."

"I would not ask you to."

"It's difficult enough raising a child, but to think of . . . " She sighed loudly. "Ryan's mother must believe she is doing the right thing, and I know she tried to raise her children right. But I know, because I had to live with it, that there were ideas instilled in her home that damaged my home. I will not even consider allowing Allison to be raised with that influence."

"Emily, leaving Allison behind is not even a consideration. You're doing the right thing. Give it time. It will work out."

"I wonder," she said cynically.

"Where is that undying faith of yours?"

"I think it died."

Michael didn't press it further, but he felt concerned for her in a way he couldn't describe. His writing materials were a day slower than he'd anticipated, but as he began to write, stress descended unlike he'd ever known. Allison regressed into quiet solitude. Emily began to wear a permanent scowl of concern, like the one she'd worn when he'd arrived to find her destitute. Alexa went through a bout of teething that left her whiny during the days and restless at night. And Amee seemed to sense the tension, responding to it with fits of crankiness.

The days became long and tiresome, and the nights much too

short to acquire the needed rest. One evening, barely into a fitful sleep, Michael awoke to a light knock at the bedroom door.

"What?" He sat up abruptly and attempted to orient himself.

The door opened and a beam of light streamed in from the hallway. "Emily just called," Lucinda reported in concerned tones. "The message was simply: Tell Michael I need him."

"Thank you," he said, his heart pounding. "What time is it?"

"Nearly three, I believe."

She left him to dress hurriedly, then followed him to the door. "If I can do anything, let me know."

"Thank you," he said, impulsively bending to kiss her cheek.

"We're going to the temple in the morning, but I'll be home after ten or so. If you need anything, you'll have to wait until then."

"I think I can manage."

Michael rushed to the car, wondering what could have possibly happened now. He prayed aloud as he drove the eight and a half blocks to Emily's and ran to the door. He could hear the baby crying before he opened it.

"What's wrong?" he asked, dropping down beside a weary Emily who was futilely trying to console Alexa. The baby just wiggled and cried in a way he'd never heard before.

"She's in pain," Emily said, trying to remain calm. "That's all I can tell you for certain. I suspect it's an ear infection. Feel her." She guided his hand to Alexa's little back, beneath her undershirt.

"She's burning up," Michael confirmed, his eyes narrowing.

"I gave her something for it, but it's only gotten worse."

"How high is it?" he asked.

"I couldn't get her to hold still long enough to take her temperature, but I'm guessing about 103. If I could call the doctor, I could at least find out what to do, but she won't stop crying and . . ." Emily's lip quivered.

"Should we take her to the hospital, or—"

"I don't think that's necessary. By the time they got to her, we'd be close to business hours anyway. If you'll just hold her, I'll call and see what we can do."

Michael took the baby and began to walk with her while Emily dialed a memorized number to get her doctor's answering service. She explained the situation and was connected to the doctor within minutes.

"All right," Emily announced after she hung up the phone, "he told me what we can give her to safely ease the pain, and we need to get her into the tub to lower the fever. He said to be in his office at nine o'clock."

Michael sighed. He'd never done anything like this before, and realized he was distraught.

"You undress her. I'll fix the water."

Michael followed her to the bathroom while he pulled off Alexa's clothes.

"I don't know why I didn't think of the bath. I used to have to do that for Allison all the time."

"You did?"

"She had so many ear infections as a baby that they finally had to put drainage tubes in her ears. I can't count the nights I stayed up with her, bathing her every two hours to keep the fever down."

"And what was Ryan doing?" Michael had to ask as Emily laid the baby on her back in the shallow water.

Emily gave him a brief, sharp glance. "He helped some, but he had to get up and go to work."

"So did you."

Emily ignored the comment and left Michael to watch the baby while she retrieved the medicine from the kitchen. She gave Alexa the proper dosage, then sang softly to her. She gradually began to act more like herself as the fever lessened. When she was dressed, Michael sent Emily to bed.

"I think I can handle it for an hour or two."

"Are you sure?"

"Yes, I'm sure," he insisted. "Get some sleep."

Emily walked down the hall but returned a moment later with a pillow and two blankets which she set on the couch. "If you need anything, let me know." She almost felt guilty.

"Go to sleep, Emily," he ordered, and she was in bed only a few minutes before she did. The alarm clock woke her and she threw on a robe, wondering what she had slept through. In the front room, she found Michael asleep on the couch with Alexa sleeping on his chest.

For a minute she just watched them. The scene was so tender—much like everything Michael did in her life. She was amazed at his goodness and sensitivity, and a little awed to see him taking over Ryan's role in ways that Ryan never had.

Reminding herself of the time, Emily woke Allison with an explanation of the night's events and urged her to hurry her morning routine. Emily dressed and put eggs on to boil, then decided she had to wake Michael if they were going to get to the doctor. She nearly nudged his shoulder, but impulsively bent over him to press her lips meekly to his. She felt response in the kiss before his eyes opened. Emily pulled back and Michael smiled.

"I used to have dreams like that," he whispered, "but you were never there when I woke up."

"I'm here now," she said, touching Alexa's wispy hair, "along with all my complications."

Michael kissed the top of Alexa's head. "Just so you're here."

"How did she do?" Emily asked. "I must have slept right through."

"She fussed for a while, but she's slept pretty good since about four-thirty."

"You rest a little longer," she ordered, pushing the hair back off his forehead, "and then we'll get her to the doctor. I think Amee's awake. I'd better get her dressed."

Michael eased Alexa onto the couch, where she miraculously remained asleep. He looked at the clock and decided he could stand to clean up a little if they were going out, but Sister Swann wasn't home. He went into the bathroom, where the mirror convinced him he was a mess. Impulsively he decided this was as good a time as any to get rid of some of the ghostly images in this house. With all the sorting Emily had done, what had belonged to Ryan had remained untouched, and it was beginning to get on his nerves.

He left the bathroom door open while he took what he needed from the medicine chest and began to shave. Allison came in to brush her hair and hardly seemed to notice him, but before he finished, Emily was leaning in the doorway, watching him.

"What are you doing?" she asked curtly.

"I'm shaving," he stated. "That's what we men have to do when we get this disgusting stubble on our face, and—"

"Michael," she interrupted. He splashed water on his face and rinsed off the razor.

"What?" he asked when she didn't say anything more.

Emily remained silent, wondering why it bothered her to see him use Ryan's personal things, when it didn't bother her to see him raising Ryan's children. "Nothing," she finally said, but Michael knew from her expression that she didn't like what he'd just done. Wishing he knew exactly where she stood, Michael decided to test her sentiments. He casually pulled a bottle of aftershave from the cabinet.

"Don't you dare!" she snapped. He looked toward her innocently. "Fine. Use his razor, but I cannot tolerate having you smell like him."

Michael put the bottle back and closed the cabinet. "Why is it still here?" he asked quietly.

"I've been busy. I haven't gotten around to—"

"You haven't gotten around to it, or you don't want to?" She didn't answer, and he took the aftershave back out and tossed the bottle in the garbage. "There," he said, "I just got around to it. Now, do you think there's a clean shirt somewhere in this house that might fit me? Sister Swann is out for the morning and her house is locked."

Emily looked at Michael, then at the bottle in the garbage, feeling confused but not understanding why. "I'll see what I can find," she said tersely and turned away.

She returned to find him brushing his teeth. He looked up when he was done and announced, "I used your toothbrush." He grinned slyly. "I hope you don't mind my germs." He kissed her to pass along a few more, then Emily handed him a shirt.

"Is that all right?" she asked tonelessly.

Michael recognized it as Ryan's black sweatshirt that Emily wore on occasion. Was it so difficult to allow him to wear something that Ryan had worn last?

"It's fine," he said and closed the bathroom door to clean up while Emily went to the kitchen.

Alexa was declared to have a double ear infection by a doctor who obviously knew Emily well. Emily explained it with, "You have two babies in two years, and you spend far too much time in the doctor's office."

"The girls both look good other than that," the doctor declared after looking Amee over as well. He politely glanced toward Michael, seeming to wonder who he was. "And how is the rest of the family?"

Michael saw the panic in Emily's face as she realized the doctor didn't know. "Actually," Emily stated, "we had Allison in the hospital for an emergency appendectomy. I think you were out of town. She's doing fine." She hesitated then added, "Ryan was killed in June. An automobile accident."

The doctor looked up abruptly from where he scribbled on a prescription pad. "I'm sorry to hear that," he said with sincerity. "I must have missed the obituary." He looked up at Michael with a slight smile. "Then I assume this is not your brother."

Michael chuckled. "Not hardly."

"You're not American," the doctor said, intrigued.

"No," Michael admitted. "I went to college in the states for five years, but I can't say two words without giving it away." They embarked on a brief conversation about Australia, as the doctor mentioned he had a cousin who married an Australian and they now lived near Adelaide. The doctor congratulated them on their forthcoming marriage and sent them on their way.

With prescription in hand, they returned home where Michael held Alexa while Emily did the minimal housework. She found the two sleeping again on the front room floor, and eased Alexa away from him to put her in the crib. After Amee went down as well, Emily decided she would be wise to use the time to catch up on some of the sleep she'd lost. She nearly went to the bedroom, but impulsively she lay on the floor near Michael and quickly drifted off.

Michael woke to find Emily sleeping close to him. He brushed the backs of his fingers over her face, marveling at the woman she was and the effect she'd had on his life. He eased closer to her, relishing her nearness, wishing away the time until they were married. She began to stir and he kissed her into coherency. She smiled and he eased her closer. He couldn't remember ever holding her this way before, and they watched each other with quiet anticipation. He kissed her again, then cleared his throat and pulled away.

Emily watched him closely, the desire in his eyes all too apparent. She found comfort in it, along with a sense of frustration. After being married so many years, it was difficult to be sharing all aspects of her life with Michael, except one. She touched his face and he closed his eyes, sighing her name and pressing his cheek further into her hand. He kissed her again, then took a deep breath and jumped to his feet.

"I think I hear my mother calling," he said quite seriously.

"From Australia?" she laughed.

"I forgot to take out the garbage," he added and walked into the kitchen, where she heard him exploring cupboards.

"What are you doing?" she leaned over the bar to ask.

"I'm going to bake something full of fat and calories, and maybe if I eat enough of it, it will distract me from . . ." He cleared his throat but didn't finish.

Emily chuckled. "You'd better make a double batch."

Alexa woke up and Emily went to get her while Michael looked through recipes. "She feels warm," Emily stated. "It's past time she had more of that stuff. Would you hand it to me, please?"

Michael opened the cupboard above his head where the medicines were kept. "What, this?" He held up the bottle of liquid fever reducer.

"Yes, and the dropper." Michael passed them over the bar, then turned to close the cupboard door when something caught his eye. Looking further, he found four different prescriptions with Ryan's name on them.

"What are these?" he asked Emily. Her expression told him it was obvious. "Why are they still in here?"

"I told you. I just haven't gotten around to it."

"Or is it that you don't want to get around to it?"

"Michael, I have been taking care of three children and living under a fair amount of strain ever since he died. One of these days I'll get around to it. Obviously I've got to do it before we move."

She dismissed the subject so curtly that Michael felt certain a part of her was holding on to Ryan in a way he didn't consider healthy. "Memories and keepsakes are fine, Emily, but his things are around this house like he was here yesterday. Have you moved anything at all? Did you pick up the dirty socks he left the night before he died?"

He'd meant to give her a light analogy, and hardly expected her to answer with a tearful, "Yes, I . . . washed them and . . . put them away."

"Emily!" he said in a combination of empathy and disgust.

"I'm sorry, Michael." She held up a hand. "I can't talk about this right now."

"That's what you said weeks ago, and I let it drop," he retorted. "But it's getting a little ridiculous. You've gone through nearly everything in this house that you can go through until we shut down the house and stop living in it. What seems to be the problem?" Michael wondered, though he couldn't bring himself to ask, if Ryan's last weeks of life had made her somehow idealize him, keeping her from facing the reality of what they had shared. "Well?" he pressed when she didn't answer.

"I said I would get around to it," she insisted. "This is not easy for me, Michael."

"Why?" he asked strongly. "Tell me why it's not easy and let's get on with our lives."

"I said I don't want to talk about it."

"When are you going to talk about it?" he retorted, and for the first time ever, he shouted at Emily. "Sooner or later, you have got to stop living with a ghost!"

Michael immediately regretted his remark as Emily's expression turned to fear. He felt a dull pounding in his head while he wondered where those words had come from.

"I'm sorry, Emily." He moved toward her, wanting to take them back. "I don't know why I said that. I—"

"Here!" She handed Alexa to him abruptly. "You give her the medicine. I think I need to be alone."

Emily hurried to the bedroom and knelt to pray in silence. She prayed for guidance and discernment, strength and the ability to see herself clearly. Then she listened. With her head bowed against the bed, she left her mind open to the Spirit. Several minutes later, she returned to the front room with no definite impressions. Michael was sitting on the couch with Alexa cuddling against his shoulder, his eyes full of regret.

"I'm sorry," he said again. "I don't know where that came from. I told you I would give you all the time you needed. I have no right to get upset over something so trivial."

"It's all right, Michael," she spoke solemnly. "I'm certain there is much I need to deal with that I'd rather not." She turned toward the kitchen.

"Where you going?"

"I'm going to wash dishes," she announced. "I need to think."

Emily filled the sink with sudsy water and loaded it with glasses and silverware. While she washed, tears began to fall. It was difficult to know how to feel when there were so many aspects of her life, past and present. Should she only remember Ryan for his good traits, that had rarely shown until the final weeks of his life? Should she only remember him for the changes he had made, the hope she had felt on his behalf? Was it possible to forget and disregard all he had done to hurt her, and the difficult life she had led because of his insecurities directed toward her? The results were all around her, and yet she loved Ryan. A part of her ached for the tragedy of his untimely death. But if he were alive, she would never know the joy she was now finding with Michael. For all the stress they were experiencing, he was a boon to her. He lifted and rejuvenated her. His attitudes were gradually bringing her to believe in herself again. She could not imagine her life without him. But where should she draw the line? Something held her back, and she didn't understand what. Was it fear? Guilt? Or just too many unvented emotions? Perhaps a combination. But at the moment, her most prominent feeling was confusion.

Her thoughts took her through the dishes, and she glanced around the kitchen to find one forgotten glass. The confusion weighed heavily as she immersed it in the water and reached into it with the dishrag to loosen the dried milk from the bottom. Her next conscious realization was the water turning red, and the broken glass fell from her hands. She felt light-headed, but whether it was from shock or abrupt loss of blood she didn't know. Instinctively she pressed her forehead to the counter in front of the sink in an effort to regain her balance. After a few seconds, she lifted her eyes to see blood gushing from her hand into the dishwater.

"Michael!" she called, hearing a panic in her voice that she didn't consciously feel until she said it.

He set the baby down and ran to her. "What? What is it?"

"I cut myself," she stated, her head against the counter, her eyes closed.

She felt Michael's hand grip her wrist while he muttered breathily, "Mercy! What happened?"

"A glass . . . broke in . . . my hand . . . and . . ."

"All right," he said calmly. "Stay put. Just a second here." She heard the linen drawer open and felt him wrap her hand tightly in a towel. His arm came around her waist from behind. "All right. Let's get you to a chair. Take it easy."

Emily lifted her head slowly and saw stars. Unwillingly she fell back against him. He scooped her into his arms as if she weighed nothing and set her carefully in a chair next to the table.

"Hold this here." He pressed her good hand over the wound. "And keep your head against the table." Emily did as he said, hardly able to think of anything except the pattern she was beginning to see in all of this. Amee's stitches. Allison's appendix. Alexa's ears. And now this. Was someone trying to tell them something?

Michael found Penny's number and punched it out quickly. "Guess what?" he said after a minute. "Penny's not home."

"Great," Emily muttered sarcastically. "Doesn't she know it's her sole mission in life to sit around and wait until I need her?"

"She ought to by now." Michael slammed the phone down. "Who else can I call to watch the babies? We've got to get you to the doctor."

Emily tried to think. "Try Launa Wright. It's on the list. But we'll have to take the babies there . . . if she's home."

Michael called the number and felt relieved to hear Sister Wright's kind voice. He quickly explained, and she eagerly told him to bring the babies over.

"Oh," he added, "Alexa has an ear infection, but—"

"It's all right," she assured him. "I've dealt with such things before."

Michael then dialed the doctor's number that Emily recited

from memory. "They said they'd be ready for you," Michael said. "You stay put. I'll get the babies loaded."

"Don't forget to put diapers in the bag," she called.

He came back for Emily and found the dishtowel soaked red, but he didn't say anything for fear she would panic. He was panicked enough for both of them. He just wrapped a clean towel around her hand before she lifted her head, and grabbed a few more just in case.

Emily walked, leaning heavily against him, until she nearly collapsed in the car seat and he buckled her in. The throbbing in her hand matched the pulsebeats in her head that seemed to be draining away her coherency.

"Put some pressure on it, darlin'," he said calmly, and she attempted to direct her strength to the effort. "Where we going?"

"Around the corner, three houses down, this side," she mumbled.

Michael found it easily as Launa walked out to meet them, quickly taking Alexa and the diaper bag while he retrieved a sleepy Amee.

"Thank you," he called and ran back to the car.

"Don't you worry," she called back. "They'll be fine."

"Oh," he added quickly, "Allison will be—"

"I'll pick her up from school while Ellie stays with the babies. What's the code word?"

"The what?" He narrowed his eyes in question.

"The code word?"

"Emily." He leaned into the car. "What's the code word?"

"Chocolate mousse," she reported blandly, "but please don't shout it to the whole neighborhood."

Michael ran back up the walk and stated, "Chocolate mousse." Launa nodded and he returned to the car, without a clue what they were talking about.

"Chocolate mousse?" he questioned, turning the car toward the highway. Emily nearly appreciated the distraction, even if it was one of her least favorite topics. "It's a requirement for raising children these days. Allison is not to get in a car with anyone except Penny or Bret, unless they give her a code word that only family would know."

"But surely if it's someone she knows . . . " he began to protest but she interrupted.

"Actually, more than eighty percent of the horrible things that happen to children are done by someone the child knows."

Michael's eyes widened with this new revelation of parenthood. "You're joking," he nearly gasped.

"No," she stated, "I'm not joking. These days, teaching our children such things is the same as teaching them not to play in the street or to play with matches."

"I'm glad you know all this stuff," he said. "Some parent I'd make without you."

Emily looked over at him, her head resting wearily against the seat. "I love you, Michael."

"I love you, too. And if you feel better with Ryan's ghost around, that's fine with me. But . . . " he smiled, "let's not take it to Australia."

"All right," she closed her eyes, "but . . ." She hesitated too long

"Are you okay?" he asked almost frantically.

"Just a little slow on the brain," she replied. "I was just thinking that . . . maybe it's time I . . . dealt with it and . . . " She opened her eyes, and he saw a subtle pleading there. "I need you . . . to help me, and . . ." Her words trailed off.

Michael nodded firmly and put a hand briefly to her face. "You take it easy. We'll talk later. Do you want me to carry you?" he asked, opening the car door for her.

"No," she insisted. "I'm not that bad off."

They were ushered into a back room intended for treating lacerations. The nurse helped Emily lie back on the table and provided Michael a seat where he could hold her good hand and apply pressure to the injury. A few minutes later the doctor entered with a jubilant, "I thought I'd gotten rid of you people earlier today."

"We're not necessarily pleased to be here," Michael stated. Emily didn't make a sound.

"What happened?" he asked, carefully unwrapping three blood-soaked towels.

"She was washing dishes," Michael explained. "A glass broke in her hand."

"Oooh," the doctor grimaced at the sight of it, "you must have been pushing pretty hard. It's deep."

Michael looked warily at the wound while the doctor examined it more closely and Emily winced. His nose wrinkled at the sight of the deep, diagonal cut in the fleshy part of her lower hand, just off the thumb.

"I don't think there's any serious damage," the doctor stated, continually stopping to blot the blood away with sterile gauze. "And I dare say it's bled plenty to get rid of the dishwater. We'll stitch it up and go from there."

Emily came to life as the doctor shot painkiller in and around the wound. "That's not very nice," she said when he was finished.

The doctor chuckled and put a fatherly hand to her shoulder. "I've seen you suffer through much worse, Emily. I think you'll survive this."

"There is no comparing this to childbirth," Emily retorted weakly.

"From what I hear," the doctor replied, apparently waiting for the medication to take effect while he kept pressure on the gauze over the wound, "nothing compares to childbirth. And I've heard about it a great deal in my career." He chuckled again, then added to Michael, "I've talked to a few pregnant women in my time."

"I bet you have," Michael smiled.

"So," the doctor said casually while he poked the wound to test it. Emily winced and he relaxed again. "What part of Australia are you from?"

"It's a rural area in the southern part of Queensland. It's not near anything most Americans would recognize, but it's a beautiful part of the country."

"Is it as flat as the central regions?" he asked.

"Much of my family's land is flat and dry, but we're on the edge of the Great Dividing Range, which adds some diversity. It's a beautiful place to live, but we get some very strange weather."

"Yes, I've heard Australian weather can be unpredictable."

Michael chuckled. "Downright deadly at times. I've seen storms settle into those mountains that could kill the best horseman."

The wound was tested again for readiness and Emily still reacted, so he shot a little more painkiller into it.

"Do you use horses much?" he asked Michael.

"Well, *we* do," Michael chuckled. "We're in the business of breeding and racing. Horses have been our life for more than a hundred years."

"Fascinating," he replied and they embarked on a conversation that left Emily hardly aware of the many close-knit stitches being put into her hand. It was carefully wrapped, two prescriptions were written out, and instructions given to keep it elevated for a while, keep it dry until the stitches were removed, and to put Emily on an iron supplement to help compensate for the blood she'd lost, as she was prone to anemia.

Michael took Emily home and settled her on the couch. "I'll get the children and pick up the prescriptions. Is there anything else you want?"

"I'll be fine," she smiled, "but . . . "

"What?"

"I want a homemade root beer float."

"You got it." He kissed her brow. "I'll see you in a while."

Emily closed her eyes and let the weariness relax her further, enjoying what time she had left before the anesthetic wore off.

CHAPTER NINE

As Michael pulled up in front of the Wright home, Allison ran out the door.

"Where's Mom?" she asked. "What happened?"

The panic in her voice evoked Michael's compassion as he squatted down to face her. "She's fine, sweetie. She's at home resting."

Allison threw her arms around him with a sob of relief, and Michael felt choked up. For the first time since he'd become involved in their lives, he stopped to try and imagine the impact of those first moments of losing Ryan. Allison's fear now was obviously the result of the shock of her father's death, which Michael knew he could never understand. Despite the difficult loss of his own father, the sickness had come on slowly, and the death had been anticipated for months.

He put comforting arms around Allison, whispering gently, "It's all right, baby. She cut her hand, that's all. It was kind of bad, but the doctor stitched it up and she's just fine."

Allison drew back and sheepishly wiped at her tears. Michael gave her an accepting smile and added, "Nothing is going to happen to your mom. I'm going to take very good care of her."

Allison hugged him again, and Michael felt the reality of parenthood. He loved and cared for this child as much as he loved and cared for Emily. His heart was not divided by having to love the children. It was only added upon.

"Come on," Michael said, "let's get the babies and go to K-Mart. We've got to get some prescriptions for your mom, and maybe we can get her something else, too—something to cheer her up."

"Okay," Allison agreed, perking up. "But don't spend too much money, or she'll get mad at you."

"I'll try to restrain myself," he laughed and followed Allison into the Wrights' house to retrieve the babies and give the latest tragedy report from the Hall household. By the time they returned from K-Mart, dinner had been brought in by Emily's visiting teachers, and all signs of the accident had been cleaned away.

The phone rang, and Michael answered it to hear Lucinda Swann say in perfect cockney, "So, what was the emergency?"

"Which one?" he retorted, then proceeded to explain.

"Good thing you weren't staying in that nasty hotel," she said in her normal voice.

"Yes," he agreed, "it's a good thing."

"Can I expect to see you this evening?"

"Actually," he said, "despite the risk of gossip, I think I'll take tonight on the couch here. With Alexa sick and Emily down, I think I'd better stay. But I promise I'll be a good boy."

"Oh, all right," she agreed with mock reluctance. "Do you need any of your things?"

"I think I can manage tonight. I'll come by in the morning."

"Is there anything I can do?" she asked with genuine concern.

"I think it's under control, but thank you anyway . . . Mother."

"Now," she chuckled, "none of my guests have ever called me that before."

"You couldn't understand them if they had," he replied, and she had to agree.

Michael kept the household under control while Emily spent the evening barely coherent from the pain medication. When the children were in bed and the house tidied, Michael went to the bedroom to write while Emily slept, oblivious to his presence. Exhaustion sent him to the couch near midnight and soon after, Alexa woke up. He gave her the necessary medicine and rocked her back to sleep, then he went to check on Emily and found her awake.

"How you doing?" he asked gently, the light from the hall illuminating a path to the bed.

"I'm all right," she said groggily. "I think I need another pain pill. It throbs clear up my arm."

"I can imagine. I'll get it for you."

"That's all right. I need to get up anyway."

When Emily came out of the bathroom, Michael met her with the pill and a glass of water. She smiled and took it, then went back to bed. Michael stood in the hall for a moment, feeling a little lost, though he couldn't figure why. He switched off the light and returned to the couch, where he slept until morning.

As Emily became free of the pain and the need to dull it, the routine settled again. Allison grudgingly helped with the dishes, and talked of little else but wanting to go to Idaho, when she talked at all. When Emily felt she could bear it no longer, she snapped at Allison to be quiet, then went to the bedroom as a habitual effort to find solace. Instead, she found Michael at the computer.

"What's wrong?" he asked, turning immediately toward her.

Emily sat on the edge of the bed and put her forehead into the hand that wasn't bandaged. "If that child says 'Idaho' one more time, I'm going to scream." She looked at her damaged hand scornfully. "It's not bad enough that I can't do anything normal without help; now I have to listen to that. I can't take it, Michael. I just can't take it."

"Listen to me." Michael sat beside her. "I told you we would not leave the country without Allison, and I meant it. Just try not to let it get to you, and we'll work it out somehow." Emily only sighed. "Maybe we should get out," he offered. "We haven't done anything since you got hurt. Would you like to go to—"

"Actually," she said, "there's a ward social tonight. I suppose we should go. We're supposed to take a salad."

"Why didn't you say something?" he asked.

"You've been busy," she justified, "and you've already had to help so much. I can't even change a stupid diaper without—"

"Emily." He stopped her with a firm embrace. "I have obligations to meet, but none more important than my family. Come on. I'll help you make a salad, and we'll go to the church social. You'll feel better."

The cultural hall was decorated with an autumn motif, and a potluck buffet of the finest cooking in Orem spread over long tables to celebrate the harvest moon. Emily felt better quickly as acquaintances socialized and gave empathy. Michael fit comfortably into the surroundings, and Emily's mind wandered as she watched him. The last church social Ryan had attended was when Allison was three months old. In the years since, Emily had always gone to these functions alone, plagued by a certain emptiness as she observed other couples who were active and apparently happy. Now, she wondered if Michael had any idea how completely he filled her life.

They returned home with sleepy babies who were soon put down, and Michael helped Allison with her homework for half an hour before she went to bed. While Emily sat on her bed and read from the Book of Mormon, Michael sat to write until his curfew, when he knew Lucinda Swann would call if he wasn't in her house.

"How's it coming?" Emily set a warm hand on his shoulder and leaned over to look at the screen.

Michael leaned back, folded his arms, and took off his glasses to rub his eyes. "Slow. Very slow. I prefer to write from inspiration. I don't much care for this pressure of contracts."

"But you told me yourself the story was inspired."

"I know, but . . . I guess I'd rather do it because I want to, not because I have to."

"It will come," she encouraged, pressing a kiss to the side of his neck.

"Eventually." Michael turned to look at her and found himself wishing, as he often did these days, that a lack of matrimony wasn't standing between them. She bent over to kiss him softly. He smiled up at her, then from the corner of his eye he saw a common fixture of the room that suddenly made him angry. Abruptly he stood, picked up the dust-covered shoes off the floor, and tersely threw them into the closet.

"What are you doing?" Emily asked.

"Something you should have done a long time ago," he stated.

Emily swallowed her rising anger and said calmly, "As soon as I get these stitches out, I will go through his things."

"And in the meantime, I am not going to sit here and try to be inspired while I work at your late husband's toy with your late husband's belongings strewn everywhere I turn."

"Haven't we argued about this enough?" she asked.

"Not until the problem gets solved, we haven't."

"Michael, I am in mourning here. You have no idea what I am going through."

"Death has touched my life before, Emily. I lost my father when I was eleven."

"Yes, I know; and I know it was difficult for you. But this is different. I lost my spouse, Michael. However unsteady the relationship may have been, I loved him. He was the center of my life. It's difficult to even know how to function when the center of your life is suddenly gone with no warning. So, don't stand there and try to tell me how I should feel, when you have no idea what you're talking about or—"

Michael grabbed her arm to interrupt her. "Don't you dare," he said through clenched teeth, "tell me that I don't know how it feels to hurt because the center of your life is suddenly gone with no warning. You have no idea what I went through after you left me, Emily. You turned and walked out of my life without a trace, and I mourned. I *mourned*."

Her eyes narrowed skeptically and he pulled her toward him, tightening his grip. "Yes, I mourned. And I would have far preferred that you had died. I didn't go out of those four walls for days. I could barely eat. I hardly slept. My life fell apart. When the term started I forced myself to go through the motions, but my grades crumbled. I crumbled. Everywhere I turned, all I could see were memories of you, and you were off merrily planning a wedding—a wedding that should have been mine. Until you left for Idaho, there had not been a day in months that you and I had not shared. We were as close as two people could be without sharing a bed. It took me months to even think clearly, and I *never* got over it."

Emily opened her mouth to protest, but he held up a finger to stop her. "Now that it's over," his voice softened, "I understand why all of that was necessary. But don't you dare try to tell me that I don't know how it feels to hurt and to mourn. Our suffering has come in different colors, Emily, but it was suffering just the same."

Michael let go of her arm, but before she had a chance to respond, the phone rang. Michael glanced at the clock and sighed. He took out the disk and turned off the computer while Emily went to answer it.

"Just a minute," she said, "I'll get him and—"

"Tell her I'm on my way," Michael said and left without another word. Emily gave Sister Swann the message and hung up the phone, wondering what was happening in their lives. Hearing his car drive away, she sat down and cried.

As Michael drove the short distance, he puzzled over what was wrong with him. He didn't understand the discouragement he felt, any more than he understood why the issue they were arguing over bothered him so intensely. He wasn't the type to get so easily agitated, and yet he was doing it frequently. Emily proved to him continually that she loved and accepted him as her husband-to-be, and as a father to her children. So why did the presence of Ryan's earthly belongings make him so angry?

By morning he still didn't have any answers, but he was determined to get this in the open once and for all.

"Good morning," he said to Emily, then opened a cupboard and started pulling out all prescription bottles belonging to anyone deceased. Emily didn't pay much attention as he flushed their contents down the toilet and threw the bottles away. But her interest perked considerably when he started going through magazines and tossing in a box anything that was obviously Ryan's. When she opened her mouth to protest, he cut her off.

"You're wounded. You can't do it. I'll do it, because I can't stand it any longer."

"Michael, it is not your place to determine what happens to my husband's things."

"In a few weeks I will be your husband, Emily. If you don't want me to take charge of this, then I suggest you help me."

"I don't want to do it right now," she insisted.

"Well, you have to!" he shouted. "Because I cannot concentrate until it's done, and we are not going anywhere until I get those chapters finished."

"I don't understand why this is getting to you so badly. I know I'm a procrastinator, but—"

"This has nothing to do with procrastination, Emily. You are holding onto him for reasons I do not understand."

"He's only been dead a few months. What is wrong with—"

"If you're not ready to put it behind, just say so. I'll come back next year and we'll try it again."

"Don't you dare threaten me, Michael Hamilton, because I won't stand for it."

"And I won't stand for you putting Ryan Hall on some kind of pedestal because he's dead. I couldn't compete with the man when he was alive, and I certainly am not going to compete with him now that he's dead."

"Is that what this is all about? Competing?"

"No! It's about getting on with our lives, getting rid of the garbage and starting over."

"Yes," she agreed, "it's time to start over. But we both have to accept that life is different. Like it or not, Michael, Ryan has a lot to do with this relationship, and—"

"Now you listen to me, Emily Ladd, I will not—"

"I am not Emily Ladd! My name is Emily Hall. I am not the schoolgirl you fell in love with, Michael. Things have changed. I've changed."

"Yes, you've changed all right. You've changed because you spent the last ten years living with a man who didn't even have the decency to treat you as his equal, when he should have been treating you like a queen."

The compliment, however boisterous, forced Emily to stop and absorb what he was trying to tell her. In a softer voice she replied, "But he was different before he died, Michael. He was doing so much better."

"Yes, he was doing better, and I'm glad. I'm glad for him. But facts be faced, Emily, the final weeks of his life could not undo the consequences of ten years just like that." He snapped his fingers. "What I see before me is the result of those years. In many ways you *are* the schoolgirl I fell in love with. But there is something missing, Emily; something that's not quite right. However subtle, there is a lack of vibrancy in you, of self-worth. I cannot believe that it doesn't still exist in there, and I'm going to find it. If getting rid of some of this stuff doesn't help, maybe it will at least get you to start feeling and facing up to what you feel. The only answer I've gotten from you so far is that you feel confused. Now, why don't we get down to business and start talking about what is really going on here."

Emily felt a painful throbbing penetrate between her eyes. She pressed her fingers there in a feeble effort to hold it back. Michael recognized the gesture as a reaction to pain and wondered if they were finally getting somewhere.

"What are you feeling, Emily?" he asked gently. She shook her head and moved her hand to cover her mouth. Michael turned his attention away to break up a fight between Amee and Alexa, then he hurried to help Emily pick up the magazines that the babies were suddenly interested in now that they'd been distracted from their previous play. When it was under control, Emily looked up at Michael and a sob escaped her. He urged her to the couch and put his arms around her, whispering with a soothing voice, "It's all right, darlin'. Cry it out. Feel it. Talk about it."

Emily wondered how she had managed to live with Michael all these weeks and not face this long before now. But she felt certain this time he would not let it drop, and it was likely just as well. Still, the confusion was difficult to face as she attempted to shape it into recognizable emotions.

"You're right, Michael," she uttered tearfully, "he did change before he died, but not enough to rectify the circumstances he'd created. But still . . . I was . . ." She bit her lip in an effort to maintain a degree of control. "I was . . . falling in love all over again, Michael. The timing of this whole thing has been . . . so . . . confusing."

"I think that's understandable."

"I suppose the confusion has been the most difficult thing to face," she admitted.

"Define 'confusion,'" he stated.

"I knew you were going to say that."

"So I'm predictable," he said lightly, "but at least I'm cute."

Emily hugged him and pressed her face to his shoulder. "When Ryan died," she sobbed, "I thought I would die, too. I had felt so much hope. I loved him, Michael. I did."

"I know."

"I finally felt impressed that it had been his time to go, and I felt peace, but still . . . I missed him. It was all so tragic. I felt so empty." Michael stroked her hair and brushed his lips over her brow. "And then when I had to face up to the reality, I . . . became so . . . angry with him." She cried several minutes before she could continue. "How could I be so angry and miss him so much at the same time?" she asked like a child.

"Why were you angry?" he questioned gently.

Emily quickly told him about the financial situation, and his lack of trust in her that had left her ignorant and destitute. Then she told him about Kathy Gibson's visit and the disturbing things that had been revealed by this woman Ryan had worked with—the expensive lunches, their after-hours personal conversations, his sociable nature at work that seemed to automatically shut off when he walked through the door of his own home. "And then," she added, "when I think how I nearly left him, and what happened between you and me, I just feel so . . ."

"Guilty?" he provided.

"Yes."

"Yet you just told me how Ryan behaved with another woman, so why should you feel guilty for what little transpired between you and me?"

"What Ryan did does not excuse my actions," she insisted.

"Perhaps not," he said vehemently, "but it makes them understandable, Emily. You told me in your letters that you talked to the bishop about what happened between you and me, and I did the same before I was baptized. It's cleared away, Emily. One passionate kiss and some stray thoughts do not warrant your feeling guilty for any reason."

"But, Michael," she sobbed more strongly, "sometimes I . . . feel like we're . . . being . . . punished . . . for . . ."

"Punished?" He was appalled.

"Look at the trials . . . and all . . . we've been . . . through."

"Emily! Someone's putting nonsense into your head. You know as well as I do that God does not work that way. We have both suffered the consequences of our actions, and much of this has not been easy, but it has nothing to do with Ryan getting killed, or any other hardship we've had to face."

"I know," she had to admit, then she looked up at him as a fresh reality struck her deeply. Her eyes went wide as her mind was enlightened. "Michael," she nearly laughed, "you and I are supposed to be together."

"I'll go along with that, but I'm afraid you've lost me."

"You said that someone was putting nonsense into my head, and the other day when you got angry, you said you didn't know what had come over you, and . . ."

Michael took a deep breath as he began to perceive the implication. The discouragement and tension he'd been feeling suddenly made sense. In his studies of religion, he was well aware of the concept that Satan was as real as God, and very capable of influence and pressure. But until now, he had never consciously recognized such blatant evidence of the opposition working on him personally, attempting to manipulate his life. There had been confusion and difficulties prior to his baptism, but nothing like this.

He looked at Emily and saw a fear in her eyes that only deepened the evidence. What she had said brought a whole new perspective into view. This evidence of Satan's hand only deepened his conviction that they were doing the right thing. Instinctively he drew Emily close, as if he could shield her from the enemy's onslaught. With conviction he whispered in her ear, "It's likely to get worse before it gets better. But we won't let him win, Emily. We won't! We are going to make it through this. We will keep this family together. We will be married, and we will dedicate our lives to what we know is right. We will not let him win!"

Emily clung to him and cried, finally feeling her guilt and confusion fall away in a purging of tears. Once the emotion was drained, a mutual rejuvenation of spirit filled them.

"Michael," she spoke with hope in her voice, "will you help me? Let's go through his things and get it over with. You're right, we need to do it. Let's do it now."

Michael embraced her warmly. "Emily, I'm sorry for the way I've behaved. You need to do what's best for you."

"And that is to do exactly what you said. Come on." She stood and urged him along. "Let's get started, and then you can go buy me a roast beef Subway sandwich for lunch."

"Okay," he grinned. "No peppers or onions."

"You do love me," she smiled.

"Yes, I do."

By the time Allison got home from school, most of Ryan's things had been sorted and removed. The following day, while Allison and her high-strung emotions were at school, the task was finished. Most of it had been boxed up and put in the basement with all else that wouldn't be kept. A box of things was set aside for Ryan's mother to keep or distribute to other members of his family, and Michael took it out to be mailed the minute it was taped shut. A few items were put into a small box to be given to the children when they were older, and in the meantime were placed in the bottom of the cedar chest with what few things Emily had decided to keep for herself. A photograph of Ryan with the girls, taken last Christmas, was left on Allison's dresser, which Allison later declared to be 'neat'. It seemed to somehow make her feel better.

Over the next few days, as Michael continued his writing, Emily checked through the house carefully, mentally tallying where they stood. All of it, combined with long talks with Michael, made the past fall more easily into place. She wondered if it was wrong to admit that it was easier to let go of Ryan, knowing that the stress he had created in her life was finally being alleviated. She thought of the changes he had been making and felt grateful for what might have been had he lived; but now she could be honest with herself and not deny the consequences of his years of being less than fair with her in many respects. Though there were eternal implications that she didn't fully understand, Emily felt peace as her memories of Ryan became as positive as the prospect of her life with Michael.

"It's all ready," Emily announced one day when Michael surfaced from his work long enough to heat up leftover stroganoff for lunch.

"What is?"

"What we're sending to Australia."

Michael smiled. "We'll get it shipped out tomorrow."

"And don't tell Allison, but I'm shipping what's worth keeping of hers along with it. I consider it an active display of faith."

Michael smiled again.

While they were eating, Amee brought a doll to Emily that she hadn't played with for weeks. She firmly requested, "Put da dress on, Mommy."

Emily fumbled with it for a minute, then declared quietly, "I can't do it with this bandage on my hand, sweetie. Have Daddy do it."

Michael looked up, both surprised and touched as Amee brought it to him without hesitation. "Put da dress on, Daddy."

Michael did as requested and sent Amee on her way.

"Did she just call you Daddy?" Emily asked.

"You said it first," he replied.

"I did?"

Michael nodded.

"Oh." Emily shrugged her shoulders and smiled, as if it were the most natural thing in the world. "I guess I did."

CHAPTER TEN

Michael reached across the table to kiss Emily, then nearly wished he hadn't when she looked up at him with warm desire showing in her eyes. As the tension concerning Ryan's death dissipated, a new tension surfaced. It was apparent every time he touched her or looked at her. He knew Emily shared his desires, and they had discussed briefly their sentiments concerning it. But it was difficult in these days of waiting to remember that yielding now to what would soon be right and good within their marriage, would only bring more pain and difficulty into their lives. It soon became evident that the adversary was well aware of the tension; and though it wasn't voiced between them, Michael and Emily both felt the whisperings of temptation regularly.

Michael found that sticking close to the scriptures helped considerably, even when it was a challenge to find the time. And to his surprise, he also found that the blessings of service kept him closer to the Spirit. He first noticed it when Penny mentioned that Launa Wright was down with the flu. While Emily and Penny took the children to the park, Michael fixed double of a quick dinner and quietly took it over. The feeling it left him with was incredible, and even his writing seemed to improve slightly. After that, he began to see a pattern develop. The more time he took to serve, even to serve Emily and the children, the better his work seemed to go, despite an obvious battle with the opposition that never seemed to cease completely.

As autumn deepened, Michael felt his faith being tested. He found it a challenge to literally put his life in God's hands, expressing through prayer and active faith that he meant it. He fasted for the second time in his life, the first being prior to his baptism. Allison remained headstrong in her desire to go to Idaho and live, and the tension in the home was still evident in varying degrees. But remarkably, he found evidence of an additional blessing that he might not have noticed if Emily hadn't.

One afternoon, she tiptoed into the bedroom to look over his shoulder at the words silently filling the screen at the command of his fingertips. "Wait a minute," she said, but he didn't stop typing. "I thought you were a slow writer. You told me every word had to come from the tips of your toes. It looks to me like you're doing seventy words a minute."

Michael stopped and looked at his hands as if he'd never seen them before. He read what was on the screen and wasn't certain where it had come from. "It must be your inspiring influence," he said. But later, when he counted the words he'd produced, he had to give credit where it was due. He'd written an incredible amount in the last few days, and it was some of the best work he'd ever produced. If he could keep it up, he'd have his deadline met in another two days.

Emily's delight in the miraculous progress of Michael's work somehow eased the dread of facing whether or not Allison would hold to her threat. One morning, she put a cassette into the player on the kitchen shelf as she often did. While the babies slept she worked in the kitchen, feeling the motivation of the music, and dancing back and forth from counter to stove to fridge. Realizing that her hand was doing much better added to her positive outlook. She started to sing along and felt even better, until an arm came around her waist from behind and she gasped.

"I thought you were writing," she said as Michael turned her around and put a hand to her back.

"I thought you were cleaning the kitchen," he retorted, leading her into an easy dance step that she followed without having to think.

"I was."

He turned her quickly to make her dizzy, then danced more slowly to let her gain her balance. The song ended and another began, but Michael kept dancing through the silence between. Emily knew he was familiar with the music as he'd demonstrated to her once before, but she was surprised when he began to sing along, close to her face, as if he were serenading her.

Emily became mesmerized by the words, his voice, his expression. Her eyes filled with mist. The dancing slowed, then stopped, but the music played on while Michael kissed her. Any fear dissipated beneath this tangible evidence of his love, but it made her ache to put the past behind and move ahead.

Later, reality crashed back down when Allison came home from school, hurt because Ashley had done another turnaround. All she could talk about was going to Idaho and the things she intended to take with her. Thankfully, no mention was made of the few things missing that had already been shipped to Australia.

After a stressful evening with Alexa's teething and Amee's two-year-old perception of her independent rights, Emily felt a wave of discouragement that left her weak from the inside out. When the house was in order, she counted days on the calendar since they had applied for the visas. She went to the bedroom to find Michael typing furiously. He stopped and looked up when he sensed her presence.

"It's getting late. I suppose you want me to get out of here so you can go to bed."

"No, you're all right," she said. "Finish your thought."

Emily sat on the edge of the bed and knew she should pick up the scriptures and read, but she decided she was too tired. She lay down on the bedspread and relaxed, letting her mind drift into an oblivious void. Michael's lips on her brow brought her eyes open.

"Good-night," he said. "I'll finish my thought in the morning."

"Wait." She took his hand and sat up, urging him to sit beside her on the edge of the bed. She put her arms around him and rested her head on his shoulder. "Just hold me for a minute. I need you."

Michael hesitated, but put his arms around her, trying to keep his mind on something else. He felt her soften within his embrace and her nearness became too real. He was willing himself to pull away when she touched his chin and urged his lips to hers. He allowed himself to indulge for just a moment, and felt his willpower slipping.

"Emily," he heard himself say, barely aware that he was getting carried away. She relaxed so completely that the next thing he knew she was lying on the bed and he was looking down at her. How beautiful she looked with her hair spread around her head. She reached a hand around his neck as she urged him to kiss her.

Michael couldn't recall ever allowing himself to be in such a position before in his life; and now that he was here, it was difficult to figure how it had happened. But what surprised him most was that he had no desire to get out of it. Nagging voices of logic whispered somewhere in the back of his mind, but they were quickly drowning in the present. His entire perspective changed, and he only wanted one thing.

"Michael," Emily whispered with an unfamiliar huskiness in her voice, igniting something inside him that he almost didn't understand, but longed to explore. He'd never held a woman this way before; never wanted so badly to just rationalize away the time left until they were married, and . . .

The phone ringing in the distance was like a warning buzzer going off at the same instant in both their heads. For a startled moment they looked at each other. Emily's face was flushed. Michael's breath was labored. The phone rang again. And again. With great effort, Michael rolled away from her and lunged for the receiver on the bedside table.

"Is this Mr. Hamilton?" A phony Australian accent came through the receiver.

"Yes," Michael chuckled dryly as he came to his feet, "this is he."

"This is Zanni Poon calling on behalf of Lucinda Swann. She wishes to inquire as to whether or not you are minding your manners, as it is past your curfew."

"I'm minding them now," he said lightly, while the reality of what had almost happened left him weak and frightened for a moment. "I'll be out the door in a minute, I promise."

"Then I shall inform Mrs. Swann that she can expect to see you in less than five minutes. I'll have the butler leave milk and cookies on the table."

"That won't be necessary, but thank you for calling."

"It's my pleasure, mate," she finished. "G'day."

"G'day to you too, mate," he replied, "and give my regards to Mr. Dundee."

Michael hung up the phone and let out a long sigh. He turned to see Emily standing on the other side of the bed, tears showing in her eyes.

"I'm sorry, Michael."

"You don't have to apologize to me, Emily. I'm at least as much to blame."

"I don't know what's wrong with me," she said. "There are moments when everything just seems so wrong, that I have to wonder if it's right for us to be together or . . ."

A familiar pain hit Michael between the eyes, and he rushed around the bed to take hold of her arms with a sense of desperation. "After what you and I have been through, don't you dare even think this is not right. I will not lose you again for any reason. I know it's right and you know it's right. You know as well as I that there are forces out there fighting to keep us apart. But we will not let them win. Do you understand me? We will not!"

Emily cried against his shoulder, grateful for his strength when hers seemed to have gone dry. "Keep fighting for us, Michael. I'm not sure I have much fight left in me. Sometimes I feel as dead inside as the leaves on the ground."

"It's spring in Australia, Emily." Michael looked into her eyes. "I will never stop fighting. We are going to make it, and we are going to do it right." Emily nodded eagerly. "Now, you get some sleep. We'll talk in the morning."

Emily nodded again. Michael headed down the hall, then turned back. He took both her hands into his and went to his knees. Emily followed, and he squeezed her good hand tightly as he prayed aloud for strength, direction, and the softening of hearts. When he left, Emily felt hope and peace.

The phone rang, and she picked it up to say without greeting, "He's on his way."

"I see him pulling into the drive now." The phony Australian accent made Emily giggle. "G'day, mate."

"Lucinda," Emily said.

"Yes, dear," she replied in a normal voice.

"Thank you."

"I'm not even going to ask what for, but you're welcome anyway."

"G'day mate," Emily said, then laughed at how ridiculous her attempt at Australian sounded.

"You need practice, dearie," Lucinda said.

Emily agreed and went to bed, exhausted. She was physically, emotionally, and spiritually spent.

Michael came the next morning to find Emily unshowered and an hour behind with the morning routine, unenthusiastically feeding Alexa breakfast.

"Good morning," she said, but he knew she didn't mean it.

He went to Allison's room and knocked at the door; she appeared within a few moments. "Are you nearly ready?" She nodded. "I'll take you to school, but I want to leave in just a minute."

"I'll be right back," he called to Emily as he ushered Allison out the door.

In the car he said quietly, "Allison, you're growing up and you have the right to think for yourself. That's why I want you to think about one thing today when you're not supposed to be thinking about your school work. Your father loved you very much, and he loved your mother, and Amee and Alexa, too. He didn't choose to die when he did. That was in our Heavenly Father's hands. If Heavenly Father had a reason to take your father home, do you think he would have left your family to be abandoned or separated?" He let her think about that for a minute and felt some hope when he could see that she was.

"Your father's spirit lives on, Allison. That's what is so wonderful about the gospel, and knowing what we know. But while your father's spirit is in heaven, he can't be here to ease the loneliness or provide a living for you. I can do that, and that's why I believe Heavenly Father had your mother and me meet back in college, so that I would know her well enough to come back into her life now to help her, and you. But all the help I can give will mean nothing if I should be in Australia, and you want to go to Idaho, and your mother is left feeling torn in between. I told her I would stay here with her, if that was the right thing to do. But we have prayed about it, Allison, and we believe we should go to Australia. I want you to pray, Allison. You have as much right to feel the Holy Ghost as I do. Maybe more. You've been a member of the Church longer than I have."

Allison looked out the car window at the schoolyard.

"I only want to say one more thing," he continued. "I can't promise you that you'll like Australia. I can't promise that you'll have friends, or that it will be easy. But I can promise you that I will keep your family together, and I will take good care of you—all of you. And really, I think *you* will like it, if you give it a chance. It will be different from what you're used to, but it's a good life. You think about it, and when you get a chance, pray about it, and then I want you to have a talk with your mother. Think about the reasons you really want to go to Idaho, and if you still want to go, we'll see what we can work out. Okay?"

"Okay," she said quietly.

"Have a good day, Allie. You look pretty in that sweater."

"Thanks," she said. "It's the one you bought for me."

"I remember," he smiled.

Allison got out of the car and Michael watched her walk away. He prayed inwardly that she would feel what he had felt this morning when that little speech had come into his head.

Returning to the house, he found Emily picking up Cheerios off the carpet.

"Got any plans today?" he asked.

"Other than picking up Cheerios, you mean?" She sighed. "Not that I can think of. Why?"

"Go take a shower and put on your best. I'll watch the babies."

"I thought you had to write."

"I'm ahead of schedule. It can wait."

"Are we going out?"

"No, but you are."

"I'm sorry? You lost me somewhere."

"I woke up this morning and thought to myself, if I could just go to the temple, maybe I could get past this and make it through. Well, I can't go, but you can. So go take a shower."

Emily stood up, looking disoriented. She put the Cheerios into Michael's outstretched hand.

"How long has it been since you've gone?" he asked.

"Not since Ryan died," she said, as if it had never occurred to her. Michael turned her around and urged her down the hall.

The morning seemed to get steadily worse. The phone kept ringing, little accidents kept happening, and Allison called to say she'd forgotten her library book and she *had* to have it. Michael took it to her while Emily attempted to choke down some toast so her stomach wouldn't growl through the temple session.

When Emily finally got to the temple, the oppression that had overpowered her life and kept her from coming here, was the very thing that fled when she walked through the doors. A slow replenishing came over her, and she sat in the celestial room longer than she ever had, looking forward to the day when Michael could share this with her. She felt a twinge of sadness to think that she and Michael could not be sealed, but it was immediately replaced by a warm peace that everything would be all right. Surely they would be together forever, and God would see that Ryan, too, was happy through the eternities.

She wondered about the temple in Sydney. How far was it from her new home? How did it differ from this one? But there was peace in her thoughts. However different all of it was, it would still be the same gospel, the same love. And she would be with Michael.

She felt apprehensive to leave, afraid of the world and the opposition it pressed against her. But a sense of peace left with her, and she felt anxious to share it with Michael.

The house was quiet when she returned. The babies were napping, the kitchen clean, and the toys were picked up. Michael was writing.

He looked up to see her leaning in the door, much as she had last night. He might not have recognized the darkness of discouragement that had been with her then, if he hadn't been able to compare it to the light surrounding her now. Leaning back in his chair, he wanted to just absorb it.

"You're a genius, Mr. Hamilton," she said, tossing her purse onto the bed.

"No, just inspired. How do you feel?"

"Better," she admitted. "Much better."

"Do you still want to marry me?"

"Emphatically!"

Michael took off his glasses and rubbed a thumbnail along his bottom lip. "You look radiant," he smiled.

Emily sat on the edge of the bed and he turned in his chair to face her. "Can I tell you something?" she asked carefully.

"I'm listening."

She leaned forward and took his hand. "You know, Michael, I told you I'd marry you before I knew you'd been baptized. And I would have done it willingly. But I have to say now, I am grateful that . . . " Her voice began to crack and she looked at the ceiling. "As I sat alone in the celestial room, I got to thinking how much time I had spent there alone, watching people pair off, holding hands, sitting close, speaking quietly together of sacred things. And I wanted you there so badly. To think that you might never share those things with me could be heartbreaking, Michael. But I want you to know I would have done it, because you give me so much that compensates. Still, when I realized it was only a matter of time before we could be there together, I felt an incomparable joy."

Emily touched his face and absorbed the emotion in his eyes. "I long for the day when I can share a piece of heaven with you, Michael Hamilton. Two people will never know such perfect happiness as we will, just being together within temple walls."

Michael gave her a warm smile that expressed how he shared her longing. There were other things about the temple he wanted to discuss with her. There was so much he wanted to know. But he knew now wasn't the time. The fact that they couldn't be sealed was something he was still having trouble with, but he felt confident that eventually he could come to terms with it.

"I just wanted you to know that," Emily said and kissed him lightly.

She took some clothes to Allison's room to change, and left Michael to write while she laid on the couch and took a much-needed nap. When the babies woke up, she felt rejuvenated in body as well as spirit. Everything felt better—until Allison came home from school. "Mom," she announced, "I don't want to go to Idaho, but I don't want to go to Australia either."

Michael overheard but decided to stay out of it for the moment. He was glad he had made that decision when it turned into the closest thing to a fight that Emily and Allison had ever shared.

Emily listened to Allison rant about how she wasn't going to leave her home and her friends, and she didn't want Michael trying to be her father. Emily began to wonder why she had felt such peace earlier, and she tried futilely to hold on to that peace as she struggled to make Allison understand.

As the conflict wore on, with Emily becoming more upset and Allison becoming more indignant and demanding, Michael decided he'd had enough. He took a deep breath, said a quick prayer, and stepped in with his first attempt to govern in a way he felt sure Allison would not appreciate.

He found Emily sitting on the couch, looking as if she might sink into despair, and Allison standing with her hands on her hips, as if she could take on the world. She reminded him of Emily in college.

"Allison, would you please sit down?" he requested. Emily looked up in surprise. Allison ignored him. "I said sit down," he repeated firmly, and she did. "I'd like to ask you a question, young lady." He put his hands in his pockets and looked directly at her. "How did it make you feel when your father and mother used to argue?" She said nothing. "I'd like an answer, please. I assume they did argue." He glanced at Emily and she rolled her eyes.

"I hated it," Allison admitted.

"Why?"

"I don't know. I just hated it."

"Do you love your mother?"

"Yes."

"Is it possible," Michael shifted his weight to the other foot, "that you hated it because of the way your father treated her? Did you like the way he talked to her?"

"No."

"Well, that's interesting, Allison. Because I hear you talking that way to your mother right now. You must have learned that tone of voice from your father, because I've never heard your mother use it."

Michael got the reaction he'd hoped for sooner than he'd expected. Allison's expression fell into obvious regret. "You see, Allison," he continued in a gentle voice, "I love your mother, too, and I'm not going to allow you to talk to her like that. If you have feelings you want to express, you are welcome to do so, but not at the expense of someone else's feelings."

Michael glanced at Emily, who gave a grateful nod. He then looked at Allison, who was looking at the floor. "That's all I have to say," he said and turned to leave the room. He was barely out of sight when he heard Allison start to cry. His nerves tightened as he wondered if that was good or bad.

Emily was aware of Michael hovering in the doorway as Allison fell into her arms and began to sob. As the pain began to spill out, Emily wondered if Allison's anger was the true answer to her prayers. Had her daughter finally been able to get in touch with her own pain? Night came with still no conclusion on Allison's part, but Emily felt they had made progress. For the first time since Ryan's death, Allison had expressed the true depth of her loss. Emily believed it was important for Allison to feel that she wasn't being forced to go to Australia. But at the same time a sense of desperation was rising in Emily. Her life here was hanging in the balance, and it would not settle into place until they had this move behind them and she and Michael were married. At this point, she could only pray that it would all come together.

Michael went to the Swanns' home early, but he called Emily and they talked on the phone until nearly midnight, working every-thing through carefully without the distraction of children or affec-tion. They decided to fast together, and Emily counted days on the calendar before she read in the Book of Mormon and went to bed.

The October morning came with a drastic drop in temperature. Emily dressed warmly and went out to get firewood so she could take the chill off the house before the children woke up. She came in with an armload of wood to find Michael looking for her.

"What are you doing?" he asked as she set the wood down and

began to build a fire in the wood burning stove.

"You've got eyes, Mr. Hamilton. I'm building a fire. It's cold in here."

"What about the furnace?"

"It costs too much to . . . " she began a well-rehearsed fact, then stopped. "Oh, well, I don't know if it even works. I've been doing it this way for years. I'm used to it. And we've got plenty of firewood. My home teachers brought me three truckloads of wood in the summer. Most of it still needs to be split, but it's there. They said they'd do that when I needed it. I'm sure they can find somebody who can use it after we're gone."

"Here," Michael moved her aside, "let me do that. Your daughter wants to get out of her crib."

Emily went to get Alexa while Michael wondered how often Ryan had carried wood into the house and built the fire. He checked the thought and reminded himself that the past was over and the future was bright.

CHAPTER ELEVEN

The morning went more smoothly than the last several had. Emily discovered that Alexa had cut two more teeth, Amee didn't spill her breakfast, and Allison got ready for school and did her jobs without needing any reminders.

"Do you want a ride, Allison?" Michael asked. "Or are you going to walk with your friends?"

"I'll take a ride," she said and Michael picked up the keys. "Mom," Allison added, "when we go to Australia, are we going on a plane?"

Michael wanted to cry. Emily did. "Yes, sweetie. A very big one."

"Okay," she said. Michael followed her out the door after he winked at Emily and gave her a thumbs-up.

When Michael didn't return, Emily became concerned until she heard a familiar noise in the yard and went out to investigate while the babies actually shared the Legos. She stopped for a moment to lean against the house and watch Michael splitting wood with an axe. She had watched Ryan do it many times and found it an intriguing display of masculinity. To see Michael there now was almost eerie, as if Michael had always been there, while it felt as if Ryan were still there as well. Was it possible to love two men in such a way?

"I thought you had writing to do," she called. He looked up and wiped sweat off his brow with the back of a gloved hand. Ryan's gloves, she noticed.

"What I need is some exercise." He leaned on the axe for a minute. "All that cooking and writing and changing diapers is turning me into a blob."

Emily admired his lean form in slightly baggy jeans and a flannel shirt. "No, I don't think so. You told me yourself, all that diaper changing is hard work. It's like saddling a horse on the move."

"All the same," he chuckled, "I think I'll chop some wood."

He resumed his chore and Emily went in to check on the babies and start some laundry.

After lunch the babies napped and Michael wrote, declaring he'd be finished with what he'd promised in another hour. Allison came home in a bright mood, and Michael impulsively put the finishing touches of his work on hold to request her assistance.

Emily heard laughter from outside and glanced out the window to see Michael and Allison throwing dried maple leaves at each other and quickly making havoc of the pile they had just raked together. While Allison stopped to rake them again and begin round two, Michael glanced up and saw Emily watching. "I love you," he mouthed and she returned it, then blew a kiss, which he pretended to catch by snapping his head back quickly.

Impulsively Emily put sweaters on the babies and went out to join them. While the children were occupied in giggles and crinkling leaves, Emily put her arms around Michael and looked up to find love glowing in his eyes.

"Michael," she said softly, "thank you."

"For what?"

"I haven't told you before, because I figured it was obvious, but I want you to know that . . . " tears brimmed in her eyes, "there is so much you do that he never did. You have brought so much good into our lives that was never there before. And maybe it would have been one day. I don't know. I just wanted to tell you how much I appreciate you, and the way you love us."

Michael chuckled humbly. "Actually, it's purely selfish, darlin'." His expression sobered. "You're the most wonderful thing that ever happened to me, Emily. Sharing my life with you is nothing less than a privilege."

"A widow with three children?" she laughed. "A privilege?"

"Yes, indeed," he grinned as a handful of leaves came showering over their heads. Michael chased Allison down and threw her, giggling, into the pile.

The next morning Penny spent much of her time loitering about in a typical way, but Emily sensed a subtle tension as they both realized their time as neighbors was rapidly drawing to a close. To Emily, it was the only gloomy spot in a bright future, but she knew it had to be, and so did Penny.

Later in the day, Emily felt a thousand emotions as an envelope from the Consulate General in San Francisco arrived in the mail. Several other envelopes were tossed onto the table without regard, and she hurried down the hall to lean in the doorway until Michael noticed her. When he finally looked up from the computer, she waved the envelope like a carrot in front of a starving rabbit.

"'Down Under', here we come," she purred, and suddenly found herself suspended off the ground with Michael's arms around her, laughing quietly to avoid disturbing the babies' naps.

"Ah," he breathed, setting her down, "I don't believe it. Yes, I do. I believe it. I believe in miracles, Emily. Do you think you're ready for this?"

"As ready as I'll ever be." She smiled in a way that couldn't begin to express the pounding joy in her heart. The waiting was over.

"How long will it take us to be ready to leave?" he asked. "I mean, really ready?"

"Two days," she said easily.

"I'll call a travel agent today."

"Michael, after we're married, will I be an Australian?"

"What you will be is a permanent resident," he stated. "I assumed you would want to keep your American citizenship. After all, it is the promised land."

"And we will come back once in a while, won't we?"

"Of course. One of these days we have to take Allison to the Grand Canyon."

"And we can visit Penny?"

"And the Swanns."

"Let's get packing."

"As soon as I finish up here."

"I don't know if you thought of this, but what exactly are we going to do on a plane for that many hours with two babies?"

"I thought of it," he smiled. "Now let me finish this. I'll copy these diskettes and send them off this afternoon. They'll beat us there, and Douglas will love me for another few months."

A whirlwind of excitement carried them through the next three days. Even Allison seemed caught up in it. She'd hardly been beyond her hometown except for an occasional trip to Idaho, and the adventure seemed to intrigue her now that she'd gotten used to the idea.

Now that their plans were tangible, Emily took the time to call her sisters and let them know she was getting married again. Her oldest sister, Julie, had married and moved to Chicago long before Emily had even gone to college. Becky had married a military man and was currently living in Virginia. Though the sisters had never been particularly close, they had stayed in touch through letters over the years. Both Julie and Becky were surprised to learn that Michael Hamilton had come back into Emily's life, and they were pleased about the marriage, especially in view of the fact that Michael had joined the Church. Emily wished they could somehow be there for the wedding; but even if traveling to Australia hadn't been a problem, Julie was expecting a baby in the next few weeks, and Becky was preparing to move—again. Still, it was good to talk to them, and they promised to keep in close touch.

Through the day prior to their leaving, the house was a bustle of activity and nervous energy, while friends and acquaintances stopped by to share farewells. As Michael watched Emily pack her things into a piece of luggage he had purchased a few days earlier, he verbally went over his mental checklist.

"You got everything you need?" he asked.

"You said we could buy what we needed there. We have what we need to get there."

"Okay, but let me put it this way. We *can* get anything you need, but some things are not as easily available. Is there anything personal you might need that you would rather get before we leave?"

Emily thought hard a minute. "Good idea," she said. "I'll do that now."

He followed her to the front room, where she picked up her purse and headed for the door. "Is there anything else we need while I'm out?"

"I don't think so, but what are you going to buy it with?"

"I have my checkbook, and . . ." She stopped when she remembered that the account had been closed.

He handed her two hundred dollars out of his pocket.

"I don't need that much."

"Take it anyway," he insisted, and was pleased when she didn't try to argue.

"Speaking of closing accounts, did you arrange for all the utilities and—"

"Yes, darlin', everything's done."

"You took your gifts to the Swanns?"

"No, but I'll see them tonight. Go shopping, Emily. I'm going to call my mother."

Emily returned with a supply of new underclothing and a few other miscellaneous things. Michael was on the phone, apparently finishing up with his mother.

"Yes, I left the Cruiser in the hangar. Yes, we'll be careful. We'll see you the day after tomorrow. Well, actually it will be two days after tomorrow, but only because it's still yesterday here and it's tomorrow there. Good-bye, Mother."

"You weren't on the phone all that time," Emily said.

"No, I just got through to her a few minutes ago. Now, do you have what you need?"

"Yes," she smiled, and took her purchases in the bedroom to pack them. She paused to admire the lavender nightgown she'd bought and felt a tingle of excitement to think of wearing it for Michael on their wedding night.

"Isn't it a little thin?" he said from behind her. She nearly jumped out of her shoes.

"Michael!" she scolded, hurriedly folding it.

Michael chuckled and touched the flush rising in her cheek. "What were you thinking just now, my love?"

Emily was tempted to avoid his gaze, but something about his nearness outdid her timidity and she had to look at him. She felt no need to explain herself. It was obvious he knew where her thoughts had been.

"I have no doubt you'll look stunning in it."

She smiled meekly and continued with her packing. "What are you doing in here anyway, while I'm packing my private things?"

It took him a moment to remember. "I was wondering if you were keeping that skirt."

"What skirt?"

"The black one that you wore to the mall—and, if I'm not mistaken, the same skirt you wore when we were dating."

Emily smiled. "It's already en route to Australia."

"Good." He kissed her quickly. "I think we're about ready."

The next morning, Michael took Allison with him to do some last-minute errands. Emily took the babies to Penny's house so she could finish up the packing and check through the house without interruptions.

With suitcases on the porch, Emily walked through the house to survey it. It looked so clean and orderly, almost clinical in the way that nearly everything was left in place. But the spirit seemed absent, like Ryan that last time she had touched his lifeless face. Tears came and she let them fall, weeping over the memories, the friendships, the love and the trials, all spent here in good faith.

When she could bear no more, Emily locked up the house and walked the few steps to Penny's house. She placed the keys gently in her best friend's hand, then squeezed it. They embraced and cried.

"You know," Penny said as they sat together on the porch while the babies played in the carpet of crisp leaves on the lawn, "it's not going to be easy getting rid of the tidbits of life you've left behind over there."

"Not easy, but perhaps fulfilling," Emily consoled. "Give the firewood to someone who needs it, and the food. There's meat in the freezer and a lot of food left in the cupboards. Just use your judgment with the rest. I gave you the papers on the house so you can take care of the—"

"We already went over all of this three times, Emily. I'll take care of everything."

"And like I said, I want you to keep the car. With Heather driving now, you can use it and—"

"We've discussed this, too."

Emily's chin quivered. "You will write?"

"I told you I would."

"And I will, too. What we have shared is too precious to lose. Promise me we'll always keep in touch."

"I promise," Penny barely managed to say. "And I want you to remember to be happy. You've earned it, so enjoy it."

"I will."

They sat in peaceable silence until Michael pulled up to load the suitcases into the trunk, then he moved the car in front of Penny's house. Allison played with the babies in the leaves. Michael stood in front of the porch with a shopping bag in his hand, watching Emily expectantly.

"What's that?" she asked.

"It's an entertain-three-children-on-an-airplane kit," he said, handing it to her for approval.

Emily peered inside and smiled. "Looks good to me."

Michael handed an envelope to Penny. "Open it later," was all he said. Penny only cried as she threw her arms around him and they shared a warm embrace. He waited patiently for Penny and Emily to express their good-byes, though no words were exchanged. They had all been spoken already.

Penny hugged each of the children, and Michael put the babies into their car seats. With the children buckled in and everything loaded except Emily, she turned to Penny for one last embrace, then quickly got into the car. Michael closed her door, winked at Penny, and walked around to get in.

As they drove away, Michael reached over to take Emily's hand. "It's not easy, is it?"

"I feel like I've just closed a door on part of my life."

He squeezed her hand firmly. "It's spring in Australia, Emily. We're opening a new door."

Emily looked over at him and felt peace.

Before heading to Salt Lake City, they stopped for lunch at a buffet restaurant. Allison thoroughly enjoyed the concept of something she'd never experienced before. She especially liked the dessert bar and went back three times.

The babies slept in the car and were wide-eyed with interest as the little family filed into the busy airport. Allison was quietly fasci-

nated by everything, but especially the huge airplanes they saw
landing and taking off. Amee began to chatter about the 'pwanes,'
but she would not allow Michael to put her down. With time to
spare, they browsed the gift shops and explored the escalators and
electric walkways. When it was finally time to board, Allison began
to show a visible, nervous excitement.

Once in flight, Alexa slept in Emily's arms, while Amee wanted
to do nothing but wiggle. Michael remedied her condition with
animal cookies and a new story book from his "magic bag," as Emily
had dubbed it.

Los Angeles brought to Allison's view an even larger airport
where they had dinner, killed time, prepared the babies for bed, and
boarded an even bigger plane. Allison had tried to memorize all the
airlines while in Salt Lake City, and found many similar ones here,
but she declared she'd never seen and couldn't pronounce the name
across the side of the plane that would take them to Australia.

"Qantas," Michael stated. "It's an Australian airline."

"That's a funny word. Do they speak a foreign language in
Australia?" she asked fearfully.

"Just Australian English," Emily answered. "There are a few
differences, but you'll catch on."

"I'll interpret," Michael claimed. "Just don't ask for a napkin in
a restaurant."

The plane rose into the dark city sky soon after ten-thirty, and
the babies quickly fell asleep to the gentle hum of jet engines. Allison,
too, was soon sleeping after an exhausting day. Michael shifted Alexa
into the small bassinet provided by the airline, then he turned to
watch Emily quietly organizing her bag by the light of a reading lamp
in the darkened plane's interior. She pulled out the plane tickets
Michael had handed her once they'd boarded, and curiously looked
them over.

"Nonstop to Sydney?" she questioned. "Didn't we go to
Brisbane last time?"

"Yes, but since I've started traveling more, I found it's easier to
get flights in and out of Sydney, nonstop. If you'll recall, we had
stopovers in Hawaii and New Zealand. A fifteen-hour flight is long
enough without having to stop for a couple of hours here and there."

"That's true. But isn't Sydney further from your home?"

"*Our* home," he corrected, and she smiled. "Yes, but not dreadfully when I use a private plane to get there anyway."

"I'd forgotten about that."

He leaned over and kissed her cheek. "It's about time you remembered." He brushed some straying hair from her brow. "How you doing so far?"

"Fine. And I must admit, the children are doing better than I expected."

"I prayed," he grinned.

"So did I, but don't speak too soon. We're a long way from Australia yet."

"Have faith, Emily. We wouldn't have gotten this far without it."

"How true," she admitted, then her eyes caught something on the papers in her hand and she held it closer to the light, certain she'd not read it correctly. "Michael!" she insisted quietly. "You can't possibly have paid . . . " She squinted to read it again. "Michael, these tickets were more than the price of a new car—a nice one."

"That's the going rate," he stated.

"But, Michael, that's . . . " she couldn't finish. "Surely we could have gotten by with less if we hadn't gone first class, or—"

"Emily," he squeezed her hand, "I generally fly coach, if you must know. But fifteen hours on a plane with three children could stand some extra comforts. The difference was worth it to me. Besides, it's only money. If I didn't have it, we'd have to live on love and stay in one spot."

"I somehow think we could manage."

"I know we could manage," he said firmly. "That's why I can say it's only money. I'd give it all up in a minute to have what has come into my life the last few months."

"And what is that?" she smiled, just wanting to hear it.

"The gospel, and my new family."

"I love you, Michael," she whispered intently.

"I love you, Emily. Now, why don't you get some sleep while you can. I have a feeling tomorrow will be exhausting."

"You're probably right," she admitted.

After a fair amount of sleep, Michael was adjusting his watch to the eighteen-hour difference from Utah time when Amee woke up. She acted disoriented and briefly frightened until he took her into his arms and held her. Gradually she settled into a wiggly coherency. Alexa woke soon after, and the plane became a bustle of activity that mostly surrounded the children. The stewards were helpful and seemed to enjoy the little travelers, and several passengers took turns holding babies to read stories or occupy them with other entertainments.

Allison became gradually more quiet as she watched the view out the window. Emily sensed she was beginning to comprehend the enormity of the distance they were traveling by counting the hours they had been in the air, but for now she could only keep a close eye on her and try to buffer it as much as possible. She and Michael had carefully explained what the transition would entail, using maps and photographs to assist. But Emily knew that when she had visited Australia, even at the age of twenty-one, it had seemed overwhelming and incomprehensible to her. She couldn't fathom how a child as sensitive as Allison would perceive all of this as a permanent arrangement.

When it was finally announced that they were approaching Sydney, Emily sighed audibly and Michael said, "I guess I can tell you now that the magic bag is nearly empty."

After more airport exploring to have a chance to walk and let the children get their wiggles out, Michael took them to board a six-passenger plane that would carry them home.

"What's B-D & H?" Allison asked about the bold letters on the side of it.

"That's Byrnehouse-Davies & Hamilton," Michael explained while loading luggage. "That's my family's business title. I'm the only remaining Hamilton, except my mother."

"When you get married," Allison said to Emily, "will my name be Hamilton, too?"

"Until you get married," Michael took it upon himself to reply, "your name will be Allison Hall, because Hall is your father's name. It will be the same for Amee and Alexa. If you choose to, you can use the name Hamilton for convenience, but that is up to you."

"Okay," Allison said after contemplating it.

Michael began helping them into the plane and Emily asked, "Where's the pilot?"

"Do we need a pilot?" he asked in perfect innocence. "I thought these things flew themselves."

"We had a pilot last time," she insisted.

"But last time," he gave a semi-phony grin, "it wasn't my plane."

"You mean—"

"Yes, darlin'," he said, and opened his wallet to prove it, "I am a certified pilot and I will get you safely to your destination."

"You've kept busy all these years," she said.

Michael nodded toward the children buckled in their seats. "So have you."

The first little while in the air again, the children were restless and Emily found herself anxious to get there. It seemed they'd been flying forever. She was grateful when the babies fell asleep, but she was concerned over Allison's silent contemplation of the view out the window.

"How long till we get there?" Allison asked.

"It's about a four-hour flight," Michael told her. "We've been in the air nearly an hour and a half." Allison sighed.

"Is something bothering you, sweetie?" Emily asked.

"I don't know," was all she said.

"If you have something on your mind," Michael said, "you have to say it or no one will know how you feel and we can't help you out." He hoped that eventually she'd get tired of him telling her that and start to talk without prodding.

"I'm okay," she insisted, but the sharp glance Emily gave Michael let him know she likely wasn't.

The babies had been awake a short while when Michael announced, "There it is." Allison perked up and pressed her nose to the window. He flew low and circled over the station to explain from a bird's-eye view. "There is the main house, though you can hardly see it for all the trees. You can see the stables and the race track."

"Is that where the horses race?" Allison asked brightly.

"We don't have official races there like they used to in generations past, but we use it to train and practice."

"Why are there so many stables?" she asked, noting the four huge buildings.

"Because there are a lot of horses. I'll tell you more about that later when we go look at them."

"What's that?" Allison pointed.

"That's the carriage house. I'll show you that later, too."

"And what's that big building by the house?" she asked.

"That's the boys' home. For a hundred years my family has taken care of boys who don't have homes, or whose families don't treat them very well."

Michael pointed in another direction and said, "You can see how the land gets more mountainous that way, and more flat over there." He headed toward the flat portion and pointed down to apparently nothing. "About there is what was once the border between Byrnehouse land and Davies land. In 1890, the two were united by marriage and an unusual court case concerning a will. Before that time, my great-grandfather was struggling just to survive and keep his land. After that he became one of the wealthiest men in Australia. His daughter, Emma, married Michael Hamilton. They were my grandparents."

"He had the same name," Allison perceived.

"So did my father," Michael said proudly.

He brought the plane in for a smooth landing over a flat stretch of land that had obviously been cleared for an airstrip. The plane was put into a hangar where another smaller plane was also parked, along with two road vehicles, both Toyota Land Cruisers.

"They have those at home," Allison remarked, pointing to the brand name as Michael transferred luggage to one of the vehicles.

"I think you'll find we have a lot of things here that you do. They're just a little different, that's all."

"But the steering wheel is on the wrong side," Allison said with a wrinkle of her nose.

"That all depends on whether or not you're an Australian."

"I'd say it's on the wrong side," Emily teased.

"Are we going to be Australian now?" Allison asked her mother.

"We will be residents, but we're still U.S. citizens."

"Okay." She seemed pleased.

When everyone was settled, Michael opened his door and took a low, flat-brimmed hat off the seat. He brushed it off and settled it on his head as he sat down and fastened his seat belt. "What?" he said when Emily smiled at him.

"You look like an Australian."

"Don't be ridiculous," he said soberly, then he cracked a warm smile.

"A very handsome Australian," she added.

"With a beautiful American wife," he replied. "Almost."

They were soon on their way, and in a few minutes they came to a road that was smooth and well groomed, despite not being paved.

"We'll be home in ten minutes," Michael smiled peacefully toward Emily.

"I think I'm nervous," she admitted.

"There's no need to be. I'm sure it will take some adjusting, but you'll all fit in beautifully, I can assure you."

It seemed no time before they drove beneath an iron archway that said "Byrnehouse-Davies," where the road became paved. The Cruiser drove past the yard of the boys' home, through a cluster of trees, and past the house.

"It's a mansion," Allison declared.

"I don't know if I'd call it that," Michael said. "It's big, but then it was built for a traditional old-world purpose, to house an entire extended family."

"What's that mean?" Allison asked.

"At one time, my great-grandparents, my grandparents, all my aunts and uncles as children, and their uncle and aunt and cousins, all lived here."

"Wow. Who lives here now?"

"Besides us? There's my mother, my sister Katherine, her husband Robert, and their two children, Stacy and Wade. Then there's the housekeeper and cook, and a few others that help us out. All of the stable hands live in the bunkhouse."

Michael pulled the Cruiser around the house where the trees moved back and the yard sloped down for a perfect view of the stable-yard and racing facilities.

"It's just like I remember," Emily smiled, and Michael squeezed her hand. He parked near a side door and got out to unbuckle Amee and set her free on the lawn.

"Will you watch her, Allison?" Emily asked and Allison followed her sister to explore the close proximities of the huge yard. Emily held Alexa, who was whining crankily, while Michael unloaded the luggage. He closed the back of the Cruiser and turned to take Alexa, embracing Emily as he did.

"Welcome home, Emily," he said near her ear. "You cannot imagine how happy it makes me to have you here."

"Even with the fringe benefits?" She touched Alexa's curls.

"Especially with the fringe benefits. If a man waited until my age to start a family, he wouldn't have time to get much of a family. I think it's perfect."

"You're good to me . . . to us," she corrected.

"It's no sacrifice," he admitted.

"Michael!" LeNay Hamilton rushed out the side door and down the steps to embrace him, taking care not to disturb the child in his arms.

"Hello, Mother," he laughed with obvious pleasure.

"And what is this?" She smiled and eased the baby from his arms to survey her with a sparkle in her eyes that reminded Emily of Michael. "Oh, she's beautiful."

Hearing LeNay speak, Emily could see what Michael meant by his voice becoming Americanized. There was a difference.

"Hello, Emily." LeNay turned to her and held out a hand. Emily took the welcome squeeze. "You look as young and pretty as the last time I saw you."

"Thank you," Emily said timidly. Michael smiled.

"She really is adorable." LeNay looked again at the baby. "And didn't you say her name is Alexa?" she asked, and Michael nodded. "Is that coincidence?" she asked Emily.

"No, I'm afraid I stole the name from your genealogy."

"Well, I'm glad you did." She looked around. "But where are the others?"

"Just getting some wiggles out." Michael pointed across the

lawn and LeNay nodded.

"I'm certain you must be exhausted," LeNay said with empathy. "I've got rooms all ready, and Millie's going to put out a late lunch. Shall we go inside?"

"Allison," Michael called, "let's go see if we can dig up something to eat, shall we?"

Allison efficiently scooped up her sister, who giggled as they ran toward the house. Michael and Emily each picked up bags and headed for the door, but LeNay held back and sat on a step to talk to Allison.

"You must be Allison." Emily and Michael paused to listen. "And is this Amee?" Allison nodded. "I'm Michael's mother. You can call me LeNay, unless you want to call me grandma. That's up to you. I'm so glad you decided to come and live here with us, because if there's one thing this house doesn't have enough of, it's pretty girls. And we just happen to have some bedrooms upstairs that I think will be just right. Would you like to go see?"

Allison nodded with a degree of enthusiasm. LeNay stood and ushered the girls into the house, still holding Alexa, who had ceased her whining for the moment.

Michael led the way up some stairs and turned into a long hall. Emily didn't remember the house seeming so big. Allison was wide-eyed with wonder. The bags were set down in the hallway, which was illuminated by a huge window at the far end.

"Now," Michael announced, "this will be our wing of the house." He pointed to a door. "That is Emily's room, which I will move into after we are married." He winked at her. "That," he pointed to the next door down, "is the sitting room, and—"

"What's a sitting room?" Allison asked.

Michael looked at his mother. "I don't know. What's a sitting room?"

"I suppose it's to sit in," she answered. "That's just what they've always called it."

"It's to sit in," he answered Allison, then proceeded to point out a door for each of the girls, a playroom, and a bedroom for someone called Mrs. Pace.

"Who is Mrs. Pace?" Emily asked.

"She has been a nanny in this house since Katherine was born," LeNay explained. "When there haven't been children, she helps out wherever she can. She's just like part of the family. When I told her Michael was bringing home babies, I had to hold her down to keep her from jumping through the roof."

Emily smiled, but Michael caught the concern in her eyes. "Don't worry," he said. "She's just there to help out when you need her. Nobody's going to take anything over. She'll only do what you ask her to."

Emily betrayed relief by her eyes, but she had to admit this all felt rather strange.

"Which room should we look at first?" LeNay asked.

"Amee's," Allison requested, then she gasped as she opened the door at Michael's request. Alexa's room was equally as inviting, and Allison was obviously pleased with her own room. All had been decorated femininely with the appropriate furnishings and some added touches of a few toys and stuffed animals to give the children something to occupy them through the transition.

Allison liked Emily's room almost as much as Emily did. It was bigger than the room she had stayed in on her previous visit, and, by its furnishings and bigger closets, was obviously meant to be shared by a couple. Allison declared the sitting room had plenty of places to sit, but she thought it was a stupid thing to use a room for. Michael agreed. Emily unpacked what they had brought and stayed with the babies until Mrs. Pace, who Emily dearly liked, said she would be happy to watch them for a while and get them something to eat. Michael added assurance as he demonstrated the intercom that could be used to help shrink distances in the big house.

"It's going to take some getting used to," Emily said as they went down the front staircase with Allison walking just ahead.

"I hope I'm worth it," he said too seriously, but a quick embrace assured him that he was.

Allison's quiet mood deepened as they were seated in the large dining room and the meal was served by a young maid who assisted LeNay. Emily tried to think how Allison might be perceiving all of this and felt concerned for many reasons.

CHAPTER TWELVE

"Where's Kate and the kids?" Michael asked when the meal was underway.

"They went into town," LeNay reported. "Robert's with them. I suspect they'll be back before dinner."

A lull of silence preceded a terse question from Allison. "Where is the school?"

Michael and Emily exchanged a concerned glance. Emily gently explained what Michael had told her concerning the situation. Allison made no reply, and her expression did not change.

When the meal was finished, Michael announced, "I think we should go see how the horses are doing. I hope they've missed me as much as I've missed them."

"They told me they couldn't wait for you to get back," LeNay said with a straight face. Emily was reminded of Michael's satirical humor.

After changing clothes and checking on the babies, Emily walked with Allison down the back stairs. She asked questions and tried to get Allison to talk, but the young girl said nothing to indicate how she felt.

They met Michael in the main stable. Allison surveyed him skeptically, while Emily soaked in his appearance with silent approval. Only during her visit to Australia had she seen him dress this way, but here it was common. The classic jodhpurs were worn and well accustomed to him, tucked into high, black riding boots, much like those he'd given Emily years ago. He wore a deep cream-colored shirt with pinstripes, sleeves rolled to below the elbows, and leather suspenders, or braces, as she knew he called them.

Michael smiled in response to her studied appraisal, and a fluttery rush of intrigue filtered through her. The reality gave her genuine joy. Michael Hamilton was going to be her husband.

He took Allison's hand and led her through the stables, showing her the difference between the racing horses and the ones they used for work or pleasure. "When the station was first established, and for many years after, horses were mandatory to accomplish the work and to get from one place to another," he explained. He showed them through the carriage house, which was more like a museum as it still housed several wheeled vehicles that had been in the family for generations. He helped Allison into what he called a "trap." She smiled but said nothing.

"What are those stables for?" She pointed to a building they had not explored as they walked back to the main stable.

"Those horses belong to the boys that live in the boys' home. They spend time each day working with their horses. It helps them learn how to love and care for something that will love them in return. It's a very important part of helping them adjust to a normal life."

Allison looked at him deeply, seeming to contemplate his words, though it was difficult to know whether she was contemplating the children who were unloved or orphaned, or wondering how it was possible for a horse to make such a difference.

"Do you remember how to ride?" Michael asked Emily.

"No," she insisted without hesitation.

"Sure you do. Once you learn, you never forget."

He led a mount from its stall and proceeded to saddle it while he explained to Allison what he was doing. He saddled another horse then held out a hand to Emily, who looked apprehensive.

"Come on," he urged, "she's as gentle as a lamb." He took her hand and bent his knee beneath the stirrup for her to step onto his thigh as he hoisted her into the saddle. She situated herself and he put the reins into her hand. "Okay?" he asked and she nodded. It didn't feel as awkward as she thought it might after all these years.

"You want to try it?" he said to Allison. She hesitated, but he could see the intrigue in her eyes. Michael knew well his family's age-old approach to adapting children to horses, a technique he'd used successfully with Emily. "Come on," he said. "You ride with me and you can get used to the feel of it while I keep everything under perfect control. What do you say?" He left her time to think about it. "You don't have to, but I think you'll like it."

Allison nodded firmly, and Michael took it as enough permission to lift her into the saddle. He quickly mounted behind her before she had a chance to feel nervous. With a firm arm around her and the reins held deftly in his other hand, he urged the horse into a walk toward the wide stable entrance. "You coming?" he smiled at Emily.

Recalling a few of the basics, Emily barely made the proper move and the horse responded immediately.

"You all right?" Michael asked Allison and she nodded. They rode for better than an hour. Emily quickly felt in control and the confidence she had earned years ago came back to her. Allison gradually seemed to relax as Michael went step by step through the horse's capabilities, and Emily occasionally caught a smile from her. "Now," Michael said cautiously, "how about trying a gallop?"

"Okay," Allison agreed, indicating if nothing else that she felt secure with Michael's ability.

"It'll be fast," Michael warned.

"I'll hold on," she said. Emily held back and watched as Michael heeled the stallion into an easy gallop. He circled around and came back toward her, lifting the horse into a canter until he stopped beside her.

"How was it?" Emily asked.

"Fun." Allison grinned.

"She laughed," Michael announced. "I guess that's better than screaming."

They returned to the stable yard where LeNay walked out to meet them. Michael unsaddled the horses and Emily helped him brush them down and reward them for their efforts. He smiled at her often, and she knew she'd have no trouble living this way. Allison walked with LeNay past the stalls and began to carefully pat the noses of some of the friendlier-looking horses.

"Michael," Emily said when they were nearly finished, "before we go in, why don't you show Allison how a horse races?"

Michael looked surprised. Emily didn't want to admit that it was she who wanted to see it. She had a clear memory of watching him fly on the back of a well-trained gelding.

"I seriously doubt that Allison—" he began.

"Oh, don't be so modest and just do it," LeNay urged.

"Do you ride horses in the real races?" Allison asked.

Michael chuckled. "Not hardly. A jockey has to be—"

"What's a jockey?" she questioned.

"Someone who rides a horse in a race. And they not only have to be very well trained and in good shape, they have to be built small enough to not weigh the horse down. I passed the standard height and weight before I was fourteen."

"But he is well trained," LeNay stated. "When he's not writing, he spends a lot of time with the jockeys. He has the natural feel for it."

"If you're going to tell lies about me, you could at least do it behind my back," he quipped humbly while he brought out a horse that had a different look about it. He saddled it with racing tack, explaining to Allison the differences and their purpose.

With a riding crop in his teeth, Michael hoisted himself into his custom-made racing saddle and lifted his long legs into the high stirrups. The women followed him to the track where he carefully warmed the animal up, then situated it at an apparent starting point. The horse began slower than normal without a starting gate, but Michael leaned forward and the animal responded. He took it twice around the four-furlong track while Emily watched with the same awe she might feel while looking at a Rembrandt or a Picasso and trying to comprehend the artistic insight behind the creation. She glanced at Allison and caught the intrigue in her eyes.

"You know, Allison," LeNay said quietly, taking the child's hand, "with some practice, you could be riding like that one day."

Allison smiled but said nothing. "Now that you've had a chance to ride," LeNay said, "I wonder if you would mind helping Millie and me decide what to prepare for dessert. Millie likes all the help she can get, and we have a lot of fun in the kitchen. Would you like to come and help us out for a while?"

Allison looked up at her mother for permission. "If you want to, I think that would be fine. I'll come and check on you in a while."

Allison went with LeNay, who added to Emily as she walked away, "And we'll check on the little ones. Take your time."

"Thank you," Emily called, appreciating some time alone with Michael. She thought of the way Penny had helped so much with the children, and missed her.

She watched Michael canter the horse toward her. He pulled back the reins to stop, but the horse continued to dance with a desire to run.

"I must have impressed her." Michael nodded toward the departing Allison.

"You impressed me," Emily said coyly. "I wish there was a way to capture it with oils."

"Just don't expect me to pose," he chortled, coming down from the horse. With no hesitance he leaned forward and kissed her quickly on the mouth. He smelled of earth and leather and horses. With her eyes briefly closed, the years fell away and the memories became vivid. A sense of peace and anticipation filled her.

"Speaking of oils," Michael distracted himself from the kiss and took her hand as they led the horse to the stable, "there is something I want to show you."

When the horse had been cared for, Michael stepped into the house only long enough to get a key from a rack inside a closet door. Emily followed him across the yard to a much smaller, older home than the one they lived in now. It had been kept up well, and had a quaint, almost cottage look to it. Emily remembered seeing the house when he had brought her here before. They had contemplated some graves near the house and their relation to his ancestors, but she had not been inside. With the key in his hand she expected him to unlock the front door, but he led her to the side of the house and up some wooden stairs to a door that apparently went into an attic-type room. He turned the key and motioned Emily inside.

The room was dim and there was no electricity, but Michael pulled back the curtains in a gabled window that faced east. Dust flew from them to match what lay over the entire room, but Emily caught her breath at what the light illuminated. A partially-finished painting sat against an easel, before a stool, with paints and brushes scattered about as if it had been worked on a few days ago. Only the dust and the fading colors of everything surrounding her made it evident that it had been this way for years, but she didn't realize how many years until Michael told her the story.

"It's kind of eerie, isn't it? My great-grandfather, Jess Davies, wrote memoirs concerning his mother and this room. She was an artist and a poet, but she was not of sound mind. This is her studio. She was killed in a fire when the big house burned to the ground. The house we live in now was built in its place, and is said to be a near identical duplicate to the one before it. To my knowledge, the contents of this room have not been disturbed since she died in the 1870s. I'd have to look up the date for certain."

"It's incredible," Emily stated, feeling an intangible fascination. "It's the kind of room that could make one believe in ghosts."

"Perhaps," he stated, and she saw a purpose come into his eyes. "I'll tell you what this room makes me think of. I always felt an . . . eeriness here, you might say, as if something were left undone, perhaps because of the painting. But I came here after I had made the decision to be baptized, and what I felt in this room became defined." He smiled, as if it were obvious, but Emily didn't grasp the implication. "They're waiting, Emily. All of those wonderful, colorful people who are a part of me, who have intrigued and fascinated me. They are waiting on the other side to become a part of what you and I are a part of. It's up to us to do it. I want to start the paperwork as soon as we're married, and as soon as I can go to the temple, you and I are going to give them the opportunities they didn't have when they were alive."

Emily felt the warmth from his words and emotion strained her voice. "Beyond marrying you, I can think of no greater privilege." She looked around again. "Why has it never been cleaned out, or used?" she asked. "I mean . . . I'm glad it hasn't. I'm simply curious."

"I don't believe anyone in the family has ever had an interest in painting, for one thing. We've had a few poets."

"And a writer," she smiled.

"But no painters . . . until now." He looked at her closely. "If you want to use it, Emily, we'll clean it out and—"

"Oh," she shook her head, "I don't think it should be disturbed, at least for now. Maybe one day we'll feel differently."

"All right, but . . . I want you to have a special place to paint. I want you to explore your gift."

"How about the sitting room?"

"Now that," he pointed at her, "is a good idea."

Together they absorbed the room again before Michael closed the curtains and slapped his dusty hands on his thighs.

"There is a feel to this room . . ." Emily said before they left and locked the door. "Did I ever tell you why I decided to name my baby Alexa?"

"No." He impulsively sat on the step and she sat beside him. "So tell me." He looked at her with interest in his eyes.

"It's nothing significant, really. It's just that the feeling in that room reminded me somehow. I was having a difficult time during the pregnancy. My health was not good, I suppose from getting pregnant again so soon. I felt run down and kept getting sick with one odd thing or another. I was discouraged about my marriage and . . . well, you know. One day I was lying on the couch holding Amee while she slept. For some reason I started thinking about what you'd told me about Alexa; how the family journals seemed to indicate she was the strength of the family. She brought about so much good, with the boys' home and all. That's it, really. I just felt better, and I decided to name the baby Alexa if it was a girl. I felt right about it. Ryan didn't particularly like the name, but I took a stand on it."

Michael smiled serenely. "I always liked to think that Alexa was my guardian angel."

Emily squeezed his hand. "She very likely could be."

"Perhaps Alexa was pulling for us."

"Perhaps she is waiting. The thought of doing her temple work is exciting."

"I can't wait," Michael said like a child at Christmas.

Emily touched his face. "I love you more than I can believe."

Michael kissed her timidly, then drew back to study her face while their breath mingled as closely as their eyes. "Let's get married soon, Emily. We're here now. The rest is behind us." Their eyes sparkled in unison. "I asked Bishop Wright about it."

"About what?" she asked, nearly dazed by his closeness and the warm spirit hovering about them.

"I asked his opinion on how long we should wait to get married; or rather, I told him we had discussed marrying soon, and wondered how he felt about that, considering your recent loss, and the children and all. I must admit I was surprised by what he said. I nearly expected him to reprimand me for moving too fast, or to advise waiting for the sake of dealing properly with the death. But he told me if you and I felt ready to share a relationship, it was far better to get married and be able to share it fully, than to put stress into our lives by waiting for formless reasons that would leave us more likely to get into trouble."

Emily turned away, blushing from the implication. But Michael took her chin and moved her face back within his gaze. "He said that such decisions were between you and me and the Lord. But he added that from what he knew of the situation, he felt that it wasn't good for you to be without a husband and a father figure for your children."

Michael stood and held out a hand. "Come on, soon to be Mrs. Hamilton, let's go look at a calendar and set a date. We'll send the Wrights and everybody else an announcement."

As they approached the side door of the house, a tall teen-aged boy came out, wearing riding attire similar to Michael's.

"Wade," Michael smiled, "how's it going?"

"Not so bad. How about you?"

"I'm great," Michael grinned. "Wade, this is my fiancée, Emily Hall."

"Hello," he nodded kindly. Emily could see a vague resemblance to Michael.

"Emily, this is Wade Sanford. My sister's son."

"The one you took to the Icehouse concert."

"Yeah," the youth's face lit up. "It was great."

"It's a pleasure to meet you, Wade."

"How's your mom?" Michael asked with some concern.

"Cranky," Wade answered. "That's why I'm going out." Michael chuckled and Wade moved on toward the stables.

"Is it bad?" Emily asked as they went into the house, recalling his briefly mentioning a problem.

"All I know is that she is having some marriage troubles. Whatever the problem is she won't talk about it, and she's not the person she used to be. Something is really eating at her. The last Mother told me, Robert was threatening divorce."

Emily said nothing, but she felt a silent empathy. Stress in marriage could turn all reason upside down. She knew not only from her own experience, but from others who had confided in her over the years.

Michael led her into the kitchen, where his mother and Millie were working busily.

"Smells good." Michael investigated and gave the cook some endearing comments on the food. He introduced her to Emily, then said to his mother, "Where's Allison?"

"She and Stacy just met and seemed quite taken with each other." Michael made a noise of approval. "Stacy took her upstairs to show her something, and then they were going to play with the little ones, I believe."

"My goodness," Emily gave an embarrassed laugh, "I almost forgot I had children for a while."

"Every mother needs a rest," LeNay smiled. "And if you must know, Mrs. Pace is in her glory with young children about again. She seemed to have everything under perfect control when I peeked in just a bit ago. Don't be concerned. We'll settle into a pattern in a few days. You get yourself acquainted and give it some time."

"Thank you for everything, Mrs. Hamilton. Your hospitality has been wonderful."

"Ah," she pushed a humble hand through the air, "it's nothing. We're glad to have you."

"You'd better believe it." Michael folded his arms and leaned against the counter. "Which reminds me. We want to get married, Mother. What day would be good for you? Tomorrow?"

It took LeNay a moment to realize he wasn't serious. The panic left her expression. "Not quite that soon, please. I do have a few things to prepare."

"Tomorrow," Emily muttered under her breath. Michael looked

at her in question. "Michael, I nearly forgot, what with the move and all. Tomorrow is Allison's birthday."

Michael looked concerned, but LeNay's face lit up almost as much as Millie's. "A birthday, you say?" the cook asked. "We don't have enough of those around here."

Michael smiled. "I guess that covers the food. Millie puts on a birthday feast you can't believe until you see it."

"We'll just have to make it a special day," LeNay stated as if it were no problem.

"Maybe we could start out with a trip to town," Michael suggested. "We can leave the babies and just take Allison. With all you left behind, I was figuring we'd need to do some shopping. We'll let Allison pick out some new things, plus something special for her birthday. We'll eat lunch out."

"And when you get back, we'll have some good food and a little celebrating," LeNay suggested.

"It sounds wonderful," Emily agreed.

"I guess we solved that," Michael said with relief. "I wouldn't want my stepdaughter's first birthday in Australia to be a tragedy."

That last word hung in the air as, a moment later, Katherine came into the kitchen with her husband close behind. Before they realized anyone besides her mother and Millie were there, she'd already let the words slip out. "My little brother becomes a Mormon, and the next thing you know, the place is crawling with them."

Following a chorus of surprised gasps, all eyes turned to Katherine in astonishment. Emily had to fight hard to keep tears from surfacing. This was not how she had imagined meeting Michael's sister. Michael broke the silence with a firm, "Was that necessary?"

"No," Katherine said, embarrassed but still terse. "I don't suppose it was. I'm sorry," she added insincerely with a quick glance toward Emily, but the words still hovered uncomfortably. LeNay looked toward Emily in a silent attempt to apologize on Katherine's behalf, but Emily was looking at the floor, trying to keep her emotion under control despite the pounding behind her eyes.

"Katherine," Michael said firmly, "this is my fiancée, Emily Hall." He put a protective arm around her. His words were not apologetic or unsure. His tone made it clear that he was proud of her, a sentiment that deepened when he added, "And she's all the more wonderful because she is a Mormon."

Emily looked up at Michael with tear-filled eyes, not because of the hurt, but because of his love for her. She realized he was continually surprising her by his attitudes, and she had to wonder if the years of indifference from Ryan had made her feel unworthy of such devotion.

"Emily," he said warmly, "this is my sister Katherine." He looked at his sister. "Or sometimes we call her Kate when we're feeling a little more affectionate. I don't believe you and Katherine had the opportunity of meeting the last time you were here. She was out of the country at the time."

"It's a pleasure to meet you," Emily said with a steady voice and a genuine smile, managing to blink back the tears before anyone but Michael noticed them.

"And this is Katherine's husband, Robert Sanford."

"Hello, Emily," he said tonelessly.

"Hello."

"It's good to see you, Robert," Michael said carefully. Robert nodded. When Katherine made no further comment, Michael said, "And since we Mormons have invaded the house, you'd do well to learn to like us. We intend to have a few more Mormons eventually." He tightened his arm around Emily's shoulders and she put hers around his waist.

"I'm sorry," Kate said, slightly more sincere. "I didn't intend to state my opinions so brashly. If Michael is happy with you here, then I'd say it's about time you got here. The man has been absolutely intolerable the last decade."

"Aren't you exaggerating just a wee bit?" Michael asked.

"Aren't you getting just a wee bit carried away with this religion business?" she retaliated.

"My joining the Church and marrying Emily have nothing to do with each other. The timing was coincidental."

"Oh, and was your not marrying her and not joining the Church coincidental eleven years ago?"

Emily winced as if she'd been struck, but Michael only held her tighter.

"Listen, Kate, I realize life is not going well for you right now, but that is no excuse to mar my happiness because you're not willing to forget the past."

"Your happiness and my problems have nothing to do with each other."

"Then why are we having this conversation?" he retorted.

"That's what I was wondering," Robert stated. Katherine glared at him.

The sound of a crying baby came from the distance, and Emily rushed past them toward the door. Mrs. Pace entered before she could leave, carrying a very upset Alexa.

"I think she just figured out she was in a strange place and couldn't find her mother," Mrs. Pace explained, reluctantly turning her over to Emily. Alexa quieted immediately, except for an occasional whimpering breath.

"Mommy's sorry," Emily whispered soothingly, then to Mrs. Pace, "Is Amee—"

"Amee is fine. Allison and Stacy are with her now. They're having a good time."

"I'll take her now," Emily said. "Thank you, Mrs. Pace."

The nanny left the kitchen. Emily moved into the hallway and Michael followed.

"Are you all right?" he asked gently. Emily nodded. "I'm sorry about that. Honestly, Kate is not usually that way."

"It's all right, Michael." They moved down a long hall toward the front of the house. "I can understand why she's hesitant to accept me."

"So can I." He pushed open the lounge room door and they sat on the sofa together. "But I'm at least partly to blame for her prejudice against Mormons. I must seem like a hypocrite to her after the memorable speech I once gave about your not marrying me because of . . . well, I don't need to explain it to you. I was pretty bitter at the time, I admit. I said some things I've regretted, but I think the biggest problem with Kate is not us, but her marriage. Mother believes the problem is more with Robert, but I wonder if she is biased. Personally, I don't have a clue what's *really* going on."

A phone rang in the distance but Michael ignored it.

"Do you think there's anything we can do?" Emily showed genuine concern.

"Pray," Michael replied, "or maybe we could—"

The door came open slightly and LeNay peeked through. "Michael. It's for you." She held it toward him with her hand over the mouthpiece.

"Who is it?" he asked quietly, not wanting to discuss the flaws of his plot with Douglas at the moment.

LeNay looked slightly dismayed. "It's Jenny."

Emily couldn't help feeling uncomfortable, knowing this was the woman Michael had considered marrying, not long before he'd come to the states after Ryan's death. The tension in Michael's eyes was evident.

CHAPTER THIRTEEN

LeNay glanced apologetically between Michael and Emily. "She called several times while you were gone," she whispered, "but I haven't told her."

Emily came to her feet. "Maybe I should go upstairs and let you—"

"Stay right where you are." Michael pushed her back to the sofa with a hand on her arm. "Thank you, Mother." He took the phone and cleared his throat, saying jubilantly, "Jenny. How are you?" Alexa took hold of the phone cord, but Michael only smiled and allowed her to chew on it. "Yes, I'm back," he continued, and Emily couldn't help hoping he'd reflect the conversation so she would know what was being said. It was impossible to not be curious. But Michael remained quiet except for a few noises to indicate he was listening.

"Jenny," he finally said, "I . . . I don't know what to say. I mean . . . we talked about this before I left, and I thought it was pretty clear where we stood, but . . ." He was obviously interrupted. "Yes, I know, but Jenny, I . . .." He glanced at Emily and she could see concern in his eyes. Emily attempted to leave again, sensing he felt uncomfortable, but he held her down firmly and covered the mouthpiece a moment to kiss her.

"Jenny, before you get into this, I have to tell you that . . ." Another long silence. "Jenny, I . . .." Alexa made a squeal of delight as she began to shake the phone cord. "Yes," he said, "that's a baby you hear. Well, actually she's not really a baby. I mean, I guess she is, but she took her first steps last week. She's a year old now and . . . That's what I've been trying to tell you, Jenny. I don't want you to hate me or anything, but I . . ." He nodded and sighed. "Jenny, will you listen to me? The baby is mine. I mean . . ." He sounded briefly panicked. "It's not *mine!* What I mean is . . . she's going to be my stepdaughter."

Through another silence Michael pressed his forehead into his palm. "Yes, Jenny, I'm getting married." He sighed. "Oh, Jenny, come on. Please don't cry. I'm not worth crying over. Listen. Hold it. Whoa, Jenny. We talked all of this through before I left. Those feelings were valid. I am absolutely certain the Lord has been directing me in this. I told you how I felt that Emily needed me, and she did need me. Her husband was killed in June, and . . . Yes, Jenny. I love her more than life."

Michael turned toward Emily and she felt embarrassed by her tears. He only wiped them away and put his arm around her as he listened. "We haven't set a date yet, but it will be soon. I wanted to marry her eleven years ago. I'm sorry if I . . . no, you don't have to be embarrassed, and . . . yes, I feel the same for you. Yes. Yes, I know, but . . . I don't care about that, Jenny." After a pause more lengthy than any of the others, he finally said with a sad voice, "Will you come to the wedding? I'd like you to meet her. I understand. Thanks for calling. It's good to hear from you. Keep in touch. I mean it. No," he smiled, "she won't be jealous." His gaze deepened on Emily. "She knows how much I love her. Good-bye."

Michael eased the cord from Alexa's hands under much protest, and rose to replace the receiver and return the phone to the hall. He gave the baby a decorative rag doll taken from a lower shelf to satisfy her, then said to Emily, "Now I know how you felt when you came to tell me you were marrying Ryan."

"But I thought it was clear you'd decided not to marry her," Emily said quietly.

"I thought so, too." He took her hand. "No one is as right for me as you are, Emily." He turned to face her and bent one knee over the sofa. "It was the strangest thing, because I really felt like I loved Jenny. I felt good about it, but I . . . well, the day after I was baptized, Jenny came over for dinner, and I told her I had been thinking about the possibility of marrying her. We decided to pray about it. Over the next few days, all I could think of was you. I was nearly angry, because I wanted to get on with my life. But the harder I prayed, the more vivid you became in my head. I felt really confused, until Jenny told me she didn't feel right about it. She couldn't explain it. She just said she couldn't marry me, and I felt peace over it. We stayed close and talked a lot. She helped me a great deal with my conversion. A few days later, I was just standing out in the stable and I felt this kind of. . . worry. I came in the house to look at your letters and realized how long it had been. I picked up the phone right then, but when I realized you would have received the call in the middle of the night, this voice inside my head said plainly, *Just go.* I told Jenny all of that before I left, but . . . I guess she never dreamed that . . . well, I never dreamed that you would be . . . " he touched her hair, ". . . free. And while I was gone, she apparently changed her mind about wanting to marry me. Now she knows everything."

Emily could say nothing. The spectrum of his story left her in awe, attempting to comprehend all of this from the heavenly perspective. The thought stayed with her through the remainder of the day as they continued to settle in.

Michael showed her and Allison through the house, explaining all they would need to know to fit in and feel at home. Emily felt disjointed memories of her previous visit fall into place, and it was easy to feel comfortable.

Michael observed Emily as she accustomed herself to her new home, and found a gratification that had only been equaled by his membership in the Church. For years he had often wondered what life might be like with Emily here, and to see it coming to pass made his heart swell. It was easy to continue the role of parent he had begun in Utah, and to see his new family become a part of the family he'd always known.

The following day as they shopped and celebrated, with Stacy along at Allison's request, Emily kept pondering the reality of her and Michael, and all that had brought them together.

They returned home with armloads of packages to find an elaborate buffet set out, and the dining room decorated with streamers of bright colors. Observing Allison, Emily began to see something in her that made her ponderings all the more significant. Emily hadn't seen Allison laugh and play like this since long before Ryan was killed. Were these new surroundings so conducive to her well-being?

Emily's thoughts were interrupted, along with the party, when Murphy knocked at the dining room door and stuck his head in. He was a gruff man in his early forties that Emily recalled meeting on her last visit. She also recalled that Michael had used him as a minor character in his novel, *Verity*.

"Excuse me for interruptin'," he spoke thickly, "but we got a problem, Michael, and I can't do it alone."

"What?" He stood immediately and Emily felt nervous.

"Irish Lady is down. It doesn't look good."

"The foal?" Katherine jumped to her feet in panic.

"Yeah."

"I'm coming, Murphy," Michael said. "Prepare the usual."

"Michael," Katherine followed him toward the door, "you know how I feel about Irish Lady. Please, you can't let her die."

"I'll do my best, Kate." He touched his sister's face and hurried out.

Katherine, who had barely uttered a word since her greetings in the kitchen, turned to her mother with tears in her eyes. Emily felt concerned.

LeNay caught Emily's glance and explained quickly. "Irish Lady has been Katherine's prize mare for many years. She's produced many a fine racer. Apparently the foal she's ready to deliver is giving her trouble."

"Will she die?" Allison asked LeNay.

"We hope not." LeNay took Allison's hand. "Michael does very well with such things. He learned at a young age about the skills necessary to care for ailing horses. Out here, we're much too isolated to depend on getting help when an animal's in trouble." LeNay's expression indicated she had an idea. "Why don't we go out there and give him some moral support? As long as we're quiet and keep out of the way, I don't think he'll mind."

Emily took Allison's hand and followed Stacy and Katherine into the hall. With the babies in bed and Mrs. Pace near them, Emily felt free to go on this excursion, but leery of what they might witness. She heard Katherine say quietly to her mother, while she put an arm around Stacy, "If we lose her, I just don't think I can bear it."

Michael barely looked up when the small group entered the well-lit stable, where the reddish-gold mare lay sprawled in clean straw. Emily wondered what Allison was thinking of the scene before her, which would not have been found in their quiet neighborhood in Utah. Michael, bare from the waist up, knelt over the horse with his arm inside the horse's womb. The animal gave indications of painful labor while he prodded carefully. When he eased away, Emily could see two tiny hooves showing, and pointed them out to Allison with a whisper.

"All right." Michael splashed clean water on his arms. "There is no way she's going to get that foal out alive." Kate made a noise of protest and he added, "But I think they'll both be fine. I'm going to cut her. There's no other way."

Katherine sighed, LeNay and Stacy looked concerned, while Emily and Allison gazed on in amazement. Emily felt almost fluttery, observing Michael in a way she'd never seen him before; yet she knew it was a big part of his life. She couldn't help admiring his skill and agility. With Murphy's careful assistance, he efficiently performed a caesarean birth that brought the little foal sprawling into the world. Michael laughed in relief, and Emily felt tears come, soon followed by LeNay's arm around her. Kate held her mother's other hand, leaving the group huddled close as the foal showed typical signs of new, healthy life. Michael hurried to put the mother in order before he stood out of the bloodied straw to wash and put his shirt back on.

"I think she'll be fine, Kate," he said as she flew to him with a vibrant hug, "but I think her foaling days are over."

"She's done her fair share, I think," Kate concluded, kneeling to pat the horse affectionately.

"Hey," Michael asked his sister, "you got any plans for the little one?"

"Nothing particular," she stated. "I just want my Lady."

"Good." Michael turned to Emily and winked, then he said to Allison, "We have a tradition around here. Every member of the family has to have their own horse." He smiled. "Happy birthday, Allison."

Her eyes went wide as she caught the implication. She looked intently at the little foal, attempting to get on his wobbly legs, then again to Michael, who clarified, "He'll be running before you know it, and when he's old enough to ride, he'll be one of the best friends you've ever had. He's got good racing blood in him, so when he gets a little older, we'll see how he does. If you want him to race, we'll do it. Over the loudspeaker at the track, they'll say the horse's name, then they'll say that he's owned by Allison Hall. What do you think of that?"

Allison hugged Michael and he briefly lifted her off the ground with a hearty laugh.

"Thank you, Michael. It's the most wonderful present I've ever had." Emily's eyes showed approval when Michael glanced her way. "What are you going to name it?" she asked.

"It can't just be an ordinary name," LeNay observed. "Race horses need unique names."

Emily smiled slyly. "How about 'Ashley's Replacement'?"

She intended it to be a joke, but Allison looked up at her with a vibrant, "Yeah."

"I think that's a perfect name," Michael concluded, and they left Ashley's Replacement in Murphy's care.

Through the night, Emily's mind wandered back to her ponderings concerning the perfection of her life. Looking over the years, it was as if an elaborate puzzle had been pieced carefully together, and she felt somehow intrigued.

The following morning, Emily took the babies downstairs for the usual buffet breakfast and found only LeNay and Katherine in the dining room. LeNay rose to take Alexa and put her into the highchair that had been brought up from the cellar and cleaned in anticipation of the children's arrival.

"Where is everyone?" Emily asked, situating Amee on a chair. "I thought Allison would be here . . . and Michael."

"Allison and Stacy managed to choke a little food down before they went out to visit Ashley's Replacement," LeNay informed them. "Who is Ashley, by the way?"

"Allison's only real friend from back home, who was not much of a friend most of the time."

"Ah," LeNay said with enlightenment. "Michael ate early. He

said to tell you he had business in the stables and he'd see you later."
LeNay systematically put bite size pieces of food in front of Alexa.
"Actually, this will give us a chance to talk. We've got plans to make
for this wedding, and—"

"Oh, please, Mother," Katherine said, "spare me. I don't think I
can take wedding plans under the circumstances. At least wait until I
have a chance to eat."

LeNay appeared to ignore the comment, but she immediately
turned the conversation to questions about all that had happened to
Emily in the last eleven years. Emily recalled Michael comparing
Launa Wright's interrogations to his mother. She just smiled and
answered the questions as best she could. When LeNay came right
out and asked about the difficulties in Emily's marriage, she felt
briefly embarrassed, until LeNay glanced unobtrusively at Katherine
and Emily realized her intent.

"I think marriage problems are more common than people
think," LeNay commented after Emily gave a brief explanation. "You
know, Katherine, with the things Emily has dealt with, perhaps she
might have some insight to your situation."

"Really, Mother," Katherine said cynically, "I doubt that Emily,
for all her well meaning, could know how it feels to have your
husband . . ." her voice cracked, "threaten to . . . leave."

"No," Emily said kindly, "but I can tell you what made me
nearly leave my husband." Katherine showed a degree of interest, and
Emily breathed a silent prayer. "Only if you want to talk about it, of
course."

Katherine said nothing, but LeNay took the liberty of briefly
explaining to Emily that Katherine and Robert had always shared a
fairly good marriage, but over the past several months, Robert had
gradually become discontented and unwilling to give in the relationship. Katherine had never been one to put up with anything less than
her due respect as a wife, but the evidence of Robert's falling out of
love with her was the most difficult thing she had ever faced.

When LeNay had gone on for some time, Katherine interrupted with an emotional, "Mother, I don't think we should involve
Emily in all of this. Perhaps . . ."

Emily sensed her embarrassment and wasn't certain how to

dispel it, but LeNay graciously said, "Emily is a part of the family now, Kate. You should know by now that I expect my family to share all joy and pain. She has a right to know, and perhaps she can even offer some empathy."

"I can," Emily said gently. "My situation was different in many ways, but I know well of the stress and heartache that comes from shattered illusions and falling out of love . . . or rather . . . loving but not feeling it, because you only get emptiness in return."

Katherine looked down and blinked several times. The meal was finished, and LeNay urged them to the lounge room where the conversation picked back up. "At this point," LeNay mused, "Robert seems determined to get a divorce, though there are moments when it seems he doesn't know what he wants."

"I know he doesn't want me," Katherine insisted. With the ice broken she began to pour her heart out, making it clear that she loved Robert very much, and though she suspected he had done something he shouldn't have, involving another woman, Katherine declared that it didn't matter. If he would only leave it behind and make a fresh start of their marriage, she would gladly forgive him. Emily hardly knew what to say, but she listened carefully, offered genuine empathy, and encouraged Katherine to let Robert know she was a woman worth having. She left religion out of it under the circumstances, but later in the conversation, Katherine surprised Emily with a sincere apology.

"I'm sorry, Emily, for what I said the other day. I will admit that some of the changes Michael has gone through as a result of attending a Mormon college have had me a little upset at times. But I can see that he is happy now, and it's not for me to question his beliefs, or yours."

"Thank you," Emily said warmly. "Your acceptance is very important to Michael, and to me. And perhaps sometime if you're in the mood, I can tell you how my beliefs got me through the trials of my marriage."

Katherine said nothing, but there was a spark of interest in her eyes that left Emily hopeful her acceptance would eventually deepen. Emily looked around to realize the babies had made havoc of the lounge room, and she said with an embarrassed chuckle, "If I'm not careful, these two will have the house torn apart before they ever become members of the family."

LeNay laughed softly. "There is nothing in this room they can hurt. These walls have seen many generations of children. See," she pointed to a very old-looking sampler, framed under glass, hanging near the door. In the midst of gathering up a number of rag dolls that served both as decoration and safe toys, Emily stopped to look at it closely, reading aloud: "This home was built to live in, not to look at." She chuckled. "That's a relief." She had to squint to see the finely-stitched signature, but her voice betrayed sentiment when she made it out. "Alexa Byrnehouse-Davies, 1897."

"Speaking of Alexa," LeNay said, but Amee interrupted.

"Lexa pwitty."

"Yes, love," LeNay smiled, "Alexa is beautiful."

Emily saw Katherine smile and felt tangible relief. There might yet be a chance for them to be close. Her prayers were being answered.

"You were saying," Katherine prodded her mother.

"Ah, yes. Speaking of Alexa, I was wondering what you had planned to wear for the wedding, Emily."

"I haven't gotten anything yet. Michael said we would get something when we arrived here, but yesterday we—"

"Well, I'm glad you didn't," LeNay interrupted. "There's something I want to show you." She looked to Katherine as she rose and picked up Amee. "Want to come, or would you rather be spared?"

"I think I'll come." Katherine stood and picked up Alexa.

After the babies were left with Mrs. Pace, Emily began to wonder what all of this had to do with Alexa Byrnehouse-Davies. LeNay took them to her sitting room, where she opened a huge chest and pulled out an antique wedding gown. Emily held her breath as the details of painstakingly-preserved features came into closer view, while LeNay explained its history.

"Alexa was married twice. Her first husband was killed, and . . ." LeNay paused as she apparently caught the distress in Emily's expression. "Is something wrong, love?"

"No, it's just . . . the parallel there took me off guard a little. I had known that, but I suppose I'd forgotten." Tears pooled in Emily's eyes and she hurried to look away.

"My dear girl." LeNay put her arms around Emily and the tears spilled. Emily clung to LeNay, reminded of her own mother and how dreadfully she'd missed her these past few years. A little sob escaped her and LeNay held her tighter. Emily wanted to explain that her tears were not from sadness as much as joy. The warmth she'd felt in relation to Alexa was just one more thing that proved how blessed she was.

"I'm sorry," Emily pulled back and wiped at her face. "I just felt suddenly overcome with so many emotions."

"You've been through a great deal in not a whole lot of time," LeNay said, offering a tissue.

"I know, but . . . it's just that . . . you're all being so wonderful. I'm just so grateful to be here, and to be a part of your lives."

"So are we, love." LeNay expressed a teary smile and embraced Emily once more. "So are we."

"I've never seen Michael so happy," Katherine interjected quietly. A moment of silence allowed Emily to absorb her statement of acceptance. They all laughed softly to ease the tension, then Emily returned her attention to the dress.

"You were telling me its history." She urged LeNay to go on.

"As I said, Alexa's first husband was killed."

"Murdered, actually," Katherine inserted and Emily's eyes widened.

"That's right, and soon after she married Jess Davies in this gown. 1890, I believe. In 1912, her daughter Emma wore this same gown when she married Michael Hamilton."

"The rogue," Emily provided and Katherine laughed.

"Well put," LeNay said.

"I wore this gown when I married Michael Hamilton the second," LeNay continued, "and . . ."

"And Katherine was too tall to wear it," Katherine added.

"But," LeNay grinned, "I think it just might fit you. What would you think of being the fourth generation married in this gown, Emily?"

For a moment Emily was too touched to speak. "I don't know if I'd dare," she said breathlessly.

"Well, it's held up pretty good. I'm certain it will survive one more wedding day," LeNay laughed.

Emily didn't know what to say, but LeNay urged her to try it on. She pulled off her sweatshirt, and the gown was lowered carefully over her jeans. It took several minutes to fasten all the buttons, but the long mirror in LeNay's bedroom declared it a near perfect fit.

"It feels so wonderful," Emily said. "I can't believe my daughter's namesake actually wore this dress."

"And the brides of two Michael Hamiltons before," LeNay added. "I think Alexa would be pleased to have you wear it, and whether or not it survives another generation remains to be seen."

"I would be honored to wear it," Emily agreed without hesitation. She was helped out of the gown and the three embarked on a long conversation of wedding plans that Katherine seemed to enjoy, though occasionally she became distant, with sad eyes.

Emily began to feel a sense of anticipation that left her fluttery. She had a desire to share all of this with Michael, and was relieved when Stacy knocked lightly on the door then peeked in. "Mom, do you know where Emily . . . oh, there you are. Michael sent me in to get you. He wants to show you something."

"Run along, love," LeNay urged. "We'll finish up the plans this afternoon."

"Where is Allison?" Emily asked Stacy on their way down the stairs.

"She's with Michael," came the reply, edged with some mischievous humor that nearly made Emily leery.

Stacy ran toward the east corral once they had come out of the house. "I found her, Uncle Michael," she called, and he turned from the fence and waved.

Emily became distracted by her feelings as she moved toward him and was greeted with a kiss. "How you doing, darlin'?" he asked.

"Good," she smiled. "I've been—"

Michael held up a finger to stop her. "Before you tell me anything, I've got something to show you that can't wait."

"All right," Emily said eagerly, and was about to ask where Allison was when Michael pointed into the corral. Emily's eyes widened to see her timid daughter riding a nearly black mare back and forth within the fenced area.

"She's a natural, Emily," Michael said, his eyes sparkling with admiration as he watched Allison carefully. "Look at her. I spent less than an hour showing her the basics, and she's taken to it like a fish to water." Emily followed her daughter closely and felt a formless peace, but Michael's question still surprised her. "Can you feel it?" he whispered, still gazing at Allison, who agilely turned the horse back and forth at an easy trot. Emily turned to him abruptly and he met her eyes. "She's only been here a few days, and she's thriving. Can you feel it?"

"Yes," Emily admitted softly, "I think I can."

Allison trotted toward them and pulled the horse to a slightly awkward halt, but she didn't seem nervous or timid as Emily might have expected. "Hi, Mom," she said eagerly. "Did you see me?"

"I certainly did. You're doing beautifully."

"I can't wait until Ashley's Replacement grows up."

"All in good time," Michael chuckled. "There are some things that can't be rushed."

"And when I grow up," Allison added, "I want to be a jockey. Can I, Mom?"

"You can be anything you want to be, sweetie," Emily said.

"That's what Michael said, too."

Allison trotted off again, and Emily's mind turned back to thoughts that had nearly obsessed her lately. Everything felt so right and good that it seemed incomprehensible—all she had done in years past to bring her to this point.

She was startled when Michael nudged her. "Are you listening to me?"

"I'm sorry." She smiled up at him.

"I asked what you've been doing this morning."

Emily gave him a quick report of the happenings. He was pleased about her progress with Katherine, and thrilled that she would be able to wear Alexa's wedding gown. "She would be honored," he said, touching Emily's chin.

"I'm the one who is honored," she insisted, then told him the other plans they had discussed, while they continued to watch Allison, who was joined in the corral by Stacy on a chestnut stallion.

She helped Allison along, and occasionally a giggle would float through the air.

Emily's mind wandered again until Michael said, "Where are you now?"

Emily looked around. "It's just so beautiful here. I had forgotten the peace, the simplicity." She touched Michael's face, then couldn't resist kissing him. "I'm glad to be here."

"That's good," he chuckled and kissed her in return, "because now that I've finally got you here again, I'm not letting you leave . . . at least not without me."

At lunch, LeNay announced that she had something to show Emily. Mrs. Pace took the babies upstairs for naps and Emily followed LeNay to the library. A memory seized her of the endless hours she and Michael had spent here poring over family journals and genealogical records.

"What you said earlier got me thinking," LeNay said while she scanned the spines of a long row of old leather-bound journals. "I've studied these books so much that I'm just certain I can find it if . . . ah, there it is."

LeNay pulled out a particular volume and began leafing through the yellowing pages covered with elegant script.

"Here," she said, handing the open book to Emily. "I think you'll find this worth your time."

LeNay smiled and left Emily alone. She pulled open the drapes and made herself comfortable in a chair near the window. She glanced back to the first page to be certain which ancestor had written this. Alexandra Byrnehouse Wilhite, 1890. This was obviously written before she'd married Jess Davies, and Emily curiously began to read.

I am overcome with poignance as I look back over these many weeks since Jess returned and became a part of our lives again. How can I deny the love I feel for him, have always felt for him, when it fills me so completely? I know that Richard sensed it, and that is the very thing that makes all of this so difficult. I have told myself so many times that Richard knew of my feelings for Jess when we made the decision to marry, but did that make it any less difficult? How could we have known

Richard would be taken at this time? It was so unexpected, so tragic that at moments I feel as if part of my flesh and blood has been torn away . . .

Emily paused and put a hand to her heart. It was almost as if her own feelings lay before her, despite the varying circumstances. Much had changed since Alexa had lived in this house, but it was evident that love and tragedy were timeless.

. . . and I want to feel despair. Just when I think I can bear no more, I look around me and I see Jess. The torment in his eyes seems to express something formless I feel inside me. I know my marrying Richard hurt him beyond words, but Richard is gone now. I'll not deny that I loved him, and I would do it no differently had I to do it again. Still, I must ask myself—am I somehow wicked to want Jess now? Is it wrong to put the past behind me and move on? Knowing that I have loved Jess all along, there is no other possibility but to accept that our futures will be crossed. What peace the thought gives me! If I could be certain that heaven exists, I might know without doubting that this was the way God intended our lives to be all along.

Emily leaned her head back and let the tears fall. The kinship she felt with this woman was indescribable. Realizing she would be wearing the gown Alexa wore to marry Jess Davies, made the words before her all the more significant. This was not just a story, it was real. She found a comforting thought in imagining Alexa as her guardian angel, just as Michael had said he did. She turned her attention back to the journal and continued to read until Michael found her there.

"Your great-grandmother is an incredible woman," she said.

Michael leaned over to kiss her. "I know. And so are you."

CHAPTER FOURTEEN

Emily hugged Michael tightly, then showed him the journal entry she'd been reading.

"Wow," Michael said quietly. He put his arm around her and continued to read while Emily's mind played through the many steps of her life that made the prospect of her future seem all the more incredible.

As the wedding date drew closer and Emily's family settled in more fully, Allison continued to thrive, and Emily continued to ponder on the wonder of it all. Allison made friends on their first visit to church, while her relationship with Stacy became easy and comfortable. They took school lessons together, and beyond regular riding instruction from Michael, Allison began piano lessons along with Stacy.

Attending church was the first real shock Emily felt with respect to the differences between her new life in Australia and the one she had left on the other side of the world. After a twenty-minute plane ride, they were met by a middle-aged couple who drove them another forty minutes, where their small branch met in a borrowed building. On that first Sunday, by the time they returned home with tired babies, Emily felt certain that one of her new challenges would be dedication to church attendance when it was not two blocks down the street. Still, the rewards were already evident as she felt the strong spirit of this little branch, and she found great comfort in the constancy of their faith.

Their first Monday evening was spent in the lounge room for what Michael declared as the Hamiltons' first official Australian family home evening. He made a point of inviting everyone, and though he didn't expect Katherine or Robert, he was pleased when his mother eagerly joined them. And Stacy came, if only to be with Allison. Michael gave a brief lesson on prayer, using some long pieces of yarn to illustrate, with Stacy and Allison's assistance, how the connection between ourselves and God must be maintained from our end, or it's like disconnected phone lines. "Heavenly Father is always there for us," he explained. "So if we lose touch, we can be pretty sure who's responsible for the communication breakdown."

While they ate cookies that Stacy and Allison had made earlier, Michael and Emily answered some questions from LeNay, leaving them hopeful that her understanding and acceptance of their religion was deepening.

The doorbell rang and LeNay rose to answer it, but they could hear Katherine in the hall. A moment later she peeked in. "Someone's here to see you, Michael," she said quietly.

"Who is it? Send them in," he said quickly.

"I think you'd better come out here," Katherine replied, and Michael rose reluctantly.

He stepped into the hall to find Jenny standing timidly near the door. He smiled and squeezed her hand. "What a pleasant surprise."

"Yes, well . . ." She glanced down and cleared her throat. "I could have called, but I . . . I have something to tell you that I would rather say to your face."

"All right." He folded his arms and leaned toward her.

"I didn't make it to church yesterday because, well . . . I didn't feel up to it, and—"

"Or is it that you didn't feel up to seeing me?"

She scowled. "Must you be so blasted perceptive?"

He chuckled. "Yes, I must."

"I was saying . . . I fasted, Michael, and I know it has to be this way. I hope my confusion didn't make it any more difficult for you. I know how you feel about Emily, and I'm truly glad that it worked out for you."

Michael grinned and impulsively hugged her. "You can't know what that means to me," he said with sincerity.

"Someday I think I will."

"Yes, I'm sure you're right." He motioned to the lounge room. "Would you like to meet her, or—"

"I was hoping you'd say that."

Emily was sitting on the floor, leaning back against the sofa while Alexa climbed on and off her lap and giggled. She looked up when the door opened, and was surprised to see a tall woman with blonde hair, all one length, pulled back and tied in a blue scarf. She was pretty in a simple way, and Michael appeared comfortable as he stepped in behind her. Emily didn't catch the connection until LeNay came to her feet with a warm, "Jenny. What brings you all the way out here?"

"I came to meet the lucky bride," she said sweetly, her Australian accent thick.

Emily felt Jenny's eyes fall on her and attempted to stand up, but Alexa crawled on her again and the effort became awkward. Michael chuckled and lifted the baby, making growling noises that resulted in a giggle. He held out a hand and helped Emily to her feet.

"Emily, this is Jenny Winn. Jenny, my fiancée, Emily Hall."

"It's a pleasure to meet you." Emily extended a hand. "Michael has told me a great deal about you. I understand you're partly to blame for his becoming a Mormon."

Jenny laughed and seemed more at ease. "I didn't do it." She smiled at Michael. "I just gave him an extra push."

"A healthy kick is more like it," Michael chuckled. "Sit down. Let's—"

"Oh, I shouldn't stay," Jenny declined. "I—"

"You don't drive this far and not stay," Michael insisted.

"Well, maybe a few minutes," Jenny said, and they were seated.

"Have a cookie or two," LeNay passed the plate over.

"Thank you, no." Jenny smiled, her eyes turning to the baby on Michael's lap who was attempting to get his glasses out of his pocket.

"This is Alexa," Michael reported, "and the short person over there destroying the decor is Amee." At the sound of her name, Amee came running to Michael with an armload of dolls that she deposited on his lap. Alexa kicked some of them off, and Amee screamed until Emily picked them up.

"Wik it, Daddy," Amee insisted, holding one of them up.

Jenny's eyes widened as she observed, but only Emily noticed.

"What?" Michael leaned toward Amee.

"Wik it, Daddy. Wik it."

He took the doll and examined it to find an apron string untied. He tied and returned it with the announcement, "All fixed, darlin'."

When Amee had scampered away, Michael pointed across the room. "And that's Allison. She just turned ten," Michael said more loudly, and Allison teasingly stuck her tongue out at him. He did the same in return. "And of course you know Stacy."

Jenny nodded. "They're beautiful girls," she said to Emily.

"Thank you. They certainly keep us busy."

Jenny smiled, then said to Michael, "It's been a long time since I've heard an American speak. It certainly is different."

"Yes," Michael grinned and took Emily's hand, "I'm finally getting even with her. In the states, I can't open my mouth without being dubbed a foreigner."

"You should have come an hour ago," LeNay said. "We had family home evening."

"Really?" Jenny seemed surprised, then her eyes turned briefly to Michael. They both knew that LeNay had not been excited about his baptism, and it was apparent that something had changed. Jenny's gaze went to Emily, as if to silently give some credit. Michael caught the look and acknowledged with his eyes that his recent experiences with Emily had made a difference in his mother's outlook.

A subtle tension remained until Jenny left nearly an hour later. Emily couldn't help watching her unobtrusively and wondering about the relationship she had shared with Michael. Jenny seemed so very different from Emily, and with just a twinge of insecurity, Emily found herself wondering what it was about this woman that had so intrigued Michael. Though the situation was much different, and Emily couldn't help liking Jenny, she pondered how Michael must have felt when he faced Ryan. Speculating over what might have been, Emily asked herself how it would feel to be in Jenny's place, standing on the outside and having to be content to stay there. A bittersweet empathy filled her as she considered the decade of anguish Michael must have endured.

After Jenny left, Michael went upstairs with Emily to help put the babies to bed.

"Jenny's a wonderful girl, Michael." Emily's tone was sincere.

"Yes, but she's not the girl for me."

"I should thank you."

"For what?"

"For letting me be the one."

Michael chuckled. "You can thank God for that. I don't think I had a lot to do with the way this worked out."

"You listened to him," she said. He set Alexa free, then bent to kiss Emily.

LeNay cleared her throat as she entered the room. Michael chuckled and Emily blushed.

"Just came to kiss the babies good-night," she announced. "I didn't know there was already kissing going on."

To Emily, it sounded like something her own mother might have said. As she observed LeNay with her children, she was grateful they would have a grandmother's influence in their lives. This kind woman had quickly taken over her role as mother and grandmother in a positive way, and it seemed natural and comfortable.

As the days passed, Katherine went in and out of bad moods, depending a great deal on whether or not Robert was around. But Emily felt a subtle deepening of closeness with her, and Michael declared their growing friendship to be the only thing keeping Katherine sane and the household in peace. Robert was tensely aloof, and Wade was rarely at home as he spent much time in town with his friends. Oblivious to any strain, the babies seemed content with their new lifestyle.

As Emily adjusted to the ways of the household, she found it easier to work with the servants and appreciate their relationship with the family. Michael told her of the concept that had come down from Jess Davies, that the servants worked with the family, not for them. Emily saw evidence of this as Michael worked hard in the stables, side by side with the hired hands. He also found opportunity to crowd Millie in the kitchen and help with the cooking. Stacy and Allison were expected to help with dishes, and each girl was in charge of keeping two rooms clean and orderly in addition to her bedroom.

Emily assisted with the laundry and kitchen work, eagerly antici-
pating her wedding while she cared for her family and nurtured the
same close bonds they had shared in their cozy home in Orem.

As days were crossed off the calendar hanging in the long hall,
Emily saw evidence in Michael of all she felt. The years, the trials, the
emotions—all seemed to be culminating in this wondrous event that
would bind their lives together completely.

Emily felt particularly close to her emotions on a warm afternoon when she was setting up a place to paint in the sitting room. As
she gazed at her nearly-finished painting on the easel, she tried to
comprehend how she might have felt when she'd started it, had she
known that she would ultimately live out her life in this very place
where the photograph had been taken. The thought almost brought
her to tears, but she was distracted by a pounding from the bedroom.

Emily pushed the door open to investigate. She found Michael
hammering a nail into the wall.

"What are you doing to my bedroom?" she inquired lightly.

"I am moving this picture," he said as he lifted it onto the nail
and straightened it carefully, "from *my* bedroom into *our* bedroom."

"I see," she said and moved closer to look at it. The tender
emotions of a few moments before now rushed to her throat as she
gazed upon a beautiful, framed photograph of the Sydney Temple.

"Do you like it?" he questioned eagerly.

"I love it," she said, barely maintaining a steady voice. "Where
did you get it?"

"Jenny gave it to me when I was baptized," he reported, looking
nostalgically at the picture. "At the time, I was thinking I might take
her there someday." He turned to Emily, his eyes glowing with affection. "Little did I know that you were on the other side of the world
with . . . " Michael stopped, and his expression sobered when he saw
Emily's distress. "What?" he asked, but she couldn't answer.

There was no logical reason why his mentioning Jenny would
make Emily suddenly think about the one big difference—if he had
married Jenny, he could have been sealed to her. But as it was . . . the
emotion overtook Emily fully, and she headed toward the sitting
room without a word. She hoped futilely to escape an interrogation,
knowing well that Michael would follow her and demand an expla-

nation.

He took hold of her arm just inside the sitting room door, and she tried to laugh it off. "It's nothing, really," she insisted. "I'm just feeling . . . emotional . . . over everything . . . and . . . "

"Emotional about what?" She didn't answer. "Emily, I said something in there that's upset you. I want to know what it was."

Emily knew better than to avoid the matter, for her sake as well as his. "If you'd married Jenny," she said with a wavering voice, "you could have been sealed to her, and—"

"I don't *want* to marry Jenny," he retorted, almost angrily.

"I know that! And I know it shouldn't matter, but . . ." Her words faded into tears and she slumped into a chair.

"But it *does* matter," he stated dryly, feeling a rush of emotion himself that made it clear he had not dealt with this; he'd only suppressed it. His concern at this moment, however, was for Emily. Kneeling beside her, he took both her hands into his and looked into her eyes. "Emily," he said gently, "why don't you tell me why this is bothering you? Let's talk about it. Tell me exactly how you feel. I want to know."

"Oh, Michael," she said, pulling a hand away to wipe at her face, "I'm just so confused sometimes. Would God expect me to live the rest of my life with you and then turn my back on all of that to spend eternity with Ryan? I want to be with you forever, Michael, I do. But then, sometimes I think of Ryan and it's so . . . sad. I mean . . . even if I chose to be with you, what about his daughters? In spite of his faults, shouldn't he have the right to be with his children in the next life? I mean . . . I am sealed to Ryan. And so are my children."

"I know."

"*All* of my children, Michael."

He glanced away and swallowed hard. "I know."

"So if Ryan has the right to be with his children, and you have the right to be with yours, then how does it—"

"Emily," he pressed his fingers over her mouth to quiet her, "let me say something. I have thought about this long and hard, and I have prayed about it. I have to admit that it's something I'm not totally . . . comfortable with, but . . . Well, I keep thinking about what Bishop Wright told me when I talked to him about it." Her eyes widened. "You didn't know that, did you?" She shook her head. "Everything he said made perfect sense to me. I believe the man is inspired. But then, you basically told me the same thing. I have to accept that in my worldly perception, I cannot try to question the infinite wisdom and omniscience of a God who I know to be perfectly just and fair. I have to live with the faith that I will inherit the rewards of the way I live. I also have come to believe that on the other side it will likely not be the way we perceive it here on earth. If it all works the way it's supposed to, all mankind should be sealed together as one big happy family anyway, right?"

Emily nodded stoically. "Still, a part of me can't help wishing it were different."

"There is no good in that," he insisted. "I believe you made the right decision, Emily. There are likely reasons beyond the ones we see, but somehow I know you were meant to marry him, to have these children of his," he looked at her deeply, "and to be mine now. In one way or another, I believe we will be together forever."

Emily gave a peaceful sigh. "I know I've said it before, but you have changed, Michael. Your faith inspires me; it lifts me."

Michael looked down at her with an ironic chuckle. "Maybe if I had been willing to let my pride go a little and change sooner, it might have all been very different. If I had humbled myself enough to develop a testimony years ago, I might have been worthy of you then; I might have saved us both a lot of misery."

"Hold on." She stopped him. "Did I not hear you say a moment ago that there was no good in wishing it had been different and that you believed I was meant to marry Ryan?"

"Yes, you're right. I guess we can't speculate over such things. If I had joined the Church then, I likely would not have had the conviction I should have had, and you might have ended up with an inactive husband either way. Perhaps these years were necessary for both of us. I know they were for me, to help me appreciate life and love, and to bring me to a point where I could never take for granted what I have been blessed with."

Emily touched his face in a gesture of admiration.

"I love you," he said. "We are going to have a wonderful life together, Emily, and we can only hope that God will give us more."

Emily nodded in agreement. But as she lay staring at the ceiling that night, she couldn't deny the confusion still hovering over her. And in her heart, she knew Michael continued to struggle with it more than he admitted. She prayed herself to sleep, hoping to finally feel peace over the issue.

She woke with a start and felt briefly disoriented. As she tried to recall the content of her dream, she was first surprised at the clarity it held in her memory, and then at the warmth she felt as the Spirit seemed to tell her there was truth in what she'd dreamt.

Consumed with a joy unlike anything she'd ever known, Emily grabbed her robe and wrapped it around her as she flew down the hall to Michael's room. Without knocking, she slipped inside and felt her way to the bedside table, where she turned on the lamp. For a moment she just watched him sleep, marveling at how much she loved him, trying to comprehend what she believed God had just shown her concerning Michael Hamilton and the part he had played in the life before this one. In her heart, Emily had no room for doubt. She knew they had been together before this life had begun, just as surely as she knew they would be together in the eternities ahead.

"Michael." She nudged his shoulder, unable to keep it to herself any longer.

He groaned incoherently until he realized he wasn't alone, then he sat up with a start. "What are you doing here?" he asked as she sat on the edge of the bed and touched his face.

"I just had the most incredible dream," she said, her eyes nearly glistening. "It was just so . . ."

"What?" he questioned when she faltered.

Emily met his eyes and suddenly felt the full spectrum of what she had been shown. She knew this wasn't the time, or the place, to share it with him.

"I can't tell you, really," she said. "It was so complicated. But I want you to know that my prayers were answered, Michael. I know beyond any doubt that you and I are meant to be together, and we will always be together. Oh," she laughed toward the ceiling, "it was incredible."

Michael sighed and hugged her. "I guess I'll have to take your word for it."

"I love you, Michael," she said and kissed him.

"I love you, too," he replied, his eyes full of wonder.

When nothing more was said, Emily came hesitantly to her feet. "I think I'd best get back to my room."

"I suppose," Michael said, exaggerating his disappointment until she laughed.

"Only two more nights," she said on her way toward the door.

"Yes," he grinned, "I know." He blew her a kiss and she returned it. "Emily," he added more seriously just before she closed the door, "thank you. I think I feel better."

"I know I do," she said and left him alone.

At breakfast, they watched each other intently across the table. Emily couldn't deny the glow of peace and anticipation in Michael's eyes that mirrored all she felt inside. Nothing more was said about her dream, but she knew it had made a difference for both of them.

The day before the wedding, Emily was almost disappointed to realize that everything was under perfect control. Michael took Allison riding in the afternoon, but Emily declined going along, feeling a need to be alone.

On her way upstairs, she overheard Robert and Katherine arguing. A once-familiar knot formed in her stomach. The only distinct words she caught before hurrying on were Robert's. "I'm sick to death of being controlled by your family's money," he complained.

"That's not fair," Katherine retorted. "Your work in the family business has nothing to do with the problems between us. You're just using it as an excuse to . . ."

Emily hurried to her room and knelt to pray on their behalf. She came to her feet, impressed to call the Sydney Temple and put their names on the prayer roll. When that was done, she returned to her room and paused to absorb the signs of Michael's forthcoming move to her quarters. Many of his clothes hung in the closet, and more recently, drawers had been filled and a miscellaneous array of his things were set out on the dresser. She idly opened a bottle of aftershave and smiled. It smelled like him. She purposely put a dab on her nose, then absently picked up the scriptures from the bedside table. She sat on the edge of the bed and thumbed through them in a different way from her usual daily study. There was a sensation of searching, though Emily wasn't certain what she was searching for. Coming across the psalm of Nephi, Emily read it and recalled the countless times it had given her comfort. Memories of the first time she'd heard Michael speak filled her with a joyful anticipation.

Searching on, Emily was surprised to find herself in the Bible. There were parts of it she enjoyed, but it was the Book of Mormon that usually consumed her scripture study. The biblical pages fell open to the story of Abraham and Isaac, and she read almost absently until her heart began to pound and she didn't understand why. Rereading the verses that had apparently brought on the reaction, Emily felt an idea begin to jell that suddenly brought all of her recent ponderings into perfect synchronization.

Nothing in the words themselves seemed to touch her, but rather her knowledge of the entire concept of Abraham's obedience, so movingly demonstrated by his willingness to sacrifice someone he loved. Years ago, had she been asked to sacrifice the love she shared with Michael, only so they could be together moments later in the realms of eternal time? Her warm tears confirmed it. In a moment's thought, Emily could nearly see the paths her life might have taken if she had chosen differently and gone against the promptings of the Spirit. If Michael had joined the Church for her sake, she believed his support would have waned with his lack of conviction. If she had married Michael eleven years ago, perhaps she would have been a candidate for complacency. And perhaps difficulties with relationship and religion would have come between them to some degree, regardless of his respect for her.

Emily could see clearly now, just how important these years of refinement and purging had been, and she believed that God had seen it this way all along. Added to her theory was Allison's progress. Emily had never seen her so vibrant, so alive. It was as if she had been born to be living this life, and had never felt quite suited to the life she had lived before. Emily felt the peace and simplicity of their new lifestyle every time she stopped to look around—and at the center of it all was the man she loved.

Settling into Michael's life had made it obvious that he was an important man. His involvement in the family businesses was evident, but far more important to Emily was the role he played in her life, her love, her future. And being a part of all he represented came as easy to Emily as breathing.

How grateful she was for a kind and loving Heavenly Father who had mapped her life out so perfectly and guided her through it with compassion and mercy. It was incredible to think that little more than eight months ago, she had come across Michael Hamilton's book at the mall. And tomorrow she would be his wife.

* * * * *

While Michael and Allison stood in neighboring stalls to curry the horses they'd ridden, Michael took the opportunity to bring up something he felt necessary.

"Guess what, Allie?" he began casually. "I'm getting married tomorrow." She gave him a glance of disgust that made him chuckle.

"You're silly sometimes, Michael," she said and returned to her chore.

"Yes, I admit it." He paused. "You like it here, don't you, Allie?"

Michael realistically expected an "I guess" or an "I don't know," but she answered him with a firm, "Yes, I do."

"Or would you rather be in Idaho?" he asked lightly, and she glared at him just like Emily might have. "Well, I'm glad you like it here." He cleared his throat. "How do you feel about . . . the wedding tomorrow? You've never told me what you think about me marrying your mom. I know how much you love your dad, and I hope you know I don't want to take his place in your heart."

Allison stopped and looked down thoughtfully.

"You miss him," Michael guessed. Allison shrugged her shoulders. "Talk, Allie," he insisted gently.

With little hesitation Allison said, "I miss him sometimes, but it wouldn't be so bad if . . ." Michael sensed the pressure of tears in her expression, and he leaned over the side of the stall to put a hand on her shoulder. "If I knew I would see him again, then maybe I . . ."

"But of course you'll see him again, Allison. You know the plan and how it works. You were born under the temple covenant, and—"

"I know, but . . ." She looked up at him, huge tears brimming in her eyes. "But what if he . . . didn't go to heaven because he . . ." She looked down, and a knot formed in Michael's throat as the answer to months of difficulty for Allison seemed to fall into place. "He wasn't very good to my mom, Michael. And he never went to church, except a little bit just before he . . . died."

Michael was stunned by the revelation of Allison's innermost concerns. He wanted to console her, but it was difficult when this religion business still felt so new to him—not to mention his own sensitivity on the subject. Instinctively, his mind went back to all he'd learned in those college classes.

"Allison, the important thing is that he was trying. The scriptures say that we are judged by the desires of our heart, and when your father died, I believe he had very good desires in his heart. Do you remember the night before he died? Your mother has told me about it. Remember how he talked about doing things together as a family? And that same night, he talked to your mother about getting some help in his relationship with her, and about getting ready to go back to the temple. Now, he didn't get a chance to do those things, but the scriptures also tell us the work that begins on earth will continue to progress on the other side. I can't tell you what's happening there, but I believe your father is doing well, and he's looking forward to the day when he can be with you and your sisters again."

Allison looked up with hopeful eyes. "Will you be with us too, Michael?"

Michael swallowed. "I certainly hope so. I'm sure that if we all live worthy, the Lord will somehow make it possible for all of us to be together. We must have faith that it will be that way, and depend on his wisdom to work it out properly."

"I love you, Michael," Allison smiled brightly. Emotion welled in Michael's eyes.

"I love you, too, Allison."

"Since you're marrying Mom tomorrow, would it be all right if I start calling you Dad?"

Michael had to take a moment to steady his emotion, but his voice still cracked when he said, "That would be more than all right with me."

Allison reached up to kiss him on the cheek, then returned to her currying as if she'd been doing it from birth. Michael watched her a moment then did the same. "I guess your Mom told you we're going away together for a while."

"Yeah," she replied easily.

"We'll be back in a couple of weeks. In the meantime, we're counting on you to help with the babies and keep up with your studies."

"Okay." Her tone became almost eager. "Mom said you'd bring us back a souvenir. Will you bring one for Stacy, too?"

"I think we could manage that."

"Will Stacy be my cousin after tomorrow?"

"If I'm going to be 'Dad,' that pretty much makes Stacy your cousin."

"Good," she declared. Michael smiled at her and felt a peace swell in him that deepened when he turned to see Emily approaching. The reality of what tomorrow would bring left him in humble awe. She went on her tiptoes to kiss him quickly, but her hand lingered against his face while a mutual sense of anticipation fluttered through them.

"How was the ride?" she asked, and Allison turned to see her.

"It was fun," Allison declared.

"If you're nearly finished," Emily added, "Grandma wants you to come in and try on your new dress so she can fix the hem."

"Okay," she said and walked past them with a mischievous, "See you later, Dad."

Emily's questioning gaze moved Michael to quietly explain their conversation. Listening to him, Emily felt certain that life could be no better. Then, suddenly, the thought kindled a memory that flooded her with panic. Michael noticed her expression change.

"What's wrong?" he questioned.

Emily's thoughts raced back to the day Ryan had been killed. She had felt such a perfect hope and joy just prior to the accident. She looked up at Michael and wondered if she could bear losing him.

"Emily?" he pressed when she didn't answer.

"It's nothing," she said. "Just pre-wedding jitters."

"Are you certain?" he prodded.

Emily forced a smile and nodded firmly. She was relieved when he didn't press it.

"I can relate." He grinned and put his arm around her as they headed toward the stable doorway. "Which reminds me, I . . ." The noise of a small plane flying close overhead interrupted. Michael looked up as if he could see through the roof, then he grinned.

"What?" she asked.

"I think your wedding gift has arrived. Come on, let's go see. I told Murphy I'd meet him at the hangar when he brought it in."

"Murphy flies, too?" she asked, running after Michael. He opened the door of the Cruiser for her, and she landed in the seat.

"Yeah, he loves it," Michael said absently, looking up through the windshield to see that the plane was still circling.

"How did you know when he was coming in?"

"I told him to fly low. And he's about right on time." Michael grinned at her, then he laughed. "You are going to love it, darlin'."

"I hope it's not going to be like my birthday surprise."

"Oh, much better than that."

"I have a gift for you, Michael," she said, "but it's not quite finished. Do you think you can wait?"

He smiled. "I've got a lifetime."

"It shouldn't take that long," she laughed, then her expression sobered as she took his hand. "I want to give you the painting I'm working on. I'll get it framed as soon as I have a chance to finish it."

Emily felt a little apprehensive when he said nothing, until she realized he was choked up.

"You really know the way to my heart, don't you, my love?"

"I try." She leaned her head back on the seat to watch him.

The Cruiser turned off the road and headed over the stretch of flat land toward the hangar, just as the plane touched down in the distance.

"I love you, Michael," Emily said and he immediately put his foot on the brake. They stopped quickly in a cloud of dust and Michael leaned over to kiss her, doing his best to express with it the anticipation of intimacies yet to be shared.

Emily felt her chest rise and fall with each breath as she drew back to meet the desire in his eyes, made all the richer by its rightness. There was peace in knowing their relationship had been chaste, and what they would share in marriage would not be tainted. Michael kissed her again, and Emily felt herself drowning in the depths of it. She reached a hand into his hair as if it might save her, then he pulled hesitantly away to whisper, "I love you too, Emily Hamilton . . . almost."

"I think we'd better get on to this wedding gift," she smiled. Michael cleared his throat and drove the Cruiser forward.

As they parked near the hangar, Emily gasped and had to blink several times to be certain she wasn't hallucinating. "Michael!" Her voice rose a pitch and she put a hand to her heart. "I can't believe it. I . . . just can't . . ."

"Well, don't just sit there. They look anxious."

Emily jumped out of the Cruiser and ran to embrace Penny. They laughed and cried, while Michael and Bret shook hands and looked on in amusement.

"I can't believe it," Emily repeated. "How did you get visas so quickly, and—"

"Ours came through right after yours did," Penny said. "Michael planned this from the start."

"You rogue!" Emily said to him, and he laughed.

"What are you wearing?" Penny looked Michael over from his boots to his jodhpurs to his flat-brimmed hat.

"Working clothes," he stated as if he were insulted, but the humor in his eyes was evident.

"He dresses like that most of the time," Emily said, and Penny made a noise of approval.

"How was the flight?" Michael asked Bret.

"Long," Penny answered for him. "I don't know how you did it with those babies."

"We had a magic bag," Michael reported. "I trust Murphy took good care of you."

"He's been great," Bret said, "and he's rather colorful."

"Oh, yes," Michael chortled. "His family has been working with us for generations, and they've all been colorful."

"You talkin' 'bout me?" Murphy hollered.

"Don't you think we could find something better to talk

about?" Michael called back. He went to help Murphy with the luggage while Penny and Emily couldn't talk fast enough to catch up on the days they'd been separated.

"Murphy showed us the estate from the air," Penny said as they drove toward the house. "But you don't call it that, do you?"

"It's a station," Michael provided.

"It's incredible," Bret said.

"And it really is spring here," Penny mused. "We left snow in Utah."

"How many acres do you own?" Bret added.

Murphy laughed. "I don't think anybody's ever counted."

"If you get bored next week, Murphy, why don't you do that?"

"I'll never get that bored."

The women chattered with excitement as they went up the back stairs. Michael and Bret followed with the luggage.

"We're putting you in the east guest room," Michael informed them at the landing. "Emily's rooms are that way," he pointed and took them the other direction, where he opened a door and Penny flitted in with a gasp of approval.

"It's wonderful, Michael," she said, while Bret comically sat on the edge of the bed to test it. "It has such . . ."

"Character," Emily provided.

"Yes, well," Michael said, "we've tried to preserve as much as possible of the original furnishings and decor. Of course, the plumbing and electrical were added quite some time after the home was built, and you can see evidence of that, but it still seems to have some . . . flavor."

"It's beautiful." Penny looked around carefully.

"How long are you staying?" Emily asked.

"What difference does it make to you?" Penny replied. "You're going on a honeymoon tomorrow."

"Actually," Michael said, "we're not leaving until the next day."

"Unfortunately we couldn't get away any sooner," Penny explained, "but Michael suggested we stay a few days and take advantage of the peace and quiet. Murphy said he'd take us riding."

"I still can't believe it," Emily said to Michael. "All this time you've been keeping this from me."

He only shrugged his shoulders and chuckled. "Come on," he said, "we'll let them get settled in while we go over that checklist one more time. Later we can show them around."

"Sounds great," Penny beamed, then she hugged Emily again before she and Michael left.

In the hall Michael said quietly, "That's the room Emma was sleeping in when my grandfather kidnapped her."

"The rogue?" she said excitedly, and he nodded.

Once assured that everything was as ready as it could be, Michael pulled Emily onto his lap and kissed her nose. "By this time tomorrow," he said, "you will be my wife."

"I know." Emily laid her head on his shoulder. "Everything seems so wonderful, sometimes I fear it won't last."

"Why wouldn't it?" Michael chuckled until he saw the seriousness in her eyes. "Emily? Whatever's wrong?"

"I don't know. I just . . . hope it's not too good to be true. Sometimes I . . ." Emily hesitated to voice something that had been on her mind more than she cared to admit. "I think how good everything felt just before Ryan died, and I . . ." Her voice faltered, and Michael put his arms tightly around her.

"Emily," he said gently, "God would not have brought us this far to allow something awful to happen now. I know it as well as I know I'm sitting here."

"Yes," she tried to smile, "but that's exactly what I told myself on the way to the hospital."

Michael sighed and looked down. "We can only have faith, Emily. I believe that you and I will have a long and wonderful life together, and there is no good in thinking anything else. We will live each day to its fullest, with the hope of a bright future." Michael hugged her tightly, wishing he didn't feel this sudden onslaught of nerves. What if something did happen now? Could he bear it?

"Emily?" he asked innocently, attempting to distract himself. Emily gazed at him in question. "Will you marry me?"

"Oh," she went along, "I suppose I could. I haven't got any other plans. When did you want to do it?"

"How about tomorrow, if you're not busy? We could just get married, have a few more kids, and live happily ever after. What do you say?"

"I'd say you're brilliant to come up with such a plan."

They laughed and he kissed her again. Their eyes met and he took her hand, threading his fingers between hers, pressing their palms together with unspoken anticipation.

"Tomorrow," he whispered, and he knew by the sparkle in her eyes that he didn't need to say more.

Chapter Fifteen

The afternoon flew quickly as Penny and Bret were given a tour. Penny was delighted to see the children, and commented more than once on the vibrancy she could see in Allison. When last-minute arrangements had been seen to, LeNay took time out to enjoy the company, and the family shared an elegant meal in the evening. The branch president arrived with his wife just before dinner, to stay over and perform the ceremony. The anticipation ran high, and even Katherine seemed in good spirits, considering the argument she'd had with Robert earlier. Robert was nowhere to be seen.

After dinner, they gathered in the lounge room while Mrs. Pace took the babies upstairs to play. They were barely seated when Penny announced, "Don't anybody leave. We'll be right back."

The conversation remained light while Michael possessively held Emily's hand. Their eyes met often to reaffirm that the excitement was mutual. Penny peeked through the door with a conspiratorial grin.

"We got you a present," she announced.

"Can't you read, Penny?" Michael scolded. "The announcement said plainly: No gifts please!"

"I can read, Michael," she retorted, "and we know you can buy anything you might want or need. But we have something money won't buy."

"I think you've already given us plenty of that in the past," Emily said warmly.

"But this can stay here with you," Penny stated. "And we can't."

Penny opened the door wide, and Bret entered with a very large wrapped package that he set in front of Michael and Emily. It covered both their laps nicely. "We custom-wrapped it to fit in the biggest suitcase we could find," Bret stated.

Emily felt the package and looked up with a quiet, "Oh, you wouldn't."

Michael was lost.

"I didn't do it." Penny lifted her hands in innocence. "Read the card."

Emily opened the envelope and Michael read aloud: "It's just not the same without you." Emily lifted the card open and they both gasped. The interior was solid with signatures, all names they recognized from the ward.

"You open it," Emily said to Michael. "I already have a suspicion."

Michael carefully tore away the paper. A flash went off, and he looked up in disgust to see Penny with a camera. "We promised pictures," she said. He stuck his tongue out and she took another. As the paper was pulled away, a huge quilt fell over their laps. LeNay squealed with delight. Emily started to cry. The fabric over the back was deep blue, and over the front were blocks of pale blue and white, alternated in a checkerboard pattern around a delicately quilted likeness of the Sydney Temple. Each block represented a family in the ward, and was hand-stitched with names and a variety of little pictures to remind them of Utah.

"It's incredible," Michael said.

"I can't believe it," Emily added. "It's the most beautiful quilt I've ever seen."

Penny took more pictures. "It's rather large," she stated. "There were so many that signed up to do blocks, we just had to keep making it bigger. But I trust you can find a way to put it to good use."

"I think we can manage," Michael laughed. He put his arms around Emily, and Penny took another picture. "Enough already," Michael said. "Save some film for tomorrow when Emily's in that century-old wedding gown."

"Really?" Penny's eyes widened, and it seemed no time before tomorrow had arrived, and she and LeNay were helping Emily into the gown and adjusting it carefully as it was buttoned.

"It's the most beautiful gown I've ever seen," Penny declared.

Emily surveyed her reflection and thought of Alexa. She could almost imagine her, more than a hundred years ago, dressing in this same gown to be married in the same place. The thought gave her goose bumps that only worsened when LeNay helped secure the headpiece of fresh, white flowers of several varieties. Heirloom pearl earrings completed the ensemble, and she was finally declared ready.

"Less than fifteen minutes," Penny stated, and Emily put a hand to her heart in an attempt to steady it. Allison and Stacy came bounding into the room in matching dresses to announce that Mrs. Pace had already taken the babies out to mingle with the guests.

"Which is where I should be," LeNay declared. "Is there anything else you need, love?" she asked Emily, clasping her hand.

"I think I'm ready. Have you got the ring, Allison?"

"Right here." She proudly displayed it.

"I'll see you there." LeNay embraced Emily carefully and left with Allison and Stacy.

"You look radiant," Penny declared.

"I'm so glad you're here," Emily said with emotion. "It wouldn't have been the same without you."

Penny made a dramatic gesture. "I'd have died if I couldn't be here today. Ask Bret. That's all I have talked about since you left." She became more serious. "Emily, I'm so happy for you," she said, her eyes glistening. "Everything you have here is so wonderful, and you deserve it. I'm going to miss you, but I'm glad I got to see all of this firsthand. I think it will help."

Emily started to cry, too, and Penny handed her a lace handkerchief that LeNay had provided. "Now, don't cry. You'll ruin your makeup." When that didn't work, Penny attempted distraction. "So, Michael says you won't be leaving for a honeymoon until tomorrow. Where are you going?"

"All he'll tell me is we're going to see Australia, and we're going by plane. But he wants to spend tonight here. Apparently, tradition has it that we eat and dance all day and into the night. Oh, Penny, I'm so nervous."

"There's no reason for that. I'd say what's about to happen is as natural as the stars in the sky."

Emily squeezed Penny's hand. "I love him so much. I only hope that . . . that . . . nothing happens now to—"

"What?" Penny insisted. Emily didn't answer, but Penny caught the implication. "Nothing is going to happen to either of you. Don't be so silly. You're just used to being miserable, that's all. Give yourself a break. You're going to live happily ever after."

"That's what Michael says."

"The man's a genius."

"I suppose we should get out there."

"Come along." Penny took her arm and they moved carefully to the upstairs hall. They waited concealed in a side corridor while the bustle of a small crowd floated to their ears, mingled with the quiet strains of a string quartet.

Allison found Michael in the opposite corridor. "I saw Mom," she bragged.

"I don't have to ask if she looked beautiful," Michael smiled tensely.

"She looked more beautiful than you could believe. You're just not gonna believe it."

"Sweetie, after what I've been through to get here, I'd believe anything. Is my tie straight?" He bent over and allowed Allison to adjust it, then she moved into the archway where she could see Penny across the way, and they exchanged a wave.

"Who are you waving at?" Emily asked from behind.

"Your daughter," she stated.

"Can you see Michael?"

"No, but . . . oh, wait. He's peeking." Penny chuckled and shook a finger at him. He stuck his tongue out. "Emily, the man's a jewel."

"What does he look like?"

"What do you mean what does he look like? He looks like he's always looked. Brown hair, kind of tall and—"

"Penny!"

"Classic," she smiled. "Black tuxedo, bow tie. Perfect."

The music ceased and Penny glanced at her watch. "It's ten straight up," she announced. "I think this is it. See you later." Penny slipped away to find her seat near Bret. Emily moved into the archway to see Michael across the way. Her heart pounded audibly in her ears. Penny was right. He was perfect.

As Emily came into clear view in the morning sunlight, Michael felt certain the joy would explode from within. Allison had been right. She looked so beautiful he couldn't believe it. He was the luckiest man alive.

The music began again and they walked slowly toward each other to meet in the center of the upstairs hall. Michael thought of the women before who had worn that gown, and he wondered if the men marrying them had felt as he did now. Her hand radiated warmth when it slipped into his. She looked up at him and the warmth deepened. Their vows were spoken with quiet fervor, and he decided he'd never been so happy in all his life.

The trembling that overtook Emily as she stepped into the hall ceased immediately when Michael took her hand. For a moment, her mind flew through all that had brought them to this day. Then everything stopped and all she could see and feel and hear was now, this moment. As the rings were exchanged, Emily thought it ironic that when she had married before it had been with elaborate, expensive rings at Ryan's insistence, and they had taken years to pay for. Yet Michael, for all his wealth, had chosen, to her delight, the simplest of matching gold wedding bands.

Michael bent to kiss her and the bonds become final. He drew back slightly to look at her, then kissed her again and started to laugh in the midst of it. Emily laughed with him, and he briefly lifted her off the floor with a firm embrace.

When Michael had told her the day would be filled with celebrating, she had never imagined it would be so festive. She'd never seen so much food in her life, never been with so many jovial people, never been so happy.

The groom spent much of the day with one baby or another, or sometimes both. By evening his jacket was left on a chair somewhere, his shirtsleeves were rolled up, and his tie hung unfastened around his neck. But Emily swore he only got more handsome as the day wore on.

The guests gradually left and the babies were sent to bed, but the celebrating continued with those remaining, which mostly consisted of family and stable hands. Penny and Bret appeared to be having the time of their lives, and Allison thoroughly enjoyed introducing herself as the bride's daughter.

Emily hadn't realized how late it was getting until she caught Michael's eye across the room. The smile he gave her sent quivering anticipation to every nerve. A minute later he abruptly set down his glass, strode toward her, and in one swift movement lifted her into his arms.

"Good-night," he called, and with no further words he carried her toward the stairs. The train of the gown dragged until she gathered it onto one arm, laughing at her seeming weightlessness as he deftly ascended and carried her into the bedroom that was now theirs. He kicked the door shut then set her carefully on her feet, leaving his arm about her waist.

"Welcome home, Mrs. Hamilton," he said softly. "Better late than never."

"Or maybe we're just right on time." She reached up to kiss him lightly, but it wasn't enough. Their eyes met with a full perception of the reality. The waiting was over. Emily put a hand to his face as Michael eased her closer. His lips came over hers with a kiss unlike anything she had ever known. She never dreamed so much love could be expressed in a kiss. He drew her closer still, and she lifted her head to gasp for breath.

"Michael," she laughed softly in his ear, "it took two women to get me into this dress. I'm not sure if . . ."

"I think I can manage," he whispered roguishly, and she giggled. "But I . . ." he added more soberly, then didn't finish.

"What?" She drew back, puzzled by his apparent concern. Michael smiled and shook his head to indicate it was nothing. Emily looked at him deeply and realized he was tense. "Are you nervous?" she asked. Michael shook his head, then proceeded to chew on his thumbnail.

"Here," she took his hand and put the nibbled thumb against her own lips, "let me do that."

He laughed tensely. "Why?"

"Because I'm nervous, too."

Michael chuckled, looked at the floor, and stuffed his hands in his pockets. Emily sensed he wanted to say something and allowed him time to find his words.

"Do you know," he began cautiously, "how many years I have wanted this, dreamed about this? And now I don't even know what to do." He met her eyes and added solemnly, "I've never done this before, Emily."

"I know."

"How did you know?"

"I just . . . had a feeling."

"What makes you want a guy like me?" he asked sincerely. Emily touched his face as a rarely-seen hint of insecurity showed itself. She knew how he felt.

"What makes you want a widow with three children?"

"Because I love you."

"There's your answer, Mr. Hamilton."

As if to apologize, he added, "You will be the first for me, Emily—and the last."

Emily smiled and lifted her face toward him. She didn't want any doubt that she meant it when she said, "I can think of no greater privilege."

Michael smiled and pulled her into his arms. He pressed his mouth over hers, and the world fell away.

Deep into the night, Michael held Emily close to him, wanting never to let her go. He was glad she slept as tears came to remind him of the countless empty nights without her, the anguish of losing her, and the contrasting joy of having her now when he had twice believed she was lost to him forever.

Absently he brushed his lips over her brow, and she nuzzled closer to him in her sleep. He asked himself how a man could reach his age and never realize how incredible life was meant to be. And then he felt sorry for all the fools in the world who made light of what he had just experienced, and expected to find happiness. "I love you, Emily," he whispered and drew her closer. He knew she couldn't hear him, but he had to say it anyway.

Emily awoke to daylight and a familiar greeting. "Mommy! Mommy, wake?" Amee bounced onto the bed, wearing red pajamas.

Emily hugged her, chuckling to see Michael stretch groggily.

"What is *that?*" he asked in mock dismay.

"It's my alarm clock," Emily reported and bent over to kiss him.

Michael made a pleasurable noise, then Amee bounced onto his chest. "Daddy, wake?"

"Yes," he grinned and tickled her, "Daddy wake." He added to Emily, "She is cute, but we don't have to take her on our honeymoon, do we?"

"No," Emily laughed, "I think your mother has that taken care of."

Allison knocked at the open door and peeked in timidly.

"Come in, sweetie," Emily called.

Michael felt momentarily uncomfortable as Allison glanced speculatively at him. "Mrs. Pace told me to come and get Amee. She got away before we knew she was awake." She put Michael at ease with a lightly spoken, "We know you want to be alone."

"That's all right." Michael leaned against the headboard and Amee sat on him, trying to provoke him into playing peek-a-boo. "She makes a good alarm clock." He tickled Amee again and laughed.

"Did you have a good time yesterday?" Emily asked Allison.

"Yeah, it was fun. That's a pretty nightgown, Mom. Where did you get it?"

Emily smiled timidly. "I bought it the day before we left Utah. Why don't you take Amee back to her room to get dressed, and we'll see you in a little while."

"Okay," Allison agreed and dragged Amee away.

Michael got up to lock the door, then returned to sit on the edge of the bed and kiss his wife. "Good morning," he whispered.

"Good morning," she replied. He kissed her again, and over an hour later they finally made it to the dining room just as LeNay, Katherine, Bret, and Penny finished breakfast. Allison and Stacy had already gone to the stables.

"We figured you'd show up here sooner or later," Bret teased, and Penny nudged him with a firm elbow.

"What are your plans today?" LeNay asked Michael as he took over getting Alexa out of the highchair.

"All I can tell you is we're flying out later this morning." He sat to eat with Alexa on his lap and winked at Emily.

"I think you'd best check the weather first," Katherine stated. "Have you even bothered to look out the window this morning?"

"Actually, no," Michael said proudly. "Is it bad?"

"Very," LeNay stated, "and I'll not have you attempting to fly out of here with skies like that. You either drive or you wait."

Michael glanced at Emily, expecting her to show disappointment, but she only said, "It's not worth the risk."

"So, which would you rather do?" he asked.

"I don't know, but . . ." She glanced toward Penny and Michael's eyes followed.

"I'd say let's wait," he suggested, and Penny beamed. "Since there's no hurry to get back, waiting around here a while won't hurt any."

The conversation turned to the success of the wedding as everyone hovered in the dining room while Michael and Emily ate. The only interruption came when Robert peeked in to tell Katherine he wanted to talk to her. A few minutes later, a stale hush fell over the room as raised voices filtered in from the hallway. Anxious glances intensified as it became evident that Robert was leaving. Michael felt irony tear at him, while Emily felt dismayed that her call to the temple didn't seem to have helped. The tears in LeNay's eyes moved Michael to stand with an intention to intervene, but she put a hand on his arm to stop him. "There's nothing you can do," she said softly. Then one set of footsteps moved toward the back of the house as the argument apparently came to its final end.

Emily felt compelled to offer Katherine some moral support, if nothing else, and moved toward the hall, expecting to find her alone there. Instead she found Robert, suitcase in hand, opening the door.

"Wait," she said impulsively, then wondered what on earth she could possibly say that would make any difference. After a quick, silent plea for help, she added quietly, "Please close the door. There's something I'd like to say to you before you go."

"All right, say it," he said cynically.

"I realize I haven't been here long, and perhaps what I have to say is of little importance to you, but I'm going to say it anyway. For

Katherine's sake, I'm not letting you leave until something is said."

"Get on with it," he spoke impatiently, and Emily felt a reminder of Ryan that made her stomach churn. She could see or hear no similarities, but there was a . . . what? A lack of sensitivity? A hard coating of pride?

"You're making a mistake, Robert."

"Katherine already said that."

"But did she tell you that there is nothing on this earth that will ever replace what you're leaving behind? The years you have invested with Katherine, your children; nothing will ever give you so much fulfillment. You can chase dreams and experiment with life, but it will only end up proving one thing: what you had to begin with cannot be bettered. One day you'll wake up and wonder what kind of stupidity made you turn your back on the only thing that could make you whole. If I were you, I'd think about that before it's too late."

After Emily's impassioned speech, she expected Robert to either walk out and slam the door or retort with something cynical. Through an uncomfortable silence he was completely unreadable, and Emily felt afraid. Her heart began to pound when he set the suitcase down and sat in one of the two chairs available in the hall.

"It's already too late, Emily," he said. She sat down across from him.

"Why?" she asked firmly.

He glanced at her then looked away, ashamed and uncertain. "I know what you say is true," he said, barely audibly, "because I've already realized it."

"What?" she persisted. "I don't understand."

Robert chuckled, a dry humorless laugh, edged with pain. "There is nothing out there to compare with Kate and the kids, but . . ." He looked down and his voice cracked. Emily sensed a truth coming to the surface that made her grateful for that call she'd made yesterday. She sensed a miracle at work here.

"It's all right, Robert. Tell me. Perhaps I'm not so biased because I'm not as involved as the others. I've lived through a difficult marriage. Maybe I can help."

"I'm not sure anything can help," he insisted. "After what I have done, I know Kate would want nothing to do with me. I have to get out of here. I can't live with the guilt. I promised her I'd stay for the wedding, but . . . now I have to go. What I have done is unforgivable."

Robert buried his face in his hands, and though he attempted to conceal it, Emily knew he was crying. The problem became very clear, and it was by no means a small one. Emily's heart ached for him, for Katherine, and for the children. But she also felt hope from the knowledge that she could share with him.

Putting a gentle hand on his shoulder, she said softly, "Robert, nothing is unforgivable. If we are talking about what I think we are, it's not going to be easy, but it's possible." He showed no response, and she wondered where to begin when she had no idea of his religious background. After quick, careful thinking, she recalled something Katherine had said and repeated it with fervency. "Robert, Katherine told me herself that she didn't care what you had done. She said if you would just leave it behind and stay with her, she would gladly forgive you."

Robert looked up with something glimmering in his eyes that prompted Emily to continue with a careful statement. "I don't know what your religious beliefs are, Robert, but—"

"I was raised Catholic, but I've had nothing to do with it since I was eighteen," he admitted, embarrassed. "Maybe if I had, I wouldn't be so bad off now."

"But surely you understand the Christian concepts you were raised with," she said with hope. "If you don't, then we should talk about it, because there is a way for you to put the past behind and be free of it forever. You can be forgiven, Robert."

The hope in his eyes increased, and the next thing Emily knew, Robert was crying against her shoulder. "Thank you, Lord," she whispered toward the ceiling.

Michael tried to keep himself from intruding on what he believed was Emily and Katherine talking in the hall. But he finally couldn't bear it any longer. His sister was hurting. With vehemence he strode into the hall, then stopped cold. He couldn't believe it. The scene before him was so miraculous, he almost expected to hear angels singing. Quickly he turned around before he was noticed, leaning on the dining room door to catch his breath.

"What is it?" LeNay questioned in panic.

He whispered loudly, "Robert is out there, crying on Emily's shoulder."

All eyes widened. LeNay gasped. "Honest," he raised his hand in a pledge. "Mormons aren't supposed to lie."

"You never did lie, did you?" his mother questioned.

"Not since I was four," he grinned. "I lied when I told you I ate that disgusting cauliflower stuff. Actually, I fed it to one of the horses."

LeNay gave him a glare of disgust, more from the absurdity of it than the confession. Emily entered the room a moment later, and all eyes turned to her expectantly.

"What happened?" Penny asked.

Emily sighed, and they all sat to hear her answer. Amee climbed onto her lap. "It seems," she said quietly, "that Robert doesn't want to leave Katherine nearly as much as he wants to be free of some mistakes he's made. He went upstairs to find her and unpack."

"Thank God." LeNay put a hand to her heart.

"How did you manage that?" Michael asked.

"I think I was just the mouthpiece," she replied humbly. Only LeNay didn't seem to know what she was talking about.

"Do you think that—" Michael began, then Stacy burst into the room.

"Uncle Michael!" He came to his feet abruptly. "Mom rode toward the mountains a little while ago, and she hasn't come back, and it's getting misty in the hills and . . ." The child was near tears, and Emily's heart began to pound.

Michael moved toward the door and her panic deepened. "Where are you going?" she demanded.

"I've got to find her," he said firmly.

"Michael, no," his mother insisted. "Katherine knows what to do if she runs into trouble. If you leave now, you'll only get lost yourself."

Michael turned to Emily, who added strongly, "Listen to your mother, Michael."

A thousand fears mingled between their eyes. Michael felt torn.

He scanned the anxious faces in the room, but a pounding in his heart told him he had to go. "That's my sister out there, Emily." He squeezed her hand so hard it hurt. "I *have* to go."

Emily followed his purposeful strides to the stables, but it soon became apparent there was no talking him out of it. He put on his hat and a long drover coat that looked out of place with his jeans and high-topped tennis shoes.

"Michael, please," she said tearfully, reaching up for his hand after he'd mounted a sturdy mare. A formless desperation made the fear of letting him go almost painful.

"I'll be careful," he said and bent low to kiss her in a way that betrayed the intimacies they had shared.

Emily stood in the stable doorway and watched with pounding heart as he rode through a steady drizzle toward the mist-covered hills. Her mind sought for some peace, but all she could hear were Michael's once lightly-uttered words coming back to her like a premonition of doom. In response to her doctor's comment on Australian weather, Michael had said it was downright deadly at times; that he'd seen storms settle into those mountains that could kill the best horseman.

"Oh, please, dear Father," she prayed aloud, "don't take him from me now. I couldn't bear it."

Numbly she ushered Allison and Stacy into the house to find LeNay, Penny, and Bret in the lounge room with the babies. No words were exchanged as she sat down and both babies attempted to crawl into her lap. She hugged them tightly and squeezed her eyes shut in an effort to block out the fear.

"He'll be all right." Penny set a gentle hand on her arm.

"Of course he will," LeNay added, but Emily could hear the strain in her voice. "They both will. They just have to be."

CHAPTER SIXTEEN

As Michael rode into a thickening mist, he counted on the instincts of the horse and his knowledge of these mountains to guide him. His mind turned to a continuing prayer that he would be guided to Katherine. He kept thinking of Lehi's dream and decided he'd give a lot for a good iron rod about now. It didn't take long to realize he was lost. The rain only worsened and the mist had turned heavy.

His mind went back to Emily mentioning her fears that something would happen to come between them. He'd brushed it off at the time, but now that fear became very real. As the horse moved in what seemed endless circles through the trees, Michael's mind wandered to their one night together. At least she had his name, he told himself. At least she'd have financial security.

Such thoughts only increased his fear, and he reminded himself of the adage that faith and fear could not exist in the same person at the same time. Michael returned his mind to prayer, but the fear wouldn't leave. Above the fear for himself was his fear for Katherine. If he was lost, she likely was too. He couldn't rid himself of the feeling that she needed him. "Please," he prayed aloud, "help me find her. You can see her, Father. I can't. Help me find her, and make certain Emily and the children will be cared for."

Michael didn't like the way that came out sounding, but before he had a chance to reword it, he felt the horse's hooves slipping in a muddy decline. The world fell out from under him in one blackening moment.

* * * * *

Emily spent the morning looking out windows, watching through the rain for any sign of life from the hills. After the babies went down for naps, she buried herself in the scriptures, trying to become distracted from the reality that this was supposed to be her honeymoon. She and Michael should have been together. She prayed for him. She prayed for Katherine. But she felt certain the fear in her heart made those prayers faithless. Penny was close by, while Bret hovered in the stables with Murphy and a few others who were watching the hills closely, waiting for the mist to lift and ease their sense of helplessness.

"He'll be all right," Penny said with confidence. "I can feel it."

"Then why do I have this awful feeling that he won't be?" Emily retorted. The mood between them was far too much like a bad dream from the past.

"I told you before. You're just used to being miserable. You probably expect it, or think you deserve it, or something."

"Maybe I do deserve it," Emily replied cynically. The tears wouldn't be held back any longer and she fell apart. "Penny, if I lost him I would die. I couldn't bear it. I just couldn't bear it."

"Come on," Penny said after she'd had a good cry, "let's pray." She urged Emily to her knees beside the bed. Together they knelt over the new quilt spread there. Emily was grateful for Penny's faith and strength as she uttered a beautiful prayer and Emily added a firm, "Amen."

They came to their feet and Penny embraced her. "Let's go outside and see what's happening."

As they reached the foot of the stairs, the side door opened and LeNay looked up at them with a smile. "The mist is lifting. Murphy just headed out with a search party of twelve." She added, looking at Penny, "Bret went with them."

Penny laughed. "He's probably in his glory, but I hope he stays close to someone who knows more about horses than he does."

"They always ride in twos," LeNay provided.

"Do you lose people often?" Penny asked.

"Not often, but we do lose cattle occasionally."

"I didn't know we had any," Emily stated, realizing she'd included herself in the ownership. The thought might have warmed her, if it hadn't been followed by a fear that something might have happened to Michael and she would be widowed again. It was little consolation that she would be a wealthy widow.

"We don't have many," LeNay reported. "We mostly keep them to use for our own beef. But in all the years I've been here, we've only had five cows and one man get killed."

"I don't want to hear about it," Emily insisted. LeNay suggested they go to the library to wait, where they could see over the side veranda to the stables. Stacy and Allison joined them there, obviously worried as well. A short while later, Robert came in and sat quietly. Emily took his hand and squeezed it, but no words were exchanged.

Over an hour later, two men were seen riding hurriedly down from the hills. The group rushed out into the warming weather to meet them. The horses drew to a halt near the edge of the lawn. It was LeNay who demanded, "Did you find them? This is not like Michael to . . ."

The look on Murphy's face made her stop. Emily put a hand to her heart while Penny squeezed the other.

"Mrs. Hamilton," he said, his eyes taking in both Emily and LeNay, "we found Katherine's horse just wandering, and . . . we found Michael's horse . . . dead in a ravine."

"No!" Emily cried.

"And Michael?" LeNay demanded.

Murphy looked carefully to the other horseman. "We can't get to his horse without some ropes, but . . . it looks like there could be a . . . body underneath it."

"No!" Emily cried more loudly and nearly collapsed against Penny.

"Mom?" Allison cried. Emily knelt to hold her.

"I won't believe it until I see it," LeNay insisted. "Find them, Murphy. And hurry."

Murphy nodded, and the two rode toward the stables where they quickly gathered some equipment before heading back toward the hills.

Penny's undying strength took over as the family seemed to crumble. She ushered them back into the house, soothed nerves with words of confidence, then announced through the chorus of varied tears, "We're going to pray. Come along." She went to her knees and motioned to the others. Allison and Emily immediately followed. LeNay only hesitated a moment before she knelt and took Robert's hand. Stacy knelt by her father and the group joined hands in a circle. With faith and fervency, Penny spoke a sincere prayer that brought the tears on stronger. The minutes ticked by and she continued to pray. By the time a mutual "Amen" was spoken, a hush had fallen over the room, though the fear was still evident.

Emily held Allison close, trying her best to whisper words of assurance. But it was difficult to console Allison, when their fears were much the same. Together they had been through so much since Ryan's death. Emily wondered if she would stay here with her children if Michael were gone. The thought of taking Allison away from here was devastating, but the thought of staying without Michael seemed worse.

Her eyes met LeNay's and her thoughts shifted. If the worst happened, they would need each other. She would stay, and like Ruth in the Bible, she would find peace with her husband's mother.

Emily shook her head and wondered what she was doing. She couldn't resign herself to this. Not yet. He was alive. He was all right. He *had* to be!

After an unbearable silence, Penny touched Allison's arm and she looked up with a tear-streaked face. "Sing, Allie," she whispered. "Remember what we learned in Primary. When we feel afraid, we should sing. You choose a song, and I'll sing with you."

Allison looked around the room at the grave countenances of her new family, then she drew her shoulders back with courage and began a shaky, quiet rendition of *I am a Child of God.*

A tangible peace fell over the room that turned expressions from fear to awe. Emily was wondering if the others could feel the Spirit the way she could, when LeNay said in a trembling voice, "They're all right. I'm not certain how I know, but I know they're all right."

A few minutes later a voice hollered from outside, "We found them!"

They ran together out to the veranda and down the steps, over the lawn and toward the stable yard where they could see a group of horses riding toward them at a slow pace. Emily looked hard in an attempt to discern Michael from the group, but the distance was too far.

"Why are they coming in so slowly?" LeNay asked Murphy, who approached them near the fence.

"Kate's got a broken leg," Murphy reported.

LeNay sighed. "And Michael?"

"Well, he—"

"Emily Hamilton!" a familiar voice shouted, and Emily wanted to collapse from the joy. "Your husband is home!"

Emily hugged LeNay, then she hugged Penny, then she lifted a giggling Allison off the ground. They saw him gallop ahead of the group and Allison ran toward him. Emily followed. Michael slid from his horse to scoop Allison into his arms with a hearty laugh. He turned to see Emily and set Allison down. She flew into his embrace, laughing and crying, kissing him wildly, oblivious to the mud spattered all over him.

"I love you," he cried softly. "I love you so much."

"You're hurt." She touched dried blood on his forehead.

"I fell off my horse," he chuckled. "I'm okay."

"I thought you were dead," she cried.

"For a minute or two," he admitted soberly, "I thought I was dead, too."

"We prayed."

"So did I."

"Oh, Michael," she held him closer, "I would die if I lost you."

"I think the Lord knows we need each other, Emily." He kissed her.

"What happened?" she asked.

"I got lost in the mist, and as close as I can figure, the horse began to slide in the mud and went into the ravine. I must have fallen as she lost her footing, and she slid out from under me. I blacked out for a minute, and when I came to, I could hear Katherine calling my name. I found her huddled under a rock. She'd had a fall and couldn't move her leg. She'd heard me praying out loud before I fell. We had a good, long talk while we waited for the mist to clear, then I splinted her leg. We started down the mountain and must have just missed the search party on their first trip up."

"Enough stories," LeNay interrupted. "We've got to get Kate into town and get that leg—"

"I'll take her," Robert said, and they turned to see him helping a tearful Katherine down from a horse. Emily briefly examined the splint and gave Michael a smile of approval.

"You want Murphy to fly you in?" Michael asked as Robert carried Katherine past them.

"No," Katherine said as they paused a moment near Michael, "I think we'll just take our time. I'm sure the splint will last that long." She reached out and squeezed Michael's hand. "Thank you, little brother, for coming to find me. I was terrified."

"Just don't do it again," Michael chuckled, and Robert carried her away.

Robert turned back to add briefly, "And thank you, Emily. When you get back from your honeymoon, we all need to have a talk."

"We'll plan on it," she called, and held Michael close while they each put an arm around Allison.

After LeNay spoke to Katherine, she approached Michael with a firm, "Don't you ever do that to me again, young man."

He chuckled and hugged her. "Yes, Mother."

LeNay looked up at him with tears brimming in her eyes. "I'm so grateful," she murmured. "Somehow I know that miracles have been at work here."

"I'm certain you're right," he replied, putting an arm around her shoulders.

"I'd like to talk to you about that, Michael," she said.

Michael felt a softening in her that made arguments they'd once had over religion seem long ago and far away.

"I would enjoy that very much," he said, pulling Emily close with his other arm. "But at the moment, I'm supposed to be on my honeymoon."

LeNay smiled and squeezed Emily's hand. "I'm certain it can wait until you get back." She looked at him firmly. "Just don't forget."

"Oh, I won't," Michael grinned. "And in the meantime, I think Bret and Penny will be around a few days. If you have any questions,

I'm sure they'd be delighted to help out."

"I just might do that," LeNay added as they moved together toward the house.

An hour later, tearful good-byes were being exchanged near the hangar. It was difficult, not knowing how long it would be before they saw Bret and Penny again; but once in the air, Emily let all anxiety fall away and concentrated on her husband. "Is this really happening?" she asked, unable to keep from beaming. Michael looked over at her, then leaned his head back with a joyful whoop that made Emily laugh.

"Where to first?" she asked.

"Sydney," he replied. "I'd like you to see a little more than the airport. I thought we'd start with a stroll around the temple grounds."

"That sounds like a beautiful place to start." Emily reached over to kiss him as the plane rose through a layer of fluffy clouds.

"Hmmm," he muttered as she pulled back and he looked around. "We must be in heaven."

"Not quite, but close." She took his hand and absorbed the view. "Yes, I'd say we're real close."

* * * * *

Emily steered the Cruiser with ease along the fifty-mile stretch of groomed dirt road. The Icehouse cassette played on the stereo, one of the few familiar things that bridged the life she'd once lived to the one she was quickly becoming accustomed to. She had taken to making the drive to town and the surrounding areas on her own, and she was even beginning to get used to driving on the wrong side of the road.

Her day had been tiresome but rewarding, and she was looking forward to sharing every detail with Michael. As she maneuvered the Cruiser around the house, a newly acquired peace made her realize that she didn't feel like a stranger here any more. It was truly home, almost as if it always had been.

While unloading packages from the back of the Cruiser, a quick glance reassured her that Allison was busy in the corral, leading Ashley's Replacement about like a puppy on a leash. If Ashley could see her now, she would hardly recognize her. Allison was quickly becoming a vibrant, confident child with big dreams and the will to achieve them.

Wondering if Michael had come in yet, Emily went in the side door and down the hall to the kitchen.

"Here are the things you asked for, Millie. I hope I got it right."

"You always do." Millie gave a congenial smile and wiped her hands on her apron. "Did ya have a good time today?"

"It was nice, yes. Have you seen Michael recently?"

"Not since he tried to force his way in here and take over makin' lunch, the rascal."

Emily chuckled and hurried upstairs. She peeked around a door and Amee immediately ran toward her with a jubilant, "Mommy! Mommy! Nanna wead a book."

The recently dubbed "Nanna" reported that the day had gone well, and Alexa was still down for a later-than-usual nap. Emily took Amee and her storybooks across the hall where she freshened up and sat on her bed to write a letter.

Dearest Penny,

I just couldn't wait to tell you this. Today I went visiting teaching. It took nearly all day. As I told you before, the branch encompasses nearly a hundred miles. The sisters I visit all live within about ten miles of each other, but it's an hour and twenty minutes to get there and back. Remember when I complained because it might take a couple of hours? Think of me next time you walk to do your visits.

Nothing much has changed since my last letter. What can happen in three days? The children are doing beautifully, and I can't express to you how much I'm loving life. I never dreamed that marriage could be so fulfilling. Honestly, Penny, every time he walks in the room, I get butterflies. I know I can't feel like a newlywed forever, but I'd like to try.

I was glad to hear you'd finished selling all my junk. When I told Michael what you made, he said he'd never dreamed you were such a shrewd businesswoman. He'd like to hire you to keep his stable hands in line. Just kidding.

I must say I'm not surprised the house was sold. Your new neighbor sounds like a wonderful woman. Her being divorced with all those kids ought to give you plenty of opportunities to get to know her better.

I miss you, Penny, and . . .

The bedroom door opened, and Emily set the letter aside. She had to smile as she was seized with a sensation just like she'd described in her letter. Michael closed the door and leaned against it for a minute, smiling as if he'd thought of a great secret between the two of them. Emily glanced away timidly, certain she knew his thoughts.

"I saw you drive in." He tossed his hat onto the bedpost and sat down to pull off his boots. Traces of sweat and dirt were evidence of the usual hard day's work. "How did it go?"

"Wook it, Daddy," Amee interrupted to point out something in the book she was enjoying on the floor. "It's a mumpmump."

"A mumpmump?" he laughed.

"That's elephant," Emily whispered loudly.

Michael nodded his understanding, and Amee crawled onto his lap for the expected hug and kiss.

"When do I get mine?" Emily asked when Amee returned to her books.

"You didn't answer my question."

"It went well. I actually enjoyed myself. I think Patty and I are going to be good friends."

"That's great. I thought you'd like her."

"And guess what I heard?" she teased.

"Oooh, gossip?"

"Not exactly. Nellie Tres told me that Jenny's decided to go to the states—BYU, to be exact."

"Really?" he smiled. "That's nice. She'll love it."

"And how are you?" Emily asked.

"I'd like you to come over here and kiss me, Mrs. Hamilton, and then I will be fine."

"That's sounds divine, *Mis-ter* Hamilton, but I think you ought to come over here."

"You don't have to ask me twice." He grinned and nearly bounded onto the bed, sending Emily into a fit of giggles until he smothered them with a kiss.

When he pulled back to take a deep breath and inhale the scent of her, Michael couldn't miss the sparkle in her eyes. How he loved her! In more than ten years of fantasizing, he never dreamed his life could be so rich.

"Michael," she asked, pressing a hand to his face, "will we always be so happy?"

"Forever," he promised firmly.

"But won't there come a day when the challenges of life could come between us, make us forget the way we feel now?"

Michael creased his brow, unable to comprehend such a thing ever happening, and not liking the logic that told him it was likely to, if they let it.

"If that ever happens, darlin', you just put those pretty boots of yours on and give me a good, swift kick. All you've got to do is get my attention."

"I think I could do that." She smiled with mischief in her eyes, then leaned up abruptly to lick his nose.

Michael laughed and pressed her arms to the bed, determined to retaliate. He paused a moment to look at her and decided he'd rather kiss her. So he did.

Photograph by Nathan Barney

About the Author

Anita Stansfield is an imaginative and prolific writer whose first published novel, *First Love and Forever,* has been an outstanding success in the LDS romance market. She has been writing since she was in high school, and her work has appeared in *Cosmopolitan* and other publications. She is an active member of the Romance Writers of America and the League of Utah Writers.

Anita and her husband, Vince, live with their four children in Orem, Utah.